AFTER MIIGAADIWIN

Anna Raddon

The Seventh Fire Trilogy - Book 1

AFTER MIIGAADIWIN
Copyright © 2018 by Anna Raddon

ISBN: 978-1-4866-1563-6

Word Alive Press
119 De Baets Street, Winnipeg, MB R2J 3R9
www.wordalivepress.ca

WORD ALIVE
—PRESS—

Cataloguing in Publication may be obtained through Library and Archives Canada

For my husband, who dares me to dream

CONTENTS

ACKNOWLEDGEMENTS

Thank you to the creators of the Ojibwe People's Dictionary for the extensive and beautiful online resource. Thank you to the University of Minnesota and John D. Nichols for providing this service.

THE SEVENTH FIRE

There will be a rebirth of the Nation and a rekindling of old flames. The Sacred Fire will again be lit.

Now, the light-skinned race will be given a choice between roads. One road will be green and lush and very inviting. The other road will be black and charred and walking it will cut their feet. The people decide to take neither road, but instead to turn back, to remember and reclaim the wisdom of those who came before.

If they choose the right road, the Seventh Fire will light the Eighth and final Fire, an eternal fire of peace, love, brotherhood, and sisterhood. If the light-skinned race makes the wrong choice, the destruction which they brought to this country will return to them and cause much suffering and death to all the Earth's peoples.[1]

---

1 *Wikipedia*, "Seven fires prophecy." Accessed: October 19, 2017. Excerpted and edited by the author from the Anishinaabeg oral tradition.

PROLOGUE

A bright spark flew across the room as a gust of wind swept around the fabric door, rustling it in the silence. The spark rose, hovering as though in suspense. The wind retreated as quickly as it came, the door falling smooth once more behind it.

Rowan watched the spark float toward him until it extinguished into grey ash on the chest of his woollen coat.

In the half-darkness, Gichi-Baawiting sat across the fire. His black hair, streaked with white, ran down his back in a tight braid. He muttered slowly and thoughtfully.

Rowan, squatting, rocked forward onto the balls of his feet so that he could shuffle sideways, closer to the elder. The elder's words were low, but clear.

"I have summoned you with a blessing, my younger brother *nishiime*,"[2] intoned Gichi-Baawiting, "for in a full millennium there has never been one of our own community who has been chosen. It is a great honour that you share with us."

Rowan ducked his head in embarrassed acknowledgment. Gichi-Baawiting held a long stick in his hand and began to pry apart the crackling logs with such vigour that Rowan scooted backward to avoid the spray of embers that rose harmlessly toward the tent's open peak. He rubbed his rough, white hands together despite feeling overheated. The space was smaller than he liked and he was unaccustomed to accepting praise.

"I did not only call you for a blessing, but a warning as well," the elder said.

The scattered flames died away entirely and the room shrank even closer about the two men. Rowan turned his face away from the glow of the charred circle to give the elder his full attention.

---

2   *Nishiime*: a younger sibling, here referring to a non-Native person.

Gichi-Baawiting closed his eyes and spoke slowly. "I have read the ancient prophecies." He exhaled heavily. "The fullness of time is upon us. A great deception is at hand."

Rowan shook his head. "The prophecies were silenced a thousand years ago. We have no further need…"

Gichi-Baawiting extended his hand to halt Rowan's words. "*Nishiime*, you are still young and do not know the Word as you should. These many years I have guided us and sought wisdom. You are right; the Word has been silent since the Ancient Ones were young. Silent—not dead."

The rippling wind moved the tent's fabric around them and a loon's forlorn cry rose on the lake. Rowan shivered despite the heat.

"The past collides with the future and we will be shaken once again. Yet there is a little time left. You must carry your burden faithfully, and maybe we will be spared." Gichi-Baawiting stirred the fire with his stick so that the flames leapt up again. "But I fear you will meet trouble on your journey. Look, the moon is already high."

He raised his face to the domed opening and Rowan followed his example. There, shining through the gap, was a perfect moon, full and pale against the charcoal night.

"The next time you see such a moon, I pray you will be celebrating at the *Naawayi!*"[3]

With an unexpected flick of his wrist, Gichi-Baawiting threw a handful of dried tobacco over the flame, smothering it instantly as a heavy smoke rose in the tent. The sweet smell filled Rowan's senses; he instinctively bowed his head.

The elder rose to his feet and his shadow filled the wall of fabric behind him. He took a step forward and placed his strong hands on Rowan's shoulders. With the weight in his lungs and on his shoulders, Rowan wondered if the man's great age had not made him stronger.

Gichi-Baawiting spoke in a low voice. "And for these gifts we remain forever grateful. Now I bless this *nishiime* you have set apart in your service. Make his hands respect the things you have made, and make his ears sharp so he may hear your voice. Make him wise, so he may understand what you have taught our people, and the lessons you have hidden in each leaf and rock. Make him ever ready to come before you with clean hands and a straight eye, so as life fades as a sunset his spirit may come to you without shame."[4]

---

3   *Naawayi*: centre.

4   Adapted from an Ojibwa prayer, author unknown.

Rowan rose, cool night air flooding his lungs as Gichi-Baawiting drew aside the tent door. An unusual clarity nearly overwhelmed his senses. Stepping into the world, he saw that Venus had risen over the lake so brightly that its reflection drew a path to the east. Rowan knew its route: past his home and family, beyond the shadowy bulk of the great Island, and straight on across the Atlantic.

chapter one

ODOODEMAN
"CLAN SYSTEM"

Gizhaa was aware of being watched. Without opening his eyes, he lay very still, detecting the familiar wash of waves on sand and the rush of wind through pine boughs. The excitement of the day began to flood his body. Heavy air, not quite rain, filled his chest. The animals smelled close this morning. He opened his eyes to the light filtering through the round window at the top of his yurt. Cloudy and bright. Perfect!

He rolled out of bed, untangling himself from a wool blanket and dropping it to the floor. He thought better of it after taking two paces toward the door and turned back to pull the fabric neatly over his bed. He would be gone for at least a half moon and Mother would be sure to send the girls over to check on the place. It wouldn't do to have them find her handcrafted blanket in a heap on the floor.

Crossing the circular room, Gizhaa hummed a lilting tune. He pulled a sweater on and shoved his feet into the well-worn shoes beside the yurt's door. On cue, the fabric moved slightly. Gizhaa reached through the wooden lattice and gave the fabric a tap. Immediately he heard a sniffing sound from under the door. He drummed his fingers on the threshold. A long, pink tongue flicked out from under the fabric and slobbered his fingertips affectionately.

"Ah, Tristen! You got me." He rubbed the stickiness from his fingers onto the canvas pants he had slept in. "Blech!"

As the door flung open, a ball of brown fuzz danced through the doorway and around his legs. Gizhaa rubbed the little alpaca's head.

"I will have to remember to bolt the door while I'm gone or you'll move right in," he murmured, sighing. Tristen pushed her head between Gizhaa's knees. "I don't know what you'll do. The girls will be good to you; don't worry. They just need a chance to be responsible." He shook himself and laughed. "Look, I even gave them my work coat so they'll smell just like me. They are my sisters, after all! So don't you even think about not eating or something while I'm gone."

He gave Tristen one final pat before straightening up.

Gizhaa's eyes rested momentarily on the sky again. To his right stood a semi-circle of three yurts much like his own, each cocooned in brightly patterned felt. To his left towered the giant white pines that made the North Shore a delight for tourists, each tree stretching eighty meters toward heaven. Beyond that he caught glimpses of blue through the trees—Lake Huron, practically on his doorstep. Unseen windmills on the beach hummed endlessly. And the pines moaned on windy nights, the yurt walls rippling while waves crashed on the nearby shore.

Gizhaa's hand closed around the smooth wood of the staff resting against his door jamb. It was an old friend that fit better every year, each finger a smooth hollow. Tristen skipped along behind Gizhaa as he walked. He heard muffled voices inside the far yurt across the clearing. Behind the richly woven red and purple felt wall, he knew his mother was already pounding down her first rising of bread and his two youngest sisters were doing their chores.

The guest yurt next to that was silent and empty. The summer tourist season was over and it was still a bit early for travellers on their way home for the fall feast; his mother wasn't expecting any guests while he was away.

Closest to Gizhaa was a large, sky-blue yurt. It too lay silent. He hummed as he walked briskly toward it, his eyes sparkling. He lifted his staff, swinging it around in time to his own music. As he walked past the blue felt, he let his staff fall gently but firmly against the fabric. He dragged it around the building, thumping against each lattice brace.

"Yow! Gizhaadan!" came a female voice from inside.

This was followed by younger voices: "We're up! We're up!"

The door flew open as Gizhaa rounded the front.

"And good morning to you, big brother," a young woman said, flipping her long blond braid over her shoulder. "Yes, I was already up. I don't look this good rolling out of bed, you know." She curtsied dramatically and spun for his approval.

Gizhaa smiled. "Well, there's a first time for everything! I think you may even find yourself a husband one of these days, if you can keep up the good work, Inaa."

She gave an exaggerated sigh. "Oh, don't you start too. It's bad enough that Mom and Dad have made it very clear they expect me to be 'prepared to woo' on this trip." She rolled her eyes for further effect. "I doubt they would let me go if there was even a hint of a suitor on the North Shore."

Tristen nudged Inaa's leg and she leaned down to give her an obliging rub before the little alpaca disappeared through the open door.

Gizhaa shrugged. "Well, it isn't every day we travel to the capital. We'll meet a lot of people for sure."

"Aha! And you don't have any ideas yourself? Perhaps someone special to meet?"

Gizhaa pushed his hand through his brown curls. "I may or may not have sent a letter ahead to Uncle Ben. It doesn't hurt to put out a few feelers."

Inaa smiled now, her blue eyes lighting up. She opened her mouth to press the topic further. At that moment, laughter spilled through the doorway and a girl tumbled out, pushed by the little alpaca's brown nose nuzzling her pockets.

"Good morning, Kris," Gizhaa said. "Did you forget to fill your pockets with treats this morning?"

"You're early," the girl complained. "I wasn't ready yet."

An older girl came out of the yurt now, holding apple slices in her hands. "Here, Kris. I'll share."

"Thanks, Abby." The two sisters sat down on the doorstep, offering their treats by turns to Tristen.

A woman emerged from the yurt across the clearing, followed by two young children. She carried a large sack in strong arms and her brown hair, tied into a thick bun, showed no signs of grey.

"Six children and a world of work to be done! Girls, stop distracting your brother!" Her voice usually sang joyfully in the mornings, but today it was edged with tension.

"Good morning, Mom," Gizhaa called over his shoulder as he turned from the circle of yurts toward an alpaca yard. Tristen stayed close behind.

Inaa hurried to take the felt-wrapped pack from her mother.

"This is the gift. Please, please keep it safe and dry," her mother instructed.

"I know, Mom," Inaa consented. Inside this pack lay her mother's most treasured work of art. Eighteen moons of work would finally travel across the country and on to *Naawayi*. It was the opportunity of a lifetime to deliver such a precious gift for such an important occasion.

Mother held Inaa by the arms a moment longer, looking into her eyes. "Little girl, you are grown and ready for this. I know, I know." She smiled and took a deep breath. Shaking away the tenderness, she added sternly, "And bring me home a son-in-law."

Inaa groaned and flipped the pack up onto her shoulder. She turned and headed for the stable.

Δ   Δ   Δ

Tristen slipped under the gate and ran to its mother before Gizhaa had even reached the yard. His pet's twin brother was already drinking his morning milk. Gizhaa stepped in to shoo the little cria away from the mother's teat so that Tristen would have a chance to nurse.

"Silly girl!" he said. "If you wouldn't escape every morning, you'd grow faster by getting the first morning feeding."

Tristen gulped the alpaca milk hungrily. She was the younger of the twins and wouldn't have survived except that Gizhaa had hand-fed her, keeping her next to him for the first few days.

He hurried through the chores, the growing morning light urging him on.

"Have you eaten yet, Gizhaa?"

He turned to see his father heading across the yard with another pack. The two were mirror images of each other: brown hair and fair skin, broad shoulders, and lanky ease. Despite the years that separated them, his father's strength equalled his own.

"I haven't had breakfast," Gizhaa said.

"Your mother must be missing you already. She said you should come over to our place. She's got a full-course dinner—I mean breakfast—on for us."

Δ   Δ   Δ

Within the hour, Gizhaa, Inaa, and their father Rowan were sitting down in the family yurt for breakfast. Together there were eight of them and the space was cramped. They rarely ate meals together anymore since the oldest children had moved into their own places. But this was a special occasion, and though none said it, they all knew it would be many weeks before they all ate together again.

Rowan bowed his head. "Good Father, we are grateful for this food. Today we serve you only. Amen." His voice was low.

As he raised his head, the older children avoided looking at him so they wouldn't see his tears. Only little Nanda stared at him, astonished at the tenderness there.

They filled themselves on the soft cheeses, fresh bread, and roasted nuts, speaking of the neighbouring families and animals. Marriage, births, and blessings were shared and noted.

It wasn't until they were drinking a final sumac tea that Mother acknowledged the coming departure.

"I will miss our evening stories most of all… sharing *gikinoo'amaagoowin*, the ancient teachings." She sighed. Each one nodded in silent agreement.

It was Inaa who broke the silence. "The sooner we go, the sooner we return."

She wrapped herself in her travel coat.

Gizhaa followed her to the door where he saw his work coat hanging. He took it down and drew the weight of it around his youngest sister Nanda.

"Take good care of the alpacas for me," he reminded her with a quick tweak of her nose. She buried her face in his leg.

Gizhaa and Inaa walked silently to the stable and began to saddle the strongest alpacas. They didn't turn back to look where they knew their parents were saying goodbye.

Gizhaa rubbed the rough fur on his companion. "You and I are going to be traveling buddies for a few days."

Inaa dropped her pack heavily on her alpaca's back. "It's not like you're going to be gone for weeks, Gizhaa!" She flipped her braid over her shoulder like a whip and turned away from him, pretending to straighten the harness.

"Not if you have anything to do with it!" he shot back. "I can't imagine the doors of hospitality swinging wide in Iqaluit to my sweet sister!"

The crackle of a step in the bed of pine needles behind them was caution enough, but their father's voice was heavy. "Gizhaadan, do not stoop to your sister's outbursts. She shows it her own way." Rowan checked his waiting harness and rubbed the gentle animal. "It's time."

chapter two

MΛΛDΛΛDIZI
"JOURNEY"

A s Inaa emerged from the shelter of the pines, the sun reflected off the clear blue of Lake Huron. She paused a moment for the alpaca she was leading to adjust to the softer footing. Inaa shielded her eyes as they trekked the length of the beach, the alpaca moving slowly in the sand. She searched the horizon for Manitoulin Island. Her father said it had once been the world's largest freshwater island. It glistened in the distance across the channel.

She had travelled there with her father last year, herding a number of alpacas to trade with another breeder. The transaction would expand the genetic base for both herds. The entire trip had taken a couple of weeks with travel to the crossing and then backtracking across the island. Sailing, her friend Jordan used to cross often to visit for a day or a week, back when they had been younger and the distance between seemed less. Even now, the thought of his battered wooden day-sailer swinging up to the beach made her heart beat a little faster.

She let her eyes rest momentarily on the location of Jordan's farm, or at least where it ought to be, invisible across the water.

But her family wasn't the seafaring type. Even before the accident, the little handmade dory they had run about in as children wouldn't have been able to handle the waves. And of course it was unthinkable to attempt such a trip after the accident. Her father had sent their boat floating free on the water in a stiff wind. In the bottom of the dory, her mother had gently draped the blanket she had woven for her lost son over his favourite seat. There was no body to bury. The family had watched the boat disappear, bobbing silently from view as they mourned their great loss. Ten years later, it was still a heavy memory.

The alpaca's gentle rhythm reminded her of how slowly they travelled. The beast's plodding was comfortingly predictable, like the lapping of the waves, the rising of the sun. It was a good thing they wouldn't need to take the alpacas all the way to Nunavut. They would never make it before winter—or even spring, for that matter. But the train line was only a two-day walk. The animals would be glad for a break by then.

Inaa scanned the horizon one last time as the alpacas stepped from the coarse sand onto a bed of hard-packed pine needles. The forest closed in around them, the animals automatically quickening their pace on the familiar path.

Rowan gave his alpaca free reign in the lead. Behind him came Inaa, her alpaca carrying their precious cargo. Gizhaa brought up the rear.

A few paces past the tree line, a weeping birch towered beside the trail, its delicate branches still laced in shimmering leaves that hung over the path as a bridal bower.

"I planted this tree the year your mother and I married," Rowan called back from the front of the pack, his voice full of warmth. "6567 was a good year."

He never missed an opportunity to remind them.

Rowan Selah had been an alpaca breeder all his adult life. In fact, the community had celebrated the one hundred fiftieth anniversary of the Selah Alpaca Farm at this year's spring festival. But it wasn't Rowan's development of Canada's finest wool that had caught the attention of international clients. It was his wife Emmy's unrivalled weaving. Together they had pioneered wool garments that moved like silk, weathered like denim, and carried the title of fine art. It wasn't uncommon to work on an item for a full year. Growing the wool, softening, dyeing, weaving, embroidering—it was labour-intensive and he and Emmy demanded excellence at every stage.

This rare combination of a couple's gifts had won them the invitation to make this once-in-a-lifetime trip.

The tribute they carried, carefully folded and wrapped, was without doubt the finest work the Selahs had ever done: a coat fit for a king. Indeed, the gold-imbued thread that ran through the piece from collar to hem was worth a full year's income alone. Intricately patterned in the vibrant shades of local blueberry and sumac dyes, it had been a labour of love. Emmy had sung many *nagamon*[5] while she worked; even when she and Rowan had been filled with sorrow, she hadn't missed blessing a single stitch.

And now she was unable to deliver it. How many times over the past months had Rowan wrapped his arms around his wife's growing belly and sighed.

"If only you could come with me!" he would say. "I almost wish I didn't have to go."

---

5 *Nagamon*: song.

But he did want to go. And she wanted him to go.

All this ran through Inaa's mind as she walked under the leafy wedding bower. Her parents' marriage had been the rock-solid foundation of her life for fifty-five years. But it was time to forge her own way.

She loved her sisters, even her brother, but she longed for her own soulmate to share life with. No one denied that the pickings were pretty slim in the backwoods of Canada. There were a handful of neighbours about, though none who struck her fancy. Other than that, the summer brought tourists, and the feast seasons of spring and fall brought travellers journeying to visit family. They would stay in the guest yurt for a night, paying for bed and breakfast, and usually purchasing a garment or blanket for themselves or as a gift. It was hardly a bustling centre of single young men!

True, the land was fertile again and the lakes teemed with life, but human activity was relatively scarce. Her father often told them of the days before *Miigaadiwin*. There had been towns and cities scattered liberally throughout the region. Newcomers had poured in by the thousands in the days when untouched forests were the fuel of society. And when the forests had been decimated, prospectors had even taken to digging kilometres deep beneath the earth's surface in search of rare elements.

The thought was so ludicrous that Inaa would have laughed out loud, except a low-hanging tree branch snapped past her alpaca's shoulder and hit her in the face.

"Ouch! Heads up, bro!" she called as a warning to those behind her. The alpaca plodded ahead, unfazed.

She decided she would ask her father to tell them about the days before *Miigaadiwin* at tonight's storytelling, *gikinoo'amaagoowin*. Even when traveling, that was one tradition they would honour.

△ △ △

It was still broad daylight when they stopped for the night. They chose a clearing beside a river. The nuts and dried berries they had brought provided a quick meal, and the river water was refreshing to drink and wash in.

They quickly strung a wool blanket across two branches as shelter from the night dew. Then, as dusk began to settle, they eased themselves into warm clothes and drew a trio of log seats into a circle. A pile of stones served as a hearth.

Gizhaa carefully set the *waazakonenjigan*[6] atop the stones. It was a small metal cylinder, perforated by holes all around and open on top. At the bottom of the container, a glass jar was separated into two compartments, one filled with clear liquid,

---

6 *Waazakonenjigan:* light.

the other with red. With a flick of a switch, the two liquids flowed together, a swirl of red diffused to pink.

Gizhaa quickly pulled his hand away, seating himself around the circle. Moments later, a burst of flame emanated from the cylinder's holes and settled into a warm yellow glow that illuminated the clearing.

Inaa handed around the sticks she had gathered and whittled into roasters. They each shoved a hunk of cheese on their sticks. As the *waazakonenjigan* glowed and they turned their cheese patiently near it, the time had come for the *gikinoo'amaagoowin*.

Rowan's voice was deeper and more grave than usual. Its weight implied the hundreds of years of custom wrapped in this ritual, the great importance of passing on to each generation the lessons of shared history.

"Tonight, we remember our ancestors who lived here before us, who suffered so that we could learn a better way of life, so that we could harvest the riches of the earth and return them to our children and our children's children as a gift.

"Tonight, we remember the days before *Miigaadiwin*, the war to end all wars."

chapter three

GIKINOO'AMAAGOOWIN
"TEACHINGS"

"For millennia before our ancestors ever set foot on Canadian soil, Creator gave this land to our *Nisayenh*[7] brothers to harvest its first fruits. Indeed, we have gleaned much from their inheritance! That history is less well known to me than I would like, but perhaps I will know it better by the end of this journey. I have heard that Prime Minister Waaban is the best keeper of the *gikinoo'amaagoowin*[8] this country has ever seen. I may have the opportunity to hear him recount one of his people's histories during my time at Parliament. So we will leave that story for other nights. Let us begin then when our own family established their first home here, long before there was a Selah Family Farm."

The wind whispered its own story through the leaves as Rowan settled himself more comfortably for the telling.

"William was the first of our ancestors born and raised on this lake in the days before *Miigaadiwin*. His parents, your eleventh grandparents, had joined a movement of people flowing into the North Shore. People came like the salmon running in fall—a sudden burst of life in quiet waters. Huron was one of the largest bodies of fresh water in the world, a rare commodity. But it was not the water they sought to exploit; it was the forests. In those days, a white pine was considered full grown at just twenty meters tall! This area was covered with them.

"William's parents were young, much younger than you kids, and the family needed work badly. Like most of their neighbours, they were hard workers but had little time to hone their skills. A man might only work his trade for forty-five years

---

7   *Nisayenh*: older brother, here referring to First Nations.

8   *Gikinoo'amaagoowin*: teachings.

before dying prematurely at sixty-five years old! *Ahaaw*, if we lived before the Healing, Gizhaa would be an old man!"

They chuckled at this absurdity as Rowan continued his tale.

"William's dad worked as a logger, cutting trees with heavy tools. Wagons etched the forest with crude, muddy roads. Like the other loggers, he sold the fallen trees to mills. Over time, huge tracks of land were cleared and the wood used for buildings, paper, heat. The winters were so long and harsh that a family expected to burn fifteen trees to stay warm for the season! Eventually, the white pines were replaced by smaller trees: poplar and birch."

Inaa looked up into the canopy overhead and wondered aloud, "Do you think they could ever have imagined the forests like this?"

Rowan nodded. "Perhaps. It is said that they had found remains of very old trees, even in the far north, that had trunks two meters across at the base, more like the mature trees of today. So perhaps they understood that the earth had once been a richer place, that perhaps it could be again.

"Well, the family rented a house from the lumber mill company. It was barely a wooden shack—cold in winter and hot in summer. But William's mother sewed curtains from the traveling dress she had arrived in and his father built her a fine rocking chair. And it began to seem a home to them. Together the family worked hard during the short, dry summers to grow food and collect wood for the winter, but it never seemed enough.

"By the time Grandpa William had grown into a young man, his parents decided to build themselves their own home outside town on the ridge overlooking the lake. Young William now had a job working at the mill, but he and his father worked from spring until fall every day when he came home—sawing, hammering, lifting. They learned everything they could about insulating to keep out the deep cold. When the new house was finally done, small and tidy, Grandpa William thought they had the most comfortable home imaginable. But wrapped in layers of wood and batting and glass, they could no longer hear the birds sing in the morning. It seemed a tiny sacrifice."

"Grandpa William was a handsome young man and soon fell in love. It is said that she was so beautiful, she had three engagement offers by her sixteenth birthday! In those days, a young couple might marry at eighteen years old, so no one minded that Grandma Barbara was only seventeen years old when William took her to be his bride!"

Both Gizhaa and Inaa shook their heads, wondering how this was possible.

"They were so sure that their future would be bright and prosperous. And it began to be. William and Barbara lived in the village of Cook's Mills, just a few kilometres from our camp tonight. It was just a cluster of houses on the banks of the creek where it joined the great Huron. Towers of lumber dwarfed the neighbourhood. William had a good-paying, steady job in the lumber mill and very soon they knew that Barbara was carrying their first child.

"But they did not realize that their security was built on the mill owners' profits. The mill ground on endlessly, pushing through logs and producing the straight boards used everywhere to build the country's infrastructure, the bridges and schools and homes that made the economy tick. Yet each year the loggers had to travel further to bring back a full load of wood. Each year the logs they brought were smaller and less valuable. And each year the mill brought in less profit for its owners—owners so distant and wealthy they had never set foot in Cook's Mills their whole lives. Of course, they now owned newer mills on the west coast where the forests remained untouched and the trans-Canadian railway provided cheap transportation.

"Somehow it came as a great shock to William when he went to work one sunny June morning to be told that the mill was closed and he no longer had a job. You can imagine it was an even greater shock to Barbara, who had just finished scouring the floors and was feeling a bit crampy when her husband appeared home again carrying his unopened lunch pail. And so they celebrated the birth of their first son later that day, jobless and wondering how they would pay the rent."

The night was fully dark now, but their faces glowed palely in the light. Inaa tested her cheese and muttered angrily, "How could the mill owners do that to them? What a terrible way to treat people!"

Rowan simply nodded. "As it turned out, a pulp mill just one hundred kilometres away was hiring. Word was if you were young and strong, you'd get on immediately. So, with his newborn son just weeks old, William left Barbara and headed out looking for work. He came home every weekend to their rental house in Cook's Mills, but both hated the separation. The pulp mill promised that family housing would be built soon, but in the meantime William couldn't dream of bringing his bride and baby to the shantytown.

"Life continued as such for two full years. But with the realization that she was carrying another new life, Grandma Barbara began to pray earnestly for some way she and William could be reunited in a home of their own. Her prayers were answered in a way she would never have dreamed."

Gizhaa rose and gathered their blankets, passing them around. Each one wrapped themselves warmly in wool even as the story wrapped them in their history.

"One night she awoke to a terrible clanging just a couple hundred meters away. It was the town alarm bell being rung with such fervency that there was no wondering if it was just one of the local boys playing a midnight prank. This was real. The room was lit by the glow of red flames arching over the scrap lumber pile behind the deserted mill. The south breeze that had been blowing through the day had grown to a full-scale wind storm and veered northwesterly, placing the village directly in the fire's path. Barbara hurriedly wrapped a blanket around herself and the baby as she threw open the back door. The night air was filled with smoke. She realized the fire was closer than it had looked and wondered if those living in the houses next to the mill had escaped. But she needed to get the baby to safety.

"She hiked two kilometres in the dark. There were many other families around her on the road. A few cars drove by, loaded with refugees. All were merely grateful to escape with their lives as they left behind everything they owned. From that ridge above the lake, just beyond the tree line where we are right now, they turned back to watch the fire devour their homes. In the quiet Barbara heard a woman sobbing, a child's ceaseless coughing, and a man's angry cursing, but soon they simply drew their families together and kept walking.

"William's parents on the ridge were shocked when Barbara banged on their door, and then they were relieved that she was safe. A heavy rain began the next morning and William's father drove down to the mill. There was nothing left where the day before the village had stood as the centre of local life. The offices, school, bar, post office, and hardware store were nothing but heaps of smouldering ashes.

"Miraculously, there were no fatalities in the fire. Everyone escaped uninjured. The families scattered to stay with relatives or find new jobs. For a few months, there was revived hope that the town would recover; word came that the old mill was to be rebuilt. But as they watched workmen hurriedly slap together rotten or scorched wood into windowless, uninsulated walls, the awful truth became apparent. This 'rebuilding' was nothing more than a show, allowing the mill owners to collect their insurance money. The new mill would never open.

"Very soon rumours were circulating that the fire had been, in fact, a company job, an easy way to collect money on a useless mill—that a hefty wage had been paid to the man who set that fire. Worse yet, it was said that the arsonist was one of the *Nisayenh*. A name was never given and no charges were ever laid. But the accusation was enough. The terrible distrust between the First Nations and the settlers, nurtured by years of broken treaties, seemed to have become irreconcilable.

"And so, the remaining villagers of Cook's Mills gave up and moved away. Only a handful of families remained in the area: mostly those who owned houses outside the village, like William's parents, or those who could not find new jobs elsewhere. All that remained of the village was a graveyard on the lakeshore—in those days every village had one—with rows of wooden crosses remembering loved ones left behind, with the last tiny grave dug just weeks after the fire. A little girl had succumbed to pneumonia; perhaps it had been the cold night air or smoke inhalation. There was no hospital nearby. Even in those days, when all life was short, it was a tragedy. Barbara's enduring memory of Cook's Mills was seeing the mother at the graveyard months later, holding an infant son in her arms and weeping over the little grave of her daughter."

Rowan sighed and paused reverently, for he too knew the loss of a child. Clearing his throat, he began again.

"William and Barbara were forced to spend every penny they had saved and borrow the remainder to buy a home near William's job down the line at the pulp mill. Their new hometown, now booming, seemed like a modern haven after the months of waiting with William's parents for that infamous mill rebuilding. Never mind that the air smelled of sulphur day in and day out for twenty kilometres around. Their new town touted a library, a large school, and a brand-new hospital."

"Why would they need a hospital here?" Gizhaa asked.

Rowan smiled at the question, for Gizhaa knew the answer. It was a game to ask it every time, though usually little Nanda got to say it first.

"In those days, disease and pain were as common as the sumac bush. And giving birth was considered one of the most dangerous passages of life, a journey that was difficult and painful at the best of times. Families feared losing a baby or a mother, and rightly so, for everyone knew the story of someone who had lost one. So when the time came for Barbara to deliver their second child, William drove her to the hospital. The doctors asked her lie quietly and rest until the baby came, while William paced the lobby. *Ahaaw,* if Emmy were here she would tell you, after giving birth seven times, that she has never lain down and rested in the process!"

They laughed together, knowing exactly how vehemently their mother would express herself on this point.

"At that time, doctors worked very hard to understand the human body and did much good to relieve pain and promote healing. But the ability to spontaneously regenerate had been lost for several millennia before *Miigaadiwin.* It is believed that the gene had been turned off by some early environmental disaster, that it was likewise turned on again by disaster at the time of the Healing. But in those early days, every community wanted a hospital or clinic that employed doctors and nurses working around the clock treating a myriad of injuries and illnesses. And even that was not enough. People travelled hundreds of kilometres to see specialists who could treat obscure conditions. Despite their best efforts to capture health, disease chased them to the grave."

It was Inaa's turn to interject. "But why were they so sick all the time in the first place?"

"Perhaps nutrition or pollution, or both. It's hard to say for sure. Barbara and William and their children kept a garden, like their parents before them, but they did not rely on it to grow the food they needed year-round. Cheap, new sources of oil meant that boats, trucks, and trains delivered produce from warmer climates, such as the southern states and even from across the oceans. It could be brought so fast that it was still edible when it arrived at the table! Of course, you might not agree if you tasted it, and it didn't do half what it ought to for a body, being picked half-ripe and stored in airless delivery crates. Still, people grew less and less food here as time went on until they had nearly forgotten how to tend the land altogether. At the same time, the rains and rivers polluted by the mill leached away the soil's goodness each season."

Rowan, Gizhaa, and Inaa nibbled contemplatively on their soft cheese.

"We can be thankful we do not live in those days! No doubt we can find some of the land's plentiful harvest on our way tomorrow. Cranberries should be on now." Rowan yawned and stretched. "But here I must leave off storytelling for tonight, for we have a good distance to travel again tomorrow. *Dibikigiizis*[9] has risen high. Praise the Creator who has restored us!"

---

9   *Dibikigiizis*: moon.

chapter four

WABUNUKEEG
"DAYBREAK PEOPLE"

Gizhaa unwrapped himself from his wool cocoon and crawled out from under the low-slung canopy they had draped. Heavy dew clung to the surrounding ferns and he carefully worked around them to keep his clothes dry. His father and Inaa still slept soundly; Gizhaa was always the early riser.

He grabbed the spent *waazakonenjigan* lamp from the rock hearth. Its glow had died long ago, but the morning light would reenergize it where he was going.

He scrubbed himself off with stream water before gathering a couple of small woven bags and starting out. He was headed for higher ground.

The trees soon thinned, damp earth giving way to grey bedrock underfoot. A few minutes later he crested the rock and stood overlooking a vast panorama. Wind from the lake whipped his brown hair back. He pulled his shoulders straight and breathed deeply, surveying the scene. From this vantage, he could see the North Channel of Lake Huron stretching as far as the eye could see to the east and west—crystal clear waters dotted by green islands.

But he turned full circle, away from the vista, scrutinizing the quiet forest from which he had just emerged. Something had drawn his attention. Was it the snap of a twig, a shadow that moved, or a hint on the breeze? He stood frozen, watching, for another minute before sitting down on the granite, settling the lamp in the morning light to harvest the sun's rays.

Gizhaa pulled a bag from his pocket. In a rock crevice at his feet lay a patch of blueberries, late in the season. They weren't as plentiful or large as the early berries, but they were no less delicious. He scooped them up and dropped them into his drawstring bag. Having emptied the patch, he stretched, cast a glance once more across the channel, and headed back toward the tree line.

He spotted another crevice nestled in the rocks, filled with ripe berries, and turned aside to empty it too. In fact, he did this several more times before it occurred to him that the morning sun was now high above the lake and beginning to warm his back. Grabbing the *waazakonenjigan*, he realized Inaa and his father would no doubt be up and have tended the alpacas. He'd miss breakfast if he didn't hurry.

Before he even arrived at camp, Gizhaa knew someone new had arrived. First it was the smell of manure from fifty meters away, then the sound of voices chatting amiably. Finally, Gizhaa could see the horse standing at the edge of the stream and a rider bent low in the saddle, his black ponytail falling over his shoulder.

"Gizhaa, we have a guest for breakfast," his father called cheerfully as Gizhaa drew near.

The stranger dismounted and offered a free hand to Gizhaa. His shake was firm and confident.

"Tom. Tom Waaban," he said, introducing himself with a nod of his dark head.

Gizhaa responded, too quickly. "Gizhaa, but you heard."

Inaa appeared at Gizhaa's side. She had apparently taken a few moments to rebraid her hair, which had none of its usual morning frizziness. "Tom is on his way to catch tomorrow's train, same as we are," she explained. "We'll have a travelling companion."

For some reason, Gizhaa disliked the word companion coming from Inaa's lips.

Tom smiled. "It's been a lonely trip from Toronto thus far, so I would be honoured to accompany you."

Gizhaa untied the two bags of blueberries from his belt. "I suppose I missed breakfast, but I brought some blueberries back from the ridge."

"An excellent crop. Strange that they are still in season," Rowan puzzled. "I wonder if we are having a second summer? They say it happens every few hundred years or so." He took the bag of blueberries and poured a few into his palm.

"And breakfast is just beginning," Inaa corrected. "The famous Selah granola is served."

Rowan turned to Tom. "You are welcome to join us."

Breakfast was a treat. Cold alpaca cream had been chilling overnight in the stream, and the granola was chock full of roasted pumpkin seeds and hazelnuts. Topped with fresh blueberries and drizzled with maple syrup, the combination was delectable. And Inaa wasn't too modest to point out that she had been perfecting the granola recipe for the past year, eliciting a shower of compliments from Tom.

"And what is the purpose of your trip, Tom?" Rowan asked.

"I am taking a job as assistant to the Foreign Affairs Minister."

"Then you are traveling all the way to the capital with us!"

Rowan began to gesture toward the parcel that held the tribute, but Gizhaa spoke up. "Congratulations. A prestigious appointment! You are a man of politics then?"

"We shall see." Tom laughed, and then sobered. "I would like to think I can make a difference. There are many changes afoot in our world. Our government will need to be ready to respond appropriately." His brown fingers wrapped a little tighter around the mug of steaming black liquid in his hands.

"Changes? I haven't heard any news of this," Rowan remarked.

Tom's dark eyes met Rowan's directly. "Some things are not revealed until the fullness of time."

Δ   Δ   Δ

The group was soon storing their belongings and securing their packs before taking to the trail. The wooded path opened onto a broad bedrock plateau above Lake Huron. The tree line shrouded the sweeping view Gizhaa had found his way to earlier that morning, but something else drew their attention to the centre of the clearing. A heavy metal pipe protruded from the rock as naturally as though it had grown there. The thick pipe, a hand span in diameter, was completely covered in rust, but it still rose straight a meter above the ground before ending in a metal cap.

Tom walked his horse up to it and kicked it with his foot. The pipe was solid. "What is this thing?"

"That's a capped ventilation pipe for a mine that once operated here," Rowan replied.

"Really? What did they mine?" Tom sounded genuinely interested.

Rowan shrugged. "Lots of things: copper, nickel, uranium. There were many mines in this area."

Inaa looked around the clearing. "But where is the entrance to the mine?"

"Oh, these mines travelled many kilometres underground. We're a long way from the entrance. If I remember correctly, this particular mine tunnelled under the lake some distance," Rowan said, straightening his pack and heading back toward the trail.

"Would there be any minerals left down there?" Tom asked, hurrying to keep up.

"Of course, but they closed these mines even before *Miigaadiwin*. The mineral concentration was too low to bother with. And after *Miigaadiwin*, who would want to spend their lives underground digging up rocks? Bio-mining was the future! Once they realized that the renewed ocean waters were a bonanza of minerals, once they had refined the bacteria that could collect those minerals, it was a whole new way of life for us. There was no going back."

Tom shook his head. "But not uranium. They don't have a bacterium that collects uranium."

"No, they don't mine uranium anymore," Rowan acknowledged.

Δ   Δ   Δ

It was less of a climb now as they headed away from the North Channel's steeper bluffs and along the gentler slopes of a river. Without the lake breeze, the autumn sun was soon warming their shoulders. When they came to a series of rapids, Tom's horse, which had been walking beside them without complaint, decided that the cascading water was too tempting to pass by. As he dipped his head in for a drink, Inaa plopped down on an outcropping of bedrock at the river's edge, pulling off her coat. The rock was sauna hot. Gizhaa released the alpacas' harnesses and the sure-footed beasts stepped down into the rushing water to drink deeply.

Tom loosened the horse's cinch and gently lifted each leg, checking its hooves. "So what takes you three to the capital? Do you folks often travel?"

Inaa laughed. "'Often' might be an overstatement. This will be my first trip to Iqaluit. We do have relatives we'll be staying with, though. Uncle Ben and Aunt Nancy have been there forever, it seems."

Gizhaa began clicking to the alpacas to come out of the water.

Inaa shrugged nonchalantly. "And we have a meeting with the Prime Minister in a couple days. Father has been asked…"

At that moment, the first alpaca exiting the water brushed up against the horse's side, causing it to shimmy sideways. This in turn pushed Tom backwards two steps, where he proceeded to lose his balance on a loose rock and topple into a shallow pool at the water's edge. The sun-warmed water sprayed over Inaa. Tom jumped up dripping wet, his dark hair plastered to his forehead. Inaa instantly began to laugh and soon tears were rolling down her face. Tom began wringing out the corners of his shirt, apologizing profusely, but her laughter was infectious and he soon joined in. Even Gizhaa, who was far more concerned with keeping the wayward alpaca out of the horse's way, wore a big grin.

"All right, circus people," Rowan said, smiling as he shook his head. "Time to hit the trail if we're going to make it before sundown."

Gizhaa was first to the path, calling back, "How about you pick up where you left off last night, Father? Seems we could use some distraction for the afternoon hike."

Rowan cocked his head, studying Gizhaa a moment. "Perhaps your alpaca's distracting antics were not entirely accidental," he murmured under his breath.

chapter five

AKI
"EARTH"

"Gizhaa and Inaa, your ninth grandfather, Howard, was the son of William and Barbara I spoke of last night. When Howard was a man, the forests we see here were thinning. The days were passing when you could make a living from lumber as his father and grandfather had. He wanted a job that paid enough to start a family and he already had his sights set on marrying a beautiful girl he'd met at college. The discovery that a whole new world of opportunity was opening up, literally beneath his feet, was exactly the ticket he needed. When the mining company came to town offering contracts to young men, he was among the first to sign on.

"Minerals trapped under the earth's surface for millennia were far more valuable than gold and could now be extracted and refined. They were exactly what the new economy needed. While copper, nickel, and silver had been dug out of the earth locally for decades, a new mineral vein had been discovered. This time it was uranium, a metal that could be refined until it reached such an unstable form that its power was nearly uncontrollable. On a minute scale, it was used to treat cancer, one of the deadliest diseases of that time. On a large scale, it was used to produce electricity. And yet far beyond that, it was used to create a weapon of unparalleled force. And it is precisely here you might see that our story begins to intersect with *Miigaadiwin*."

"Because this uranium was used in the war?" Inaa asked in awe.

Rowan walked on without pause. "Not exactly, but I'm getting there. As insane as it sounds to you and me, the value of uranium was so great that the mining companies would stop at nothing to reach it. Of course, there were the holes drilled into the rock that men descended into. That was bad enough. The air was so toxic that many of those early miners died of a mysterious cancer before sixty years of age. But long before that, the darkness they were plunged into day after day eroded their spirits and many fell to addictions of all kinds. They were scheduled to work nonstop rotations of labour. Producing uranium round the clock boosted company profits. Some men worked every night and slept during the day, rarely seeing family and friends.

"But the miners didn't stop there; they learned to drill deeper. Soon the holes were hundreds of meters deep and large enough that massive machines could be lowered into them to move mountains of rock to the surface. Fresh air was pumped from the surface to keep the workers alive, but it did nothing to revitalize their stale spirits."

Tom pulled his wet shirt away from his skin to encourage it to air dry faster. "Did your ancestors understand the wider impact of their sacrifice?"

Rowan laughed. "Not a bit. At sundown, Grandpa Howard travelled an hour to the mine. There he put on multiple layers of clothing—the mine was intensely cold and damp—and a hard hat, for at any moment a falling rock might kill him. On top of the hard hat was a single light to shine into the blackness. He then crowded into a cage with fifty other men to descend into the mine. As the door shut, a cable lowered them at hundreds of meters a minute.

"Once inside the mine, Grandpa Howard's job was driving a train through the underground tunnels carrying crushed rock to the lift. He spent his night mostly alone and the work was dangerous. The rock was blasted to pieces before he arrived on the scene, of course, but many fragments could shift without warning, causing an avalanche. Or an errant rock could block the chute that loaded the train. While prying that rock loose, a torrent could rush down on him. Or the ventilation system could fail. Or the power could go out. Or a tunnel could cave."

Gizhaa shrugged his shoulders. "Why would you put up with that? Sounds murderous to me!"

"Needless to say, the pay was good, and he was soon able to marry his sweetheart and start a family of his own. Miners could afford many luxuries that had been unheard of a generation before: fancy cars, large homes, electronic gadgets, and closets full of clothes. But the costs of such affluence slowly crept up on them. Families struggled to pay for the never-ending upgrades to their lifestyles.

"Still, the area was booming and that was all that mattered. Following the mines, refineries were built to purify the raw ore. Finely tuned machines crushed, melted, and separated the rock until the purest of elements remained—at the expense of the air. Black plumes of smoke rose from these refineries, sending toxins high into the atmosphere, then raining them back down again.

"The lakes began to die, ever so slowly. One species at a time disappeared from the waters. At first no one noticed. And when they did, they didn't know why. Before the refineries came, it was said that the giant lake sturgeon fish were so plentiful that you could cross to Manitoulin Island without getting your feet wet by walking on their backs! I doubt that, but fifty years later there was hardly a sturgeon to be found. *Ahaaw*, I suppose that is why your brother Simon was so fascinated by them—such a beautiful picture of our redemption, fish!"

Rowan paused and let their minds imagine what it might be like to walk across the lake on the backs of fish. Tom laughed out loud, having never before conceived of such an abundance of life, but for Gizhaa and Inaa the image was as bittersweet as their memories of Simon.

"When it seemed they were all dead," Rowan continued, "they returned suddenly, stronger and more graceful than anyone could remember. Simon's biggest sturgeon was at least twenty kilograms heavier than the record before *Miigaadiwin*. Ah, yes, back to *Miigaadiwin*.

"Well, no one was very comfortable with all the fallout of the mining industry, but it was the backbone of the area. And everyone knew that life without it meant unemployment, poverty, and hunger. It wasn't just individuals who needed this economy. The national government had been digging itself deeper and deeper into debt to maintain the services that people had come to demand. The costs were so burdensome that the government required more and more taxes, even while the people called for more and more care. Such lucrative industries as uranium were needed to keep the whole system from going bankrupt.

"And so, you see, at that very moment in history the entire system was ripe for revolution. It had been seething beneath the surface for years—a cry for health, prosperity, and longevity. An elixir of life that could sustain them all. It was an elusive dream. And those who were watching knew the change had to come. Grandpa Howard was not one of them. He could never have imagined life after *Miigaadiwin*. It was beyond his wildest dreams.

"Well, as I said before, uranium could be purified into a form so unstable that its power was almost uncontrollable. As someone once said, absolute power corrupts absolutely. Unfortunately, the very substance fuelling the local economy also fuelled a greater revolution. Not the one just beneath the surface in our country, but one a world away in the Middle East. No, no, Canada wasn't shipping uranium to the Middle East, not even in those days, but in a way the very uranium being mined here was partly responsible. You see, a great power imbalance existed—by nature, it had to exist with such weapons in hand—and this had begun to eat away at international relations, dissolving good will. The desire to correct that imbalance, or maybe just the desire for infinite power, drove the leaders of the Middle East's powerful alliance to develop their own weapons. *Ahaaw!* Such foolish—"

"Surely they could see what would come of this race," Gizhaa interrupted.

"No doubt you are right, Gizhaa. It shouldn't have surprised anyone when the war began, not with guns or bombs, but very insidiously as a new government was formed out of that alliance. The cry that had been growing in Canada was a mere shadow of the revolution sweeping across the Middle East. When it had reached its zenith, the leadership that arose was unlike any before it. Indeed, they had finally gained absolute power and they would stop at nothing to fulfill their vision for the world."

chapter six

⊙ODENΔWΔN
"TOWNS/VILLΔGES"

T hey made excellent progress that day despite their late start. Tom's horse
could carry some of their supplies, lightening the alpacas' load and quickening the group's pace. By late afternoon, there were clear signs that Sudbury
was close. The trail broadened, and in places they could even see the old railroad
ties underfoot where the trail was well worn. They now passed occasional travellers
heading into the country. Each one greeted them traditionally: *"Aki Ishpiming!"*—
Earth, Heaven, recalling the ancient script that said "on earth as it is in heaven."

Sometimes Gizhaa was sure there were others behind them as well. But he
couldn't see them through the trees, only the occasional flight of a startled bird.

They reached the city while the sky was still bright but the sun was sliding
below the trees.

The city limits weren't much unlike the Selah homestead. Clusters of yurts radiated from the trail, each brightly coloured tent illuminated by an inner glow like paper lanterns lining the way. The local livestock were quick to greet the travellers. Flop-
py-eared goats licked their hands, a curious mini dairy cow watched them over her
gate, and a well-plumed rooster heralded their arrival. Soon they were passing places
of business—veterinarians, woodworkers, solar providers, greenhouse builders.

They hurried on until they finally reached a large building. They had passed a
handful of solid structures, but this one was entirely unique; it was rectangular, tow-
ering eight stories high, and covered in red brick. Every window was glassed over,
unlike the yurt windows which were normally rolled open and shut with a piece of
felt. Before them the two large glass doors of the front entrance invited them in. It
was clear that this building recalled an architectural era long passed.

"And here we are, just in time," Rowan announced as the sun slipped beneath the tree line on the horizon. He pulled the door wide open and Tom accordingly opened the matching one. Inaa nodded her thanks as she stepped between them, but Gizhaa stayed behind.

"I'll wait with the animals and get them their dinner while you get settled," Gizhaa said, excusing himself.

As the doors fell shut behind the three, an elderly man greeted them warmly from behind a large desk. "*Boozhoo;* Welcome. *Aki Ishpiming!*"

Rowan responded in kind and added, "We have reservations for rooms tonight and for train tickets to Iqaluit tomorrow."

"Yes, yes, you must be the Selah family!" The man could have been two hundred years old or eight hundred. It was impossible to tell, but his quick smile reminded Inaa of a child's—pure, uninhibited delight.

"Well, two out of three of the Selahs," Rowan replied. "Our travelling companion is Tom—"

"Thomas Waaban," Tom finished. "I don't have a reservation."

"There is plenty of room. Would you like to stay next to your friends?"

Tom nodded. "Thank you. That would be perfect."

"I was expecting you folks would want dinner when you arrived, so I've taken the liberty of asking the restaurant to hold several meals," the man behind the desk said. "I'm sure there will be enough for you as well, Thomas."

"Excellent! I've heard the Canadian Arctic Railways foodservice is world class," Rowan enthused.

Their host grinned and chuckled. "I believe we've set the standard quite high, to be honest. I think you'll enjoy tonight's entrée: stuffed portobello mushrooms and hickory gravy. My absolute favourite."

During this conversation, Inaa had been wandering about the expansive foyer. The perimeter of the room was lit by strings of hundreds of tiny glowing lights. The windows below sparkled with their reflection, but beyond that yurts flowed down the hill toward the darkening city in a glittering waterfall of light. A seating area had been arranged at the far end of the room where four carved wooden benches faced each other, their gently curving backs adorned with heaps of scarlet, velvety cushions. They reminded Inaa that her feet ached.

Between her and the benches, she discovered something far more interesting. In the centre of the room, a massive ball sat atop a rough stone basin, forming an impressive monument. The black ball of smooth, polished granite glistened in the room's warm lights. Inaa came closer and leaned in. A map of the globe had been etched on its surface, but she didn't recognize the coasts, for it was the world as it had looked millennia earlier.

She reached out to touch the globe's surface and was startled to find that her fingertips became wet. The basin beneath the globe carried an imperceptible stream of water which bathed the gleaming ball. She reached out again and gently traced the Canadian continent. This time it moved beneath her fingers. Intrigued, she gently pressed further and the massive sphere spun freely.

"You are wondering how it works?" the host called across the room. He came out from behind the desk and joined her at the centrepiece. "This sculpture stood at the entrance to a demonstration mine near here a thousand years ago. Granite is extremely durable, though it has needed some resurfacing. The stone itself weighs over three tonnes, but the constant flow of water beneath it is enough to bear the weight of the rock, allowing you to spin it freely in its bowl." He demonstrated by giving the ball a mighty push. Inaa wouldn't have expected such strength from this diminutive man. The ball spun wildly but smoothly, and continued to do so for several minutes. "We have maintained the sculpture here to remind us that even the most common of forces can lift the mightiest of burdens."

His eyes twinkled as he continued. "But you have noticed that the map is no longer entirely accurate. Before *Miigaadiwin*, much of the planet's freshwater was trapped as ice at the poles. That ice has been melting for the past thousand years or so, changing the coastlines dramatically, although perhaps less than you might expect. The earth was quite a dry place before *Miigaadiwin*. For instance, here," he jabbed his finger abruptly onto the spinning globe, bringing it to a sudden halt, "was once a great desert that covered over nine million square kilometres. Today it is the Sahara Steppe, a lush grassland sprinkled with a dozen or so freshwater lakes complete with islands, where once only dunes of sand stood. We have *Miigaadiwin* to thank for Earth's ring of ice particles and dust. That ring in space has done much to evenly distribute rainfall globally. With the melting of the polar ice, there has been a rapid increase in the amount of water vapour trapped in the atmosphere, a sort of canopy as it were. That has made all the difference to places like the Sahara. And it has prevented the ocean levels from rising as quickly as they may have."

Inaa began to wonder if she had just met the Canadian Arctic Rail's resident encyclopaedia. "This is a unique building," she said. "It's obviously been here for hundreds of years. Was it built as a Canadian Arctic Hotel?"

"No, no. Its history is much older than the northern rail system. I suppose you know that the original rail lines spanned the continent east to west—from sea to shining sea, as they said. But after *Miigaadiwin*, once the great riches of the far north

27

opened up, it was decided that the severely antiquated system would be replaced, with the addition of a modern north-south connection. And of course, once the capital was moved to Iqaluit, the new railway became necessary.

"This building was actually a hospital before *Miigaadiwin*, packed full of patients, doctors, and nurses on any given day. Thankfully, that became completely unnecessary. With the new line running practically past the back door, this became a Canadian Arctic Hotel!" He threw his arms open with the finesse of an entertainer. "Of course, with some major renovations."

Gizhaa had returned some time during this discussion and now spoke from behind them. "It's a huge place! Do you ever fill up?"

"We are surprisingly busy, with being at the junction of Lake Huron and the north line to Iqaluit. Many of our guests are travelling to or from the capital, as you are. Occasionally we're able to host important diplomats, as we are tonight, especially during the feast season. It is a fascinating place to work! But in answer to your question, no, we have never 'filled up.' Now then, your sister looks like she is ready for a bit of a rest."

The man smiled at Inaa, who had found her way to the cushioned benches at last and was just pulling off her second boot.

Several minutes later, they had unloaded their bags in their respective rooms, washed up, and headed back to the restaurant.

"Thank you for your horse today, Tom," Rowan said. "We may have had to travel by *waazakonenjigan* without his extra load-bearing. It's a bit farther than I remember."

As they entered the restaurant, Rowan sank gratefully onto a carved bench.

"*Miigwech!*"[10] he said to the boy who placed tall glasses of water before them.

"My pleasure," the youth responded. "We have your dinners held warm in the kitchen. I hope you don't mind having the special. The kitchen is already closed for the evening."

"Of course. Please don't let us be any trouble, and thank you for your kindness," Rowan responded warmly.

A minute later, they were eating in silence.

After some time, Inaa spoke. "I know there is nothing quite like a hot meal after a long day's march in fresh air and sunshine, but I still think this may be one of the best meals I've ever tasted!"

"You may be saying that again tomorrow night," Tom warned her. "It's true that the Canadian Arctic prides itself on serving gourmet meals for breakfast, lunch, and dinner. Prepare to be stuffed!"

---

10 *Miigwech*: thank you.

At that moment, the boy reappeared carrying a tray with four cheesecakes dripping with raspberry sauce.

"You can say that again!" Inaa exclaimed.

"I'm finished here for the evening," the boy said. "But can I get you anything before I go?"

"That will be plenty," Rowan replied. "*Miigwech* once more." He turned to Tom. "Tell us where you come from. It sounds as though you are a frequent traveller."

Tom swallowed a mouthful of cheesecake. "I've been visiting my grandparents these past few days. They live very close to where I met you this morning, so this is really my people's ancient tribal region. The horse is actually theirs. They will collect her from the stable in a few days when they're in town. I'm living in New York—or rather, I have been until now. I took a train east and then transferred to the north line. But the trip gave me a chance to stop and visit them for a couple days before I start my new job. Hence my recent experience with train dining!"

"What's New York like?" Inaa asked, tilting her head.

"The ocean on our doorstep is always the highlight for visitors. Have you ever seen the ocean? There's nothing like it. The breakers crash over the boardwalks. The beaches stretch for kilometres. You can take a boat out to sea and there's nothing but water and sky to be seen."

Rowan pushed his empty plate aside rather abruptly. "No, we're not the seafaring type, I'm afraid, Tom." His usual gentle smile was gone. His brow had furrowed. "I have never understood why anyone would enjoy boating!"

Gizhaa stood. "How about I return our dishes to the kitchen? We'll have an early start tomorrow."

Tom shrugged. "I suppose I should check on the horse before I turn in."

"You'll find him in the rear of the stables," Gizhaa said as he deftly piled up the dishes.

The group said an awkward goodnight and moved their separate ways.

Inaa and her father walked together down a long corridor toward their rooms. At the door of Inaa's room, her father stopped.

"I'm sorry, Inaa. Perhaps we will skip the storytelling tonight. I think I've said enough for one day."

She nodded, accepting this as his apology for snapping at Tom. She knew the memory of Simon's drowning weighed heavy on him.

"It's okay, Dad," she said softly. "I know."

She squeezed his hand before turning the door handle to her room. Alone inside, she sank down on the soft bed and cried.

chapter seven

ISHKODEWIDAABAAN
"TRAIN"

The sky was barely lit as Gizhaa noiselessly opened the door of his room and stepped into the corridor. He paused briefly and stretched, then turned his head toward Inaa's room and listened intently. Moving down the hall, he paused outside Tom's door, also listening. Satisfied that he was the only one up, he carried on down the hall.

Just as he was about to enter the empty lobby, he heard a soft click from one of the doors he had just passed. He hesitated but saw no one—another early riser, no doubt. He moved on through the lobby into the fresh air.

Gizhaa shook himself as he made his way around the eastern side of the hotel, where the first rays of sun were warming the red brick wall. Why did he feel so edgy, so suspicious? Inaa was always telling him to lighten up and accept things for what they seemed to be! Even his father sometimes raised his eyebrows at Gizhaa's "instincts." But he'd been right... sometimes. And this time he couldn't shake some very nasty vibes. First, Tom wasn't everything he seemed to be. Sure, his story sounded good—a dedicated grandson, an up-and-coming politician, an honoured *Nisayenh*. But what wasn't he saying? It was a hint of disdain or some allegiance or passion of which he did not speak.

Secondly, Gizhaa had felt someone following them several times—near the cliff, on the trail, in the hallway. No one could deny that Gizhaa's senses were ultra-sharp. His family relied on it daily on the farm. He was the first to know if a doe was in labour, a guest was arriving, or a child was roaming too far. But why on earth would anyone follow them? It was ludicrous.

By the time Gizhaa was brushing down the alpacas, his mind was a blur, yet one thought rose with absolute clarity: this trip was a calling, not just an invitation—a command issued by the Creator in millennia out of mind: "Celebrate the Festival of Ingathering at the end of the year, when you gather in your crops from the field."[11] He had been called to make this journey with his father to deliver the tribute as far as the Canadian capital. For some reason, he had been chosen and he would use every skill, every gift he had been given, to finish the job, no matter how crazy it seemed. If his gifts made him suspicious, then so be it.

Normally what would have taken Gizhaa half an hour to complete in the stable was done in five minutes. The alpacas may have wondered what had come over their groomer; where were their rubs and talks and treats? But a new passion had seized Gizhaa and he could not get back to his father fast enough.

The stable hands were just arriving. Gizhaa immediately subjected them to the most authoritative two-minute lecture on alpaca care they had ever received. Then he disappeared, taking long, decisive steps back to his room.

He wasn't listening for clicks in the hallway anymore. By the time he burst back into the room, he was nearly weak with relief to find his father just rising from the desk with a folded piece of paper in his hand. Beside him on the bed lay the precious gift, still wrapped snugly in its felt blanket.

"A letter for your mother," Rowan said, waving the piece of paper gently. "She'll be glad to hear how we are making out."

"Would you like me to take it to the front desk?" Gizhaa offered automatically, then thought better of it.

"*Miigwech*, that won't be necessary. I believe I'll see if there's a traveller headed out our way to pass it along quicker." Rowan sealed an envelope. "Have you seen Inaa yet this morning?"

"No. I'll go knock next door." Gizhaa hesitated, his hand on the knob. "Dad, I think it might be wise if we kept your mission, this tribute, under wraps. I don't have a good feeling about this leg of our journey."

Rowan raised his eyebrows, but Gizhaa didn't wait to hear whether it was in rebuke or appreciation.

Gizhaa walked into the hallway and knocked lightly on Inaa's door, looking up as it immediately swung open and Inaa appeared. He was taken aback. Having known his sister for fifty-five years, he had never seen her quite as she looked now. Her long, blond braid had been replaced by a sweep of golden hair that crowned her head. Her sun-drenched skin now highlighted her rosy cheeks and her blue eyes shone out from under richly hued lids. She was stunning.

"Inaa?" He caught himself. "I mean, you're up early this morning."

---

11 Exodus 23:16, NIV.

"It's an important day. I mean, we haven't seen Uncle Ben and Aunt Nancy in a decade," she said, faltering. "Is Father ready for breakfast?"

"I think so. Why don't you head over to the dining room with him? I'd like to finish packing," he said, but he silently added, *And stand guard.*

When they were gone, Gizhaa quickly dumped the contents of his backpack. He unwrapped the felt that protected the tribute. His hands hesitated as he peeled the layer back, then he breathed a sigh of relief. His mother had added a second layer of fine linen wrapping. He left the tribute wrapped in the inner lining, but carefully moved it into his backpack. It didn't completely fill the sack, so he added a pair of pants and shirt on top and a handful of toiletries. Satisfied that it was roughly the size and shape a backpack should be, he hurriedly stowed the rest of his belongings back in the tribute's original wrapping. It didn't look quite right. After several frustrated attempts to reorganize his clothes and rewrap the bundle, he decided it might pass for his mother's original gift-wrapping.

At that moment, there came a knock at the door. Gizhaa opened it to Tom, who smiled widely.

"Good morning! Are you folks ready for breakfast?"

"Actually, my father and Inaa are over there right now, but I'd be happy to join you." Gizhaa slung the backpack onto his shoulders, glancing around the room one last time.

By the time the last arrangements had been made—bills paid, rooms emptied, and luggage labelled—it was an hour later and the Canadian Arctic was flying into the station. It was a grand sight to see and a grand morning to see it. The first rays Gizhaa had seen earlier had grown into a full, sunlit cobalt blue sky, with *Didibinin-jiibizon*,[12] Earth's gas halo, clearly visible, a gorgeous silver streak that arced across the sky like a thousand clustered jet trails. The train whistle could be heard first, some distance to the south but approaching quickly; the note swelled until the engine burst over the ridge and a great sigh of air escaped. Inaa stepped back, uncertain as it slowed to a perfect stop exactly in front of the stone platform. It was a beautiful, gleaming red engine and, had Gizhaa been fifty years younger, he would have liked to have taken home a model toy.

The body of the train extended past them, each car shining like the proud engine. Curved glass arched up the sides and over much of the roof, but the centre line, facing skyward, was reserved for solar panels reflecting the rich blue sky.

After that initial moment of awe, the doors slid open and soon the platform was a hub of life as passengers exited and porters busily gathered tickets and bags.

---

12 *Didibininjiibizon*: ring.

Gizhaa dutifully handed his ticket to the uniformed woman who approached him, but he shook his head and patted his shoulder strap when she motioned toward the luggage cart.

Inaa stepped aboard and Gizhaa followed, but he immediately felt he should have removed his travelling shoes, for the floor was covered in deep carpet—red, no less. But he moved on and soon they were sliding into a cushioned booth. He was struck by the amount of light in the car; even the yurt, with its round skylight, was rather dim inside, but this was quite different as nearly the entire roof was open to the sky. The side windows and end walls were trimmed in wood mouldings and the benches they sat on matched the woodwork.

Looking back onto the train platform, Gizhaa could see that his father was still there, chatting with a passenger who had just exited the train. The man's brown curls nodded as Rowan pulled an envelope from his pocket and handed it to him, motioning to the west. Then the warning whistle was blowing and Rowan was grabbing his bag, shaking the stranger's hand warmly, and running to enter the train.

He slid into the booth beside Tom across from Inaa.

"There, I did get my letter off to Mother," Rowan said, sighing. "Nice fellow. He approached me, too, asking about travelling our direction and looking for accommodation up the trail, so it worked out perfectly."

That morning was a glorious time and Gizhaa's fears seemed far away and trivial. The train rushed across the landscape, first through dense forests, but when they suddenly emerged from the canopy at a sparkling lake they briefly saw the tall fir trees across the water, pointing like spires to heaven atop granite outcroppings. Then they plunged back under tree cover and the green needles turned into layers of gold and red and orange leaves.

A bit later, the forest gave way to marshes and the train slowed for some time as the rail curved round the wetlands. A grazing moose lifted its heavy head nonchalantly to watch them pass and a pair of mallards rose gracefully from the water and flew away. Marshes gave way to rolling glacial hills, and hills to prairies, and prairies to the limitless expanse of James Bay, and always under that open glass roof that flooded them with golden sunlight.

All the while, the foursome watched and laughed and ate to their hearts' content. By noon, Gizhaa had completely forgotten his reticence and discovered another delight about train travel: the flow of people through the car—couples and singles, children and elderly, dark and fair. When a petite Asian woman with silky black hair and bright eyes stopped beside his seat to allow another guest room to pass, she smiled at him and politely excused herself in a crisp accent. Gizhaa decided that train travel could be very interesting. At that point, he might have taken himself for a tour of the more delightful aspects of the train, but he remembered the backpack stowed under his seat and decided that hauling it through the narrow aisle would be unacceptable train etiquette.

As the supper hour drew near, he looked for an excuse to stretch his legs. An elderly Hispanic man approached their seats and stopped in front of Rowan. He held out a firm hand to Rowan and then Gizhaa as both rose to greet him.

"*On earth as it is in heaven.* I believe you are Rowan Selah? I am Santiago and I will be representing my country, Mexico, at the Fall Festival. You are also travelling to Jerusalem, are you not, Rowan?"

Gizhaa could see Tom's eyebrows lift in surprise.

Rowan laughed. "Yes, yes! We will be traveling companions, I suppose, Santiago!"

Santiago's smile broadened. "My wife and I are touring this beautiful country before my departure from Iqaluit. Would you like to join us for dinner at our table? I would love to get to know you better."

"*Miigwech.* That would be wonderful!"

As Rowan and Santiago moved off down the aisle, they chatted excitedly like children sharing a secret adventure.

"Well, I wouldn't mind a bit of exploring about this place," Tom said as he slid out of the seat. "How about it, Inaa?"

She needed no inviting, for she was already halfway out.

"I guess I'll catch a nap then while you're out touring." Gizhaa gave an exaggerated sigh and plopped himself back down. He felt so relaxed and untroubled, or perhaps the rhythm of the train was having an effect. He stretched his long legs out in front of him and closed his eyes.

"You won't mind if I have a seat?"

Gizhaa started and his eyes flew open. It was a feeling he was entirely unaccustomed to. Had he fallen asleep? Across from him sat the pretty girl he had seen earlier, now watching him with an amused expression. How had she crept up on him like that?

"*Aaniin.*[13] Not at all, please have a seat."

"*Miigwech*, I have," she said, almost laughing at his discomfort. Her playfulness quickly vanished. "Gizhaa, I need to speak with you quickly before your family returns."

---

13 *Aaniin*: hi.

His pulse suddenly jumped. Clearly this was not the chance encounter he had thought it was. "Have we met?"

"I have been following you—well, not *you* exactly—but you have noticed, have you not?" Her voice was very quiet and Gizhaa leaned toward her, his hands spreading out on the table between them.

"I knew it!" he whispered.

"You were a wise choice for this mission, but there is more at stake here than you realize. I don't have time to explain much, but I'm taking the risk of speaking to you now because I believe you may be able to help me—to help all of us."

Gizhaa's brow furrowed. "But I don't even know who you are."

"Of course. My name is Ya Min. I am the Chinese ambassador to Canada."

"Really? You seem … young for that job," Gizhaa said before he stopped himself.

She did laugh now, a musical sound that reminded Gizhaa of his little sister Nanda. "That is a very nice compliment, but looks can be deceiving! Anyway, that is my official title, but I am asking you to help me in another role. It has come to the attention of the *Ogimaa*[14] that a new group called the Revival is seeking to replace the governments he has established. Our concern is that they have set their sights on Canada, but they have already infiltrated nations around the globe."

"You are working for the *Ogimaa*?" Gizhaa spoke in astonishment.

She pressed a finger to her lips. "Are you not?" she whispered.

Gizhaa thought of the backpack and wondered how much she knew. "Point taken. Go on."

She motioned out the window while a fellow traveller passed in the aisle. "A Macaque peach orchard in Northern Quebec! You call it kiwi. I love that Canada has adopted the Chinese national fruit. How the world has grown." She leaned in closely once the aisle was clear. "We have reason to believe that your friend Tom is being courted by the Revivalists. Once he takes his new position, he would become a valuable asset to them. I have been tracking him for some time already, but your family has quickly won his trust. I believe you may be able to gather information from him that I cannot."

Gizhaa's heart sank. "Ya Min, I cannot deceive Tom, though you're right that I don't trust him."

"No, Gizhaa, I don't want you to deceive him. Please, just keep your ears open. The Revival's goals would destroy everything I have been working toward as ambassador."

"What kind of goals?"

---

14 *Ogimaa*: king.

"There are many who would like to see Earth return to the ancient days of prosperity, but they choose to forget the price it came with. I have observed the negotiation of many agreements between China and Canada over the years. Together we have shown the world that we can recover our water systems, restoring life to both land and people. But the Revival cares nothing for the land, the water. Their plans for wealth would return us to the dark ages of creation!"

Gizhaa wondered how so much passion could be tucked into such a small person, how she could whisper something in that musical lilt and make it sound like a call to arms.

"Then I will do everything I can to help," he said.

"*Miigwech*. I will be in touch soon." She rose quickly and slid into the aisle. "You have been given a gift for such a time as this. You will know how to use it."

And then she was swaying easily toward the far door of the car.

Before she was out of sight, Gizhaa heard the click of the rear cabin door and knew without glancing over his shoulder that Inaa and Tom had returned. But the shimmer of black hair was gone like a mirage and then Inaa was standing over him asking, "How was your nap, brother?"

chapter eight

NITAMOOZHAAN
"FIRSTBORN"

Santiago ushered Rowan to a table, and when he had introduced his wife they sat together over cool glasses of kiwi water.

"What a privilege it will be to celebrate the Fall Festival at the King's table!" Santiago said, a touch of awe entering his voice. "Perhaps we may even meet him in person?"

Rowan sipped contemplatively. "It certainly seems surreal, doesn't it? The Festival reminds us of the beginning of his reign, but they say it was celebrated for millennia before he arrived."

"How is that possible?" Santiago tapped the table in front of Rowan. "Now then, tell us, Rowan, how the Festival came to be celebrated by your people here in Canada."

Rowan was an expert at weaving together his people's story and the world in which it came to be.

"In time out of mind, Creator taught his children to celebrate a festival after the harvest of their crops in the fall. For the seven days of their festival they were to live in temporary shelters, to remember that they were passing through a temporary life, journeying toward an eternal home. It was a beautiful picture, a rich annual lesson in the mystery of life.

"These children of the Creator—my people know them as the *Nitamoozhaan*, the firstborn—were scattered abroad on the earth and many forgot their Father, but not all. There were some who remembered who they were, some who carried the truth with them wherever they settled, and some who came to Canada with that truth. Thankfully, over the millennia the Creator's festival migrated here."

Santiago nodded his encouragement for Rowan to continue.

"Of course, you know as well as we do that throughout history people have worshipped gods. Sometimes they gave them familiar names and forms, Baal or Zeus, but often they were simply ideas like wealth or wisdom. I suppose every age of history and every culture had its household gods. It was no different here in Canada. However, the Ancient Peoples of Canada passed on many stories of Creator. They, too, had celebrated a fall harvest for many generations, perhaps heralding from a time when all the peoples of the earth came from one family. So, there were some among them who gladly received the full knowledge of the Creator by name when it was finally made known by the offspring of the *Nitamoozhaan*. The Creator's Fall Festival became a time of great joy to them.

"But as the days of *Miigaadiwin* drew near, many people rejected their creator and a new god garnered unprecedented popularity on earth. In every nation, even in Canada, there were many worshippers of the god of the *Ohshkagoonjing Giizis*.[15] The effect here was no less influential, though less dramatic than in other places. The culture struggled to adapt. The leaders rejected discussion. The political system attempted to maintain a semblance of brave unity. Silencing dissension became the norm, until our nation lost its voice altogether.

"So the war here in Canada really began, not with bombs but with politics. *Ahaaw*, there had been so many revolutions and civil wars in the years before *Miigaadiwin* that most people hardly paid attention anymore. It was so far away and it went on for so long that no one knew what else to do. The *Ohshkagoonjing Giizis*—you may know them merely as *Ohsh*—had been fighting amongst themselves for centuries, as different factions sought for control in the world to the east. But here it was different. More civilized, people thought. We were peacekeepers, not warriors."

Santiago leaned in. "How could such a change have occurred without anyone noticing?"

"To be sure, some did notice. Even before *Miigaadiwin*, the First and Second World Wars convinced many that the world was ending. Indeed, when the first atomic bomb—which, by the way, our own Canadian uranium researchers worked on!—was dropped on Japan in the year 5705, many people thought it was the beginning of the end. After the second bomb fell, at least 150,000 people died, some immediately, but many in the months afterwards. It was hoped that the sheer terror of a weapon that could instantly destroy an entire city would be enough to settle any future wars before they began. Quite the contrary. In the seventy years following the Second World War, there were at least seventy civil wars around the world, each one ripping countries apart. It was the bloodiest season the earth had ever seen. Much

---

15 *Ohshkagoonjing Giizis*: crescent moon.

later, it became clear that many of these unrelated conflicts around the globe had a common core—*Ohshkagoonjing Giizis* was gaining power.

"After the world wars, people of the Word searched the ancient prophecies to understand the outcome of these days. Nothing seemed to add up, but the wars had unveiled one unforeseen change. As prophesied by Isaiah millennia earlier, Creator returned the *Nitamoozhaan*[16] to their land. At the very end of his prophetic work, Isaiah had written, 'Can a country be born in a day or a nation be brought forth in a moment? Yet no sooner is Zion in labour than she gives birth to her children.'[17]

"And of course that is exactly what had happened. Since the Second World War, there had been an effort to completely destroy the *Nitamoozhaan*. It was nothing short of demonic, as millions of men, women, and children were murdered. The world council agreed to restore to the *Nitamoozhaan* a national homeland. Isaiah's nation was indeed brought forth in a moment!"

"Incredible, isn't it?" Santiago murmured. "It never fails to give me goosebumps."

Rowan paused gravely. "As you well know, the creation of that nation spawned a tide of refugees—those suddenly forced to choose between their homes and a new foreign government in their land. In the decades that followed, the *Nitamoozhaan*'s land seemed to be a source of unending violence. Within days of its declaration of statehood, the *Nitamoozhaan* were at war with their neighbours, a scenario that would repeat itself dozens more times over the years. On the one hand, you had many *Nitamoozhaan* with a deep fear instilled by the genocide of the Second World War; on the other hand, growing resentment among the land's refugees pushed the two sides ever further apart. It seemed peace could never come.

"*Ahaaw*, it was perhaps not much different than the great divide that separated our own peoples in Canada, the First Nations and the settlers from the east. Yet today my people walk side by side with our honoured brothers. And even our own beloved Prime Minister is a wise elder! As it is written, 'How pleasant it is when brothers live together in unity!'"[18]

Santiago's brown eyes crinkled, almost disappearing with his smile. "We have also found the blessing of unity among our people."

"And so, too, the peace for the *Nitamoozhaan* and their brothers would come," Rowan went on. "I am getting ahead of myself. Back to the civil wars. The world to the east gradually descended into a time of turmoil. As I told my children yesterday,

---

16 *Nitamoozhaan*: firstborn.

17 Isaiah 66:8, NIV.

18 Psalm 133:1, ISV.

the availability of nuclear weapons had no restraining power over regional conflicts. Unbelievably, there were forty-eight million refugees in the world at that time, many fleeing these internal uprisings.

"Most people of the east were desperate for a solution that would allow them to once more live and work in peace. As the situation wore on for years, the world finally joined their cause, for it was not only the citizens of these countries who were suffering; the regional conflict had spilled over into a global economic crisis. Since the east was the source of a great deal of the world's oil supply, any conflict in the region meant an increase in prices. At that time, the entire economic system was built on transportation of goods powered by oil derivatives. As fuel prices went up, everything went up. Around the world, food prices hit new highs and employment hit new lows.

"Just when it looked like the global economy was about to spin into a full-scale depression, the leaders of the most powerful, and turbulent, eastern nations met in cloistered meetings for six days. When they emerged, an alliance had been formed—an alliance, no doubt, that could appease the warring factions. The world council was initially delighted, proclaiming their full-scale backing, for they had been reticent about intervening in such a volatile situation. The Alliance brought a surge of hope, promising to unite the east in a system that would bring peace and prosperity to all. Everyone knew that peace meant global prosperity, so no one minded very much that the political system of the Alliance was to be none other than the worship of *Ohshkagoonjing Giizis*.

"The Alliance's leaders were savvy men, aware of the magnitude of the problems they faced. It was no secret that the favour they enjoyed would be short-lived if change didn't sweep across the region. To avoid another round of revolution, they needed to respond to the crises without the inevitable delay of committees and systems. In fact, a charismatic leader with the power to take decisive action was exactly the cure. Remarkably, just such a leader was rising.

"Gagi, as he is called here—for later he became known as the greatest *gagiinawishki*,[19] who ever lived—began as a rebel leader of a Turkish faction. When that group joined another, he became leader of the new group. This happened several more times, each time Gagi taking control of a larger party, until he was meeting with the most powerful leaders in the world and coming out strong. When the Alliance heard that he had recently taken control of the wartorn northern region, they were astonished. Something set him apart—he could bring together the extremes and make them all believe he was one of their own. Both radicals and conservatives

---

19 *Gagiinawishki*: liar.

hailed him as their ally. The day the Alliance announced Gagi as their first *ogimaa*, the streets flooded with celebratory parades. No doubt a few bottles of champagne were consumed at the World Bank, too.

"Only days later, as the merrymaking subsided, did the international news report that Gagi was not being hailed as a great leader, but as the prophesied one who had come to restore *Ohshkagoonjing Giizis* finally as the only true faith. While people of the Word recognized him immediately, most others went back to business, trying to recover prosperity and ease in their corner." Rowan paused to sip from his glass. "Now, I'm sure you also have heard these stories since you were infants, and I suppose we keep telling them so we don't forget the lessons of history, but there is another reason to keep telling them. Each time I tell it, I learn something new. Yes, even the storyteller learns from his story.

"So here is something new. In those days, there were no prophets who carried messages from God, but there were the writings of many who had gone before. Nearly three millennia before *Miigaadiwin*, the Creator had sent prophets who warned the world that terrible days were coming, that there would be war and famine and economic woe, but to be watchful above all of the *gagiinawishki*, a leader who would deceive many by uniting his followers. Some called him Gog, others the King of Babylon, still others the beast.

"Much later, other prophets came. They, too, claimed to speak for a god, but their message was the exact opposite. These said that in a time of war and chaos a supreme leader would arise, one who would unite the ancient kingdom of *Ohshkagoonjing Giizis* and bring peace to the world. Clearly the prophets spoke of one and the same man, but one called him a deceiver and the other a supreme leader. Which prophecy was true?

"This was the key: which prophets admitted the end of the story? Only those who foretold him to be the great deceiver prophesied beyond *Miigaadiwin*. Yes, all the prophets agreed that war, famine, death awaited. Yes, the east would be united. Yes, the leader would overcome his enemies and establish his order as supreme. But prophets of the Word did not stop there. For at the height of the *gagiinawishki*, the true *Ogimaa* would return, undoing him in an instant. Let this be a lesson to us as we seek to understand our world. To discern truth from error, we must listen for the end of the story. The one who only tells half the truth is hiding the truth."

Santiago closed his eyes as though committing this to memory. His wife turned to contemplate a silver lake that rippled past the window.

Fixing their gaze on the storyteller once more, Rowan continued on. "While many followers of *Ohshkagoonjing Giizis* rightly recognized Gagi as their messiah, relatively few saw that Gagi was also the fulfilment of the more ancient prophecies, that he was also the deceiver. But the Ancient People of Canada were not easily way-laid. They had only recently discovered their Creator's name! They would not receive another in his name and they boldly opposed the spread of Gagi's followers here.

"Within months of his appointment, stories filtered across the ocean. His new laws sent throngs of truth-seekers to prison or death. At first, Canadians were hor-rified, but as the stories poured in they were in denial. Men, women, and children were fleeing for their lives as their homes were raided or confiscated. Their choice was simple: take the *Ohshkagoonjing Giizis* creed or die.

"Finally Gagi made a move that even the world council could not ignore. His tanks rolled across the border into that tiny nation of the *Nitamoozhaan*, that tract of land that could be crossed on foot in four days at its widest point from the Med-iterranean Sea. The *Nitamoozhaan* weren't exactly in the world's good books. There had been terrible news coming out of that nation leading up to *Miigaadiwin*. The refugees' conditions had continued to slide and their lands had shrivelled up, but when a child was crushed by the government's heavy equipment coming to destroy her illegal residence, the world was enraged. 'Enough is enough,' they said. 'If you will not make peace in your nation, we will not stand with you.'

"So the *Nitamoozhaan* stood alone as Gagi made his move, and he knew it. His advance was fast and furious. Everyone watching expected the *Nitamoozhaan* to counterattack in short order. Their air force was unparalleled. Their soldiers could fight with the desperation of people who had seen their own extinction burned into their grandparents' forearms. But there was no counterattack. This time, there was too much at stake. Their enemy had indeed acquired nuclear weapons. The *Nita-moozhaan* were fully convinced that the Alliance wouldn't think twice about drop-ping a nuclear bomb on them, a point the Alliance broadcast regularly in the days leading up to the raid. The only hope for the survival of millions was for the nuclear weapons to be disarmed. And so the *Nitamoozhaan* government waited patiently— suicidally, it seemed to the world—as the tanks rolled into their streets.

"Of course, the world council immediately, finally, imposed drastic economic sanctions. Too little, too late. Gagi had installed himself as *ogimaa*. Economic sanc-tions were a joke. He already owned the majority of the world's oil supply. He need-ed no one. There wasn't a nation on earth prepared to rescue the *Nitamoozhaan*."

Santiago could not contain his joy. "No one on *earth!*"

Rowan laughed. "Of course. But heaven is another matter. And so we remain ever grateful to our true *Ogimaa*, the only one willing and able to rescue! The mir-acle is that he took his throne as the Fall Festival was celebrated, as though the

Creator had planned this moment from the beginning of time. In homes all around the world, the remembrance of life's brevity began. At that very moment, the immortal king took his reign over a mortal world, and the eternal and the temporal greeted one another in time and space."

Rowan shook his head in disbelief. Santiago and his wife smiled at the irony.

"My ancestors recount how supplies were thin before *Miigaadiwin*, but that last night they celebrated anyway with a table of bright red fallen leaves, candles, sweet bread, and singing. During their meal, the room began to shake. Yes, even on the other side of the planet, the tremor from that blast lasted a full ninety seconds, a very long ninety seconds! My people thought the end had come for sure, that the bomb had finally been dropped and they would soon be surveying desolate land, dying of radiation sickness. They could not have been more wrong. *Ahaaw!* Not the end, but the beginning! For the immortal army had come, led by none other than the *Ogimaa* himself, shouting, 'Praise the Creator who has restored us in the Jubilee!'"

chapter nine

BAAPAGISHKAA AKI
"EARTHQUAKE"

"I believe you were snoring before we were out the door," Inaa laughed accusingly. "You should see this place, Gizhaa. Every car has its own world theme. My favourite was the Caribbean car—palms and orchids everywhere. It's like travelling around the globe in mere steps!"

"And we would still be lost somewhere between India and Nepal, except dinner is supposed to be served any second and I know Inaa would never forgive me if we missed that," Tom added flippantly.

"Perhaps," Inaa said. "But I wasn't the one who had to stop and sample the snack bar in every car!"

Neither one seemed to notice Gizhaa's distraction. When the famous dinner did indeed arrive, his silence was lost entirely.

At first they debated whether the gourmet cuisine placed in front of them was even edible. A layer of flowers—"Narsturtiums," the porter said—covered the entire plate. That was the bed for a layer of curly red cabbage, followed by wild rice, with the centrepiece being a large, open-leafed artichoke heart. The entire thing was drizzled in a bright yellow sauce; it was anybody's guess what it was. Eventually the delicious aroma won them over—and that was just the salad course.

By the time the chocolate truffles were served, Inaa fell back against the bench clutching her stomach. "No more! Honestly, you would think we were Immortals the way they feed us. If I were an Immortal, I would dine like this every night. I bet they never gain weight."

Tom looked at her funny, his hand halfway to a truffle. "Somehow I don't think they came for the food."

Gizhaa leaned heavily on his elbow. "You're kidding!" he gasped in exaggerated shock. "Then what did they come for?"

Inaa stopped chewing and stared at her brother. Tom didn't know Gizhaa well enough to know that sarcasm wasn't a form of humour he enjoyed. But it was effective as bait.

Tom shrugged. "Resources, I'm betting."

"Interesting," Gizhaa said, settling back in his seat as though prepared to listen.

"Why else would they have invaded when they did?" Tom continued, his voice a little lower now.

"Invaded?" Inaa sounded confused.

"Sure. What else would you call it? Before the Immortals entered *Miigaadiwin*, there was a fair fight going on between regional interests. After the Immortal invasion, they took over every nation on earth and set themselves up as rulers without any accountability! I'd call that a pretty successful invasion."

Gizhaa had a hard time controlling his breathing. His heartbeat thudded in his ears. Inaa was looking more concerned by the moment.

"Let's face it," Tom continued. "Earth is a pretty unique planet in the solar system, maybe even in the galaxy. Before *Miigaadiwin* this was an incredibly rich planet with just about every conceivable resource: water, minerals, oil, vegetation. And the best part was, the richest areas were still untouched, trapped under massive ice sheets for millennia. The Immortals must have known that somehow. They must have had some way of sensing or measuring it. So when they invaded, they also set up a mechanism by which to melt the polar ice, releasing those resources for pillaging."

Gizhaa was shaking his head involuntarily, but all he said was, "I've never heard this before."

"But the desk clerk said last night that the polar ice melted because of the halo *Didibininjiibizon*," Inaa jumped in, "that it was created by *Miigaadiwin*."

"First of all, who do you think he's working for?" Tom asked. "I'd bet my left arm he's an Immortal himself anyway, even if he wasn't working for them. Secondly, in a way he's right. The halo was created at the end of *Miigaadiwin* when the Immortal army attacked the *Ohshkagoonjing Giizis*. They managed a full-on assault from above and below. Volcanic eruptions spewed massive amounts of fine particulate and carbon dioxide into the atmosphere, while meteors falling into the ocean evaporated large amounts of water. You didn't think that was all a coincidence, did you? And I suppose the atomic bomb that *Ohshkagoonjing Giizis* supposedly set off didn't hurt the effect either, adding even more particulate to the atmospheric soup. Whether the Immortals had been counting on that one or not, who knows?"

Gizhaa thought wryly that Tom would make a convincing politician indeed.

"So, you don't think the *Ohshkagoonjing Giizis* were actually going to obliterate anyone who wouldn't bow to them?" Gizhaa pressed.

"I doubt it. How smart would that be? The Immortals chose their timing carefully. They came when we were weak and vulnerable, ready for a saviour. They told us they were rescuing us and we welcomed them with open arms." Tom folded his arms conclusively.

A porter arrived at the table with a pot of steaming liquid.

Inaa sighed. "Yes, *miigwech*, a cup of tea is exactly what I need. Let's talk of something lighter. I can't digest my supper on politics."

As the mugs were poured, Rowan returned to the booth. "Well, I must say, the only thing that would have made that dinner perfect would have been sharing it with your mother!"

But just as he was about to take his seat, the car lurched on its rails and the painful sound of metal on metal resonated through the train as though someone had pulled the brakes hard. A distinct shudder rippled through the floor for several seconds.

Gizhaa's shoulder connected painfully with the glass window. Rowan and the porter were both knocked to the ground. They seemed to be engulfed by a great roaring.

Within moments, the train had ground to a complete halt. The stillness was broken as a glass rolled across the table and shattered against the window.

Confusion erupted throughout the car. A porter hurried in, asking everyone to take a seat and attending to any who were hurt. Gizhaa was already at his father's side. The older man only needed a moment to rise. Inaa had been holding her tea and the scalding liquid had spilled over her hands. Tom was wrapping a napkin around pieces of spilled ice and applying it to her burned fingers. Train personnel ran through the cabin, presumably mechanical experts to deal with the cause of the accident.

"What was that?" Tom asked.

Rowan shook his head. "It felt an awful lot like an earthquake, but I haven't heard of one since *Miigaadiwin*. There are many stories of them in the ancient teachings, but I don't know. I suppose it's possible."

Rowan's face flinched with pain as he gently moved his ankle into a more comfortable position under the table.

The train didn't move for a full hour. Porters came every few minutes and assured them that everyone was safe and the train would continue as soon as everything was clear. Still, it was a very tense hour of waiting. The sun sank lower on the horizon, but still they saw workers moving around the train outside.

Finally, they heard the whistle that had greeted them cheerfully that morning and the car full of travellers erupted in applause. As the train began to accelerate smoothly, a porter announced that they believed it had indeed been an earthquake, Canada's first in a millennium, but the damage had been successfully repaired.

They sped on their way, the full moon rising as a golden disc. Its light reflected on Hudson Bay as the track briefly hugged its eastern shore. And then the water was gone once more and the forest returned, dark and shadowy.

Rowan turned uncomfortably in his seat, trying to stretch his legs without wincing.

"The past collides with the future and we will be shaken once again," he muttered under his breath.

Gizhaa frowned. "What did you say, Dad?"

Rowan sighed. "Nothing. I was reminded of a conversation with my old friend, Gichi- Baawiting."

Tom pulled down the window shade and glanced around at the strained faces. "I believe we could use a story tonight."

Rowan smiled tightly, whether from the pain in his ankle or the stress of the earthquake was unclear. "Perhaps you would like to tell us more about New York. I believe I cut you off last night."

Gizhaa wasn't sure if he should elbow his father or thank him. How much more of Tom's eloquence could he handle? It seemed his mysterious visit from Ya Min may not have been absurd. Another round of Tom's mind might give him the clues she needed. And that was worth something.

chapter ten

WANISHIN
"LOST"

"I moved to New York from Ontario to study law at the University of Abenaki. The school has an excellent reputation and I was very honoured to be accepted, of course. I have found my time there to be an eye-opening experience, one which I believe has prepared me well for the next phase of my life in the north.

"But I will certainly miss New York's charm and quirkiness. I suppose the transformation since *Miigaadiwin* has brought a freshness there that is unique. If you think the north has changed over the centuries, it's nothing compared to an ancient megacity! New York became a source of fascination for me, and my final project was to write a review of its disestablishment over the past millennium. Perhaps you know that it was once the second most populous city in North America, home to eight and a half million people? As beautiful as it is today, it's a shadow of its former glory.

"The city was built at the mouth of a river, but much of it covered three islands: Manhattan, Staten, and Long. I have had the pleasure of visiting each of them, although they're not as large as they once were and you must now travel by ferry to visit them. They say there were over two thousand bridges and tunnels connecting the city before *Miigaadiwin*, but the earthquakes made short work of most of those. The remainder washed away long ago. But its bridges and tunnels were feats of engineering at the time. The world's first underwater traffic tunnel was built in New York. Four of its suspension bridges were the longest ever built when they opened. One bridge was large enough to carry two train tracks, eight lanes for vehicles, and a sidewalk for hikers.

"The city's architecture was perhaps an even greater accomplishment. Several times they built the tallest building on the planet. Its last achievement, the One

World Trade Tower, reached over 540 meters to the tip of its spire. Though not the tallest building ever built, it was truly awe-inspiring. I guess that's about six times taller than some of these old growth trees. Can you imagine? That tower was covered in mirror glass panels, almost thirteen thousand of them, and from a distance it rose like a massive spear toward heaven. They say that if you stood right at its foot and looked straight up, the building seemed like a glass pyramid ascending into the clouds. You could travel to the upper deck of the building, 104 stories up, past stores and offices and condominiums, and if you looked out from that height you could sometimes see clouds below you. The effect was dizzying as the horizon curved away out of sight. I would have liked to have stood there."

Tom paused, his gaze far away.

"It sounds breathtaking," Inaa whispered.

"Sounds insane," Gizhaa complained.

"Nevertheless, after the Immortal invasion of the Middle East, the tide of global finance turned away from us. The new monetary system outlawed permanent transfers of land. That move alone allowed the Immortals to effectively gut capitalism. No real estate sales meant zero interest. Tell me, how can one acquire wealth without interest? Not very well." Tom sounded annoyed, but he checked himself. "Incidentally, although current Canadian laws reflect the law of the Immortals, it is not so everywhere. Some places are looking for ways to revitalize these great centres of civilization: Tokyo, Amsterdam, Mumbai. They have established grassroots lobbyists who are working alongside the existing governments to create a system that will once again reward those who work hard and seek the betterment of society. For example, in Saudi Arabia, the Makkah Revival is moving ahead with plans to build a tower on the very site of one of the world's greatest architectural achievements—a cluster of ancient towers centred on the third tallest building ever erected, a rare classical tower without equal, truly a wonder of the ancient world! The original tower complex was 120 stories high and could house up to one hundred thousand people. The building was capped by a clock that could be seen from twenty-five kilometres away. Over eight million tiny lights illuminated it, dancing while beams of light sliced ten kilometres up into the night sky on holidays. Such was the incredible affluence of that generation! Perhaps we will resurrect these places yet.

"But I digress. Back to New York. After *Miigaadiwin*, property values depreciated rapidly and aging buildings were never replaced, turning megacities like New York into virtual ghost towns within a few short decades. The majority of the citizens packed up and moved inland to farm. For some it was because the ocean had eaten away at the edges of their communities, for others it was because the services they had come to rely on didn't exist anymore, but for most it was simply because the life they'd grown accustomed to was gone. They were ready to escape to greener pastures, quite literally.

"But some stayed, and these hardy folks were a special breed. They redefined what city life looked like. You've seen how Canadian cities have adapted, and many of those changes you will also find in New York. Transportation is largely by foot, except for ferries and rails. New homes are simple and transient. Yards and gardens are well-tended and provident. As New Yorkers found that they were strong enough to survive in a harsher world, they also discovered that they could grow a whole new culture of innovation.

"I was able to track down the father of this movement, a remarkable old man, perhaps the oldest non-Immortal I've ever met. He initiated the innovation movement around 2200 CE—that's about 5900 by your millennial calendar—though he claims no credit for it. He told me that he simply dreamt it one night and felt compelled to act. Marcus Narragansett, born in the Bronx, a true son of the *Nisayenh*, had been working on the design for a filtration system that would provide clean water to the island of Noyack, recently cut off from Long Island by the rising sea. He already knew that ocean water contained tellurium, gallium, indium, and selenium, and while those might sound like types of fish to you, they're pretty useful metalloids—useful because they are quite likely powering this train right now in the solar cells overhead. These elements are common in nature but found in such low concentrations that it was extremely expensive to collect and refine them. The solar industry had conjured up ingenious alternatives to keep costs down for decades, such as with sulphur and the like, but at the expense of efficiency.

"So Narragansett goes to sleep working on his ocean water recovery system, but he awakes in the morning scribbling down a list of plant names—plants he's never even heard of before—and he knows these plants will trap tellurium, gallium, indium, and selenium, the proverbial solar gold mine. He soon tested the bio-mine in a lab, and just seven years later a full-scale bio-mine was in effect off the coast of New York City. It was the dawn of a new future, not only for the city, but also for the world. There's a similar bio-mine off the coast of Nunavut, though they collect different rare metals. The soil runoff released from polar ice is remarkably rich in these elements, so the Baffin Bay region has proven a source of highly concentrated waters, relatively speaking.

"Bio-mines have supplied an age of clean energy that's unparalleled in history. For New Yorkers, it has spawned an age of innovation. New ways to use rare elements are still being discovered there. And the bio-miners, the plants and bacteria that trap essential elements, are still being researched and new applications proposed."

"Do you think the Creator revealed these things to Narragansett in a dream?" Inaa asked excitedly.

Tom cocked his head to one side. "Or Narragansett tapped into some ancient collective memory embedded in our subconscious. Like how birds know where to migrate even though they've never been there before."

Inaa blinked, but said nothing.

"New York is delightful because the ocean surrounds its neighbourhoods and the ferry drivers never stop talking," Tom continued. "It's welcoming because every corner has a café that serves the darkest brew of coffee in America. It's sobering because every morning the bells ring at nine to commemorate the sinking of the Statue of Liberty. But I'm sure it's the people's thirst for knowledge and innovation that sets New York apart as a great city, for every person you meet has a story to tell of the future they're building today. These rather bull-headed people are exploring how innovation can change not only the biology and technology of Earth, but also the human systems: culture, politics, and economics.

"Now that I understand the true spirit of New Yorkers, I know that the Tokyo, Amsterdam, Mumbai, and Maakah revivals have found a partner. New Yorkers have never forgotten the great history of their city, the days when everyone worked and travelled freely, when they were never more than a train ride away from a downtown with stores lined up for kilometres, when no one had to work under the noon sun, and when buildings were cool and quiet. The restoration of such a great society may yet come in our lifetimes. Perhaps we will even see the tower rebuilt there!"

The excitement in Tom's voice grew even as his volume dropped. He leaned forward. "I believe that such progressive thinking will someday also empower Canadians to recover the prosperity that is *wanishin*[20] at present. Too long we have been content with the basics of life. Surely the Immortals can be persuaded that it's necessary to improve our standard of living. It's not to their benefit to keep the common people in such simple, provincial positions. A thriving population and economy could help further their own goals, and together we can release the riches of our planet.

"It seems to me, and to many other forward-thinking people, that the time has come to renegotiate our relationship with the Immortals. Their benevolence in the early years after *Miigaadiwin* may have been welcome, when the *Ogimaa* rode waves of praise and mutual gifts flowed freely, but those days are gone. As a matter of fact,

---

20 *Wanishin*: lost.

the *Ogimaa* hasn't been seen or heard from in several years. You won't find him at the *Naawayi*, Rowan. He was last rumoured to be travelling across Australia on foot. I suppose even an Immortal prince can't be expected to spend a thousand years just sitting on his throne. But he's been on and off the throne for centuries already, traveling in India, Romania, Papua New Guinea. He's been gone long enough to cover the whole globe! Some are saying he may have secretly abdicated his reign, or lost his mind, or maybe he's just *wanishin*. Whatever's become of him, it's time we started talking about new leadership." Tom cleared his throat. "Perhaps the Immortal invasion was welcomed at the time by the *Nitamoozhaan*—they had little choice in the matter—but today we can choose."

No one responded and the group sat in silence for some time.

"I'm guessing Gagi was less than welcoming," Gizhaa quipped much later.

chapter eleven

JNΔΔBΔM

"ΔS IN Δ DREΔM"

The amber light behind Inaa's eyes seemed to radiate pain down her neck, into her shoulders, and pool in the fingertips of her left hand, throbbing with her pulse. The earthquake—hot tea splashing onto her hand—leapt to mind. She opened her eyes, squinting into the darkness, then abruptly lifted her head. She had suddenly realized her cheek was resting on Tom's shoulder. Warmth crept into her face and she was grateful for the darkness.

In the dim light, she could see Gizhaa sitting across from her, his head leaning against the window and his mouth slightly open as he breathed evenly. Beside him, her father slumped against a pillow, a light blanket drawn across his chest and shoulders.

"It's just after five," Tom whispered in her ear.

She jumped. "Where are we?"

"I'm not sure. I'm guessing we'll be crossing the Nunavut border within the hour."

"I'll need to use the ladies' room."

Tom slid silently out into the aisle to let her pass. She rose a little unsteadily, as the unfamiliar movement of the train and the stiffness in her legs hit her. Tom touched her elbow, but she pushed his hand away.

"I'm fine," she whispered. "I'll be right back."

She opened the narrow door into the tiny room at the end of the car and instinctively shielded her eyes as light flooded down. She leaned heavily onto the vanity and pressed her eyes shut. A dream now filled her vision, not dissipating with the fog of sleep as she had hoped, but becoming clearer with her waking. She knew dreams like this: the kind that memory made stronger, colours brighter, details truer. She knew it would be exactly as she had seen. It always was.

So she let the images replay. She walked into a room, Tom leading her.

Why does it have to be Tom? she thought. *Tom, with his laughing black eyes and carefree smile.*

The room began to fill. People, mostly young people like herself, crowded in until there was standing room only. She pressed herself against the wall, trying to become invisible. A large piece of paper was tacked onto another wall: "New York Revival" was written in large black letters. A man stood at the centre of the room, perhaps on a chair, his eyes black like embers. His beard didn't hide his fierce features. She couldn't see much now, but she could hear every word.

"We have bowed to the King long enough! The Immortals have taken our great nations and made them pasture for goats and pheasants. They demand tribute, but what do they give in return? Nothing. The time has come to throw off their bonds. We will have no king but ourselves. We will resurrect the great culture that once ruled the earth! Let us return to *Ohsh!* We will join our forces and overthrow the Immortals!"

His voice was wild with passion. The passion rippled through the crowd and awakened a roar. It was the roar of the earthquake once more. She heard it reverberating through her mind.

Yet the train slid smoothly along. She opened her eyes and stared at the face in the mirror. She slowly removed her hands from her ears. Her crown of sweeping golden hair was now a tangled nest fit for a bird. Her fetching, richly hued eyes were rather soggy looking, rimmed in dark streaks.

Inaa splashed cold water on her face. Tom. His history last night, his ideas carelessly shared. He had no idea what he was into!

She splashed again and rubbed harder than necessary. She spent several minutes unpinning her hair and winding the stands back down until the horns and bobbles had smoothed into waves.

Finally, she scrunched her fingers into the whole affair and stared fiercely at the girl in the mirror.

"Inaabam Selah, what are you getting into?" She closed her eyes, dropped her head into her hands, and breathed, "Creator Father, I don't know what is right anymore, but I know what I must do. Please keep me on your path."

She exhaled and stepped back into the dim aisle, nearly colliding with Tom. She wondered briefly how long he had been there and whether he had heard her prayer. But as he eagerly grabbed her hand, she realized the sun must be close to rising.

"The porter just came by and told me that we are nearing the Hudson Strait," he said, his eyes dancing. "Since there's only a few awake, he said we can move to the engineer's cabin for the best view of the train's descent into the tunnel!"

His excitement was infectious and Inaa found herself being drawn stealthily through the narrow aisles toward the front of the train. After passing through more doors than Inaa could keep track of, they faced a smooth oak door with a brass handle. At eye level, a large red octagon warned Authorized Personnel Only.

Tom's hand gripped the handle, his shoulder already leaning into the door, but Inaa reached around him and knocked smartly.

"Yes, come in, dears," a woman's voice called.

Tom stepped back uncertainly. Inaa stepped past him and pushed the door open, peeking inside. The tiny room had large, rounded windows looking northward where a bright light illuminated a single rail hurtling toward and almost through them. The light radiated, revealing only the faintest hint of waving fields of grain to the left and right. Inside the cabin, an instrument panel glowed with a dizzying array of knobs and buttons and gauges.

An elderly woman arose from her chair with the regality of a queen. She opened her arms in universal welcome, her brown cheeks wrinkling as a smile spread like sunshine from her lips to her dark eyes.

"*Boozhoo.*[21] It is a pleasure to share my view with you early birds. Especially you, Tom, one of our very special guests this trip."

She shook his hand warmly.

Inaa glanced at Tom questioningly and saw that he shared her confusion. Perhaps political appointments carried more honour in the north than they had realized. But Inaa didn't have time to muse on this, for the engineer was gently guiding her forward through the cedar-panelled room, past the board of glowing knobs to a plush bench that wrapped around the front glass. Once seated, Inaa seemed to be suspended above the lighted rail. By turning her head to the left, she could see the entire landscape. The first rays of sun were turning the sky a delicious colour of mango. Tom slid onto the seat facing her. They sat in mutually awed silence, their hostess taking a firm stance beside them, quite enjoying the effect the vista had on them.

"We are passing the Hudson Bay now," the engineer said some minutes later, quietly as though her voice might spoil the enchantment. "You will see it in the distance to the west."

As Inaa turned to look through the window behind her. What she saw took her breath away. Distant fields had given way to the vast expanse of Hudson Bay and the first rays of the unrisen sun were scattering across the water's surface.

---

21 *Boozhoo*: greetings, welcome.

From the middle of that glorious sea rose *Didi's*[22] sweeping bow, painted red in the growing light.

"And now we begin our descent toward the Hudson Strait." The engineer's elegant hand waved their view back to the north, where the train had just crested a rocky ridge. A valley opened below them where a wide swath of water stretched across to the distant shore. The train was speeding downhill. The water drew steadily nearer. "We'll be under the strait in a minute. One hundred meters of water will be above our heads for the next fifty kilometres or so."

Within moments, the smooth, black expanse of water disappeared and a great gaping mouth opened in the earth before the train. The ever-present rail ran straight into it. The car plunged into that gaping mouth, the darkness swallowing them.

Inaa held her breath and her eyes adjusted, but the steady beam of light ahead still shone before her. She slowly exhaled as warmth crept over her hand. She was startled to realize that Tom had settled his hand over hers. She tried to nonchalantly slide her hand away, but his pressure was steady. Ruefully, she wished he had at least chosen her good hand; her burned fingers began to throb anew.

The engineer's attention was focused on the plethora of dials on her instrument panel. Not wanting to alert their chaperone to her awkward position, Inaa decided to relax and watch for the sunrise.

She turned her attention toward the dark walls of the tunnel where the light illuminated panels of rough rock. Instantly, she was mentally transported to a cave where, as a little girl, she had often gone spelunking with Gizhaa, Simon, and Jordan. They had stood together at the mouth, the sunlight revealing the path into the cave. The boys had teased her, saying that a girl couldn't explore dark caves, but they had soon discovered that she could get places none of the rest could, being smaller and lighter. And after that she went everywhere they did and no one bothered her about it.

She couldn't help thinking now, as she often did, how much she wished she had offered to go with them that tragic summer morning so many years later. If she had gone, Jordan would have gone, too, instead of staying behind to speak with her, to hold her hand in his, to ask her if…

If Jordan had gone, then Simon wouldn't have drowned.

During that very dark thought, the sunrise came. It was worth the wait. The grey light that had begun to play on the tunnel walls suddenly grew into a blinding blue that washed over the cabin. Inaa pulled her hand away to cover her eyes. She surreptitiously wiped a tear as the train exploded from the tunnel. When she looked again, she glimpsed the edge of the sun's orb above the strait.

---

22 *Didi*: nickname for *Didibininjiibizon*, Earth's gas halo ring.

She leaned forward and pressed her left cheek against the cold glass to catch the fullest view to the east. A thick morning fog hovered over the channel and the sun's rays backlit the mist, defining each smoky curl in exquisite detail. At the water's edge, she saw a large white bear ready to descend for a morning swim, and two year-ling cubs tumbling behind it, one stopping to swat the other for good measure and the second returning a playful nibble to his shoulder.

Inaa laughed out loud, momentarily cleansing the pain from her heart and hand. "Look! Just like siblings, aren't they?"

"And caribou!" Tom exclaimed as a regal group stepped from the shelter of the tree line and strolled past the cubs for a drink. The mother polar bear didn't bother about them, but continued into the deeper water; her cubs soon joined her for a refreshing dip.

"I never cease to be amazed at the wildlife in the north," the engineer said with a laugh. "The peace our Creator has placed on them is, for me, the image of the Jubilee. To think these beautiful animals were once mortal enemies! And with that lovely morning thought, I must send you back to your car."

Inaa stood as Tom thanked the engineer politely. They headed for the door.

"I will have many miles yet to travel, children, when you have arrived at your destination," the engineer said. "But you may be back my way. You're welcome to come see me again."

Inaa thought of her dream earlier and wondered where she would find herself in the future.

Wherever it is, she thought ruefully, *I can get places none of the rest can.*

chapter twelve

NAGAMON
"SONG"

Emmy straightened stiffly, her hand pressing into her hip. "Ugh! Little one, you've got to stay in there for two more months. I sure hope you aren't planning on spending that entire time pressing on my sciatic nerve." As if in answer, a little foot jabbed her in the ribs. Emmy rubbed the tiny foot. "All right, all right! We'll work it out."

The morning sun filtered through the canopy of pine needles, through the yurt window, and down to Emmy's kneading trough, full of rising dough. She had forgotten again to downsize her recipe with three fewer mouths to feed. After Simon died, it had taken her months to remember not to make enough food to feed another hungry youngster. She hurried that thought away with a two-handed shove of her arms into the soft dough. Its warmth flowed back over her hands as they disappeared inside.

Kris appeared at the yurt door with Tristen bumping hard into her backside.

"No alpacas in the yurt!" Emmy reminded her daughter firmly, turning the dough and leaning into it.

Kris braced her hands against the doorframe as Tristen butted her again, but she stumbled forward into the room. The little alpaca dancing around her legs. Kris tried to shoo Tristen back out the door, but she only succeeded in exciting the fluffy creature further and the alpaca jumped directly onto the table in front of Emmy.

"*Ahaaw*, this is too much!" Emmy cried, raising her floury hands in dismay.

Tristen leapt down and scurried behind the curtain into the little girls' bedroom. Kris pulled the curtain hastily and began laughing. Tristen dove into the bed and stuck her head under the pillow, finally still for a moment.

Emmy swept past her daughter and gathered the alpaca into her arms a little roughly, its long legs draped awkwardly around her belly.

"I don't know what got into her this morning, Momma," Kris said. "She wouldn't leave me alone! I fed her, but she wouldn't eat. All the alpacas are excited this morning, running around the yard and pushing on the gate."

"Well, it's not the weather. Wind is dead quiet today. Can't even hear the beach this morning." Emmy tried unsuccessfully to brush a piece of stray hair from her cheek by using her shoulder, as her arms were full. "All right, let's just get this beast back in her pen where she belongs." She sighed. "I hope Gizhaa is having a good time in Iqaluit by now. It's going to be a long half-moon here."

As they stepped into the yard, they both heard a voice and stopped. It was a man's voice singing with wild abandon, as one would sing if there were no one around for a kilometre. They didn't recognize the voice or its *nagamon*, but it was the kind of melody that made you want to raise your arms to the sky and join in.

This is my Father's world.
The birds, their carols raise,
The morning light,
The lily white
Declare their Maker's praise.
This is my Father's world.
He shines in all that's fair.
In the rustling grass
I hear him pass.
He speaks to me everywhere.

The man came into view, swinging a walking stick and taking long, sure strides toward the yurt. Emmy set the alpaca down and stood up faster than her hip normally allowed. Tristen ran straight toward the lean, curly-haired stranger who knelt on one knee to greet her. The alpaca fairly knocked him over in her haste, but then stood calmly while he rubbed her head and back, offering her a treat from his pocket.

"Our first guest of the feast season and I don't even have my hands clean," Emmy muttered, but she rubbed them hastily in her skirt and moved forward smiling.

The young stranger stood and extended a well-tanned hand toward her. "Emmy Selah?"

She nodded, raising her eyebrows. "Yes?"

He swung down the pack he was carrying and produced an envelope from the top of it. "I had the pleasure of seeing your husband at the train station as he was boarding. He asked me to deliver this to you."

He handed her the envelope, which she took eagerly, her eyes clouded in worry.

"Was all well with him?" she asked quickly.

"Not to worry. They are fine." He smiled. "I believe his letter will give you more details."

"*Miigwech*. Will you stay a while?"

"I would love to. I have heard much of your fine establishment and have been looking forward to a visit here."

Emmy ducked her head with pride. "That is good to hear. We are a small business, but we've been working at it for some time. Have you had a good breakfast?"

"Can't say that I have."

"Then Kris, would you please run and bring fresh eggs from the coop? And send Abigail along to give me a hand." Emmy motioned to the stranger. "And you may put your things in the guest yurt if you'd like to relax for a bit, Mister…"

"Joshua is fine. And I'd much rather take a walk around to visit the alpacas. I'm quite familiar with them."

That much is obvious, Emmy thought as she nodded in curiosity. Tristen hadn't left the man's side. "Most certainly, Joshua. I have a feeling they will appreciate your company."

About half an hour later, Joshua came back into the circle with Nanda, Kris, and Solia, each eagerly trying to be the one to show him everything about the farm. Tristen was at his heels.

Abigail peeked out the yurt door wistfully, for though she was a fully-grown young lady, her childish heart was calling.

Her mother's voice brought her back. "The eggs can be served now, Abby, and I'll bring out the tea."

A rustic and well-worn table had been laid in the centre of the circle of yurts, prepared for an al fresco breakfast with the best dishes and a huge bouquet of autumn mums. Though the four girls and their mother had already eaten, they gladly sat down for a second breakfast of tea and toast with their guest.

Joshua entertained them at length with stories from his travels: the Australian outback to the Siberian savannah. Emmy laughed so hard she wasn't sure it was good for the baby, the girls listened rapturously, and they all shed tears of empathy when suffering was shared. It was well past noon before they rose from the table.

Joshua looked around him. "I've seen many farms, but I can tell that your family is exceptionally good at caring for your livestock. Their wool is remarkable. Not to mention that the animals are really happy here. Well done!"

Emmy blushed, but it was Nanda who eagerly spoke up. "And just wait 'til you see Momma's weaving! She makes such beautiful things." Nanda pulled his arm so that he lowered his ear toward her. "She even made the *Ogimaa* a coat," she whispered seriously.

"Really?" Joshua's eyes twinkled. "Then I'd love to see your momma's work."

Emmy led them to the guest yurt. Their eyes took a few moments to adjust to the dimmer interior, but once they did the rich colours of the space enveloped them. The circular rug in the centre of the room drew Joshua immediately, a rainbow of hues that he knelt and ran his hands over.

"Amazing!" he breathed.

"It took a year to complete that piece," Emmy said. "Felting alpaca wool can be quite time-consuming."

Joshua stood and walked around the room where woven blankets hung from the lattice. No two pieces were alike, but together they produced a symphony, not cacophony. Beside the bed stood shelves with a myriad of slippers in every size and colour imaginable. And beside that, a rack hung with bags, purses, and backpacks. Finally he came back round to the door and stopped in front of a coat that hung neatly on a hanger, a simple brown jacket that tied shut at the neck and chest. He touched it very gently.

"That one is for display only. It is not for sale," Emmy quickly said.

Joshua smiled. "Yes, it is a very special piece."

"It was my son's."

They brought in Joshua's pack and set it down by the door, and when the girls saw the stretching seams they told him that Momma's backpacks could travel around the whole world if he wanted.

"You are a very gifted wool artist, Emmy," Joshua said as they moved back into the sunshine.

"*Miigwech.*"

"Well, I'd like to take a swim this afternoon, and maybe a nap." Joshua stretched.

"We don't swim this time of year," Abigail informed him. "It's too cold."

"Refreshing, I call it. No worries; I went swimming in the Pacific Ocean in December several centuries ago and lived to tell of it. I don't imagine Lake Huron can be much worse. And you have the best beach from here to Quebec, so it would be a shame to miss it over a few degrees."

As he strode away in the direction of the beach, Kris whispered to her mother, "A few *centuries* ago?"

Emmy tried to shrug nonchalantly. "He must be an Immortal."

Nanda clapped her hands. "He's wonderful! Are all Immortals like that?"

"I don't know, Nanda. I really don't know."

Δ   Δ   Δ

That evening, after everyone else had gone to bed, Emmy opened the envelope and smoothed out the letter.

Dearest Emmy,

We are just preparing to catch the train this morning. Our journey thus far has gone well.

We met a handsome young *nisayenh* who is travelling with us. Inaa seems to have taken an interest in him and I think the feeling is mutual. I sense that Gizhaa, alert as always, is wary of him. Please keep this matter in your prayers.

I miss you already. Take care of that little one until I return.

Love always,

Rowan

Δ   Δ   Δ

In the morning, when breakfast was prepared and laid out on the table in the sunshine, Emmy sent Nanda to knock on Joshua's door. Nanda called his name in her singsong childish voice several times, but there was no answer. So the family sat down at the table without him.

As they chewed their first bites of granola, the same tune they'd heard the morning before came whistling up the beach path. Little Nanda left the table and ran to greet Joshua, but the alpaca Tristen beat her to him.

Nanda grabbed Joshua's hand as the alpaca skipped along behind.

"You were looking for me?" he asked her.

"I thought you left us already."

"No, I won't do that." He pulled out a chair for her at the table and then seated himself. "But I do like to spend my mornings in prayer, and that view of Huron is a great spot to be quiet for a bit, don't you think?"

Breakfast was a long and delightful affair that lasted until late morning, and when it was well past the time they should have finished their morning chores, Joshua offered to tend to the animals so the girls could help their mother.

Emmy found herself in the quiet hours of early afternoon feeling drowsy and relaxed as she sat at her loom under a canopy. She let the shuttle fly through her fingers while her thoughts meandered far away.

After some time, a merry group came around the front of the yurts. Joshua was flanked by Kris and Solia, who chattered and giggled, and Nanda rode on his shoulders, all smiles.

"The waves go up and down like this." Joshua rose on tiptoe and then swooped down low so that Nanda squealed and grabbed his hair. "And at first you think you're going to be sick, but after a while you kind of get used to it." He laughed. "Until you step back on land and you feel like the earth keeps moving under your feet. Landsick, we call it."

While Emmy looked on, Joshua began a game of tag, which sent Nanda into gales of laughter as she bobbed wildly along. Soon even Abigail had come out of her yurt to join the fun and all five were running and panting hard.

Emmy watched for some time and wondered if this is what it might have been like had Simon lived. He had always been the playful one, getting his brother and sisters out and running, and likely as not getting into scrapes, too. She sighed, but it was not painful.

Soon the five collapsed with exhaustion on the ground and remained there until their breathing had quieted, watching the clouds sweep across the blue. Emmy brought everyone a glass of water and sat down on the earth herself to soak in the moment.

"It is time for me to move on," Joshua announced, sitting up.

No one said anything. They followed as he gathered his bag from the guest yurt's door.

Emmy whispered something to Kris and she went in and brought out a new backpack.

"It's for you," Kris said, handing it to Joshua.

"I would be honoured if you would take it on your travels," Emmy added.

"*Miigwech!*" Joshua grinned his thanks and immediately knelt to transfer his belongings to the new sack.

"Wait!" Nanda added. "We have gifts for you, too."

The four girls ran to their rooms to gather tokens of their affection.

Joshua continued repacking, kneeling on the ground, and spoke to Emmy. "I haven't only met your husband. I have met your son as well."

"Gizhaa? He is the image of his father, is he not?"

"Not Gizhaa. Simon." Joshua looked up at her.

Emmy caught her breath. "That isn't possible. He drowned a decade ago."

Joshua stood and spoke gently. "Yes, but he is well now."

Emmy took two steps and sat at the al fresco dining table. "Where is he?"

"He has gone on before you and is anxious to see you again. I like Simon. You're right. He is the playful one!"

Emmy's mind reeled and she didn't know what he could mean. She had a million questions to ask. "Will you see him again?"

"No doubt, though not for some years yet."

She walked in a trance to the guest yurt and brought out Simon's coat. "Take this. I made it for his birthday just before he died, but I never got a chance to give it to him."

"He cannot yet use it where he is."

"Then please, wear it for him."

"You did not make this coat for me."

She looked at it with a critical eye for the first time. Her skills had indeed improved in the past decade and this garment was a rag compared to the coat she had made for the *Ogimaa*. Yet this one's value came from the great love that had gone into each stitch.

"No, but Simon would be glad—I would be glad—to have you wear it for him."

Joshua put the coat on and it couldn't have fit better had it been custom-made for him. "I am honoured by your generosity," he said.

The girls ran back, bringing him, from oldest to youngest, a felt hat, a wooden ring, a shiny stone, and a drawing of himself and a little girl holding hands. Then they flung their arms around him by turns and said "*Baamaapii.*"[23] They called it until he was out of sight.

Emmy turned away as soon as he was gone and sat at her loom, but the shuttle wouldn't fly. As she sat and rubbed the alpaca weaving, a *nagamon* rose up inside her. It was one they had sung for the Feast for a thousand years, ever since the Jubilee, and maybe before. She sang it softly to herself and began to weave slowly as her hands found the rhythm.

Joy to the world, the Lord is come.
Let earth receive her king.
Let every heart, prepare him room,
And heaven and nature sing…

---

23 *Baamaapii*: until later.

Suddenly she began to laugh, quietly at first, and then she was holding her stomach as tears ran down her face. Her whole body shook with laughter. She laughed until Nanda came over to her and wiped her mother's face with her hands.

"Momma, are you all right?"

Emmy wrapped her arms tight around her daughter and took a deep breath. "Yes, yes. I am better than ever!"

chapter thirteen

WIIDOOKAAGEWININI
"HELPER"

As the sun set outside, Emmy and her daughters gathered in the family yurt. The girls draped soft throws across their shoulders and sat on the mat, wrapping their fingers around steaming, nutmeg-scented mugs. Emmy's voice tonight was solemn, but not sad. She spoke slowly, not because she was hesitant, but because she was so eager to share that she feared she might forget something important.

"Abigail and Kris, you remember Simon well because he was only a little older than you, but Solia, you were pretty young then, so I'm not sure what you remember. Nanda, you weren't even born yet. Simon was a very special boy. He was always cheerful and affectionate. Oh, how he loved a good practical joke! I remember the time he switched my sugar for salt, which might have been funny, except a large family arrived unexpectedly for dinner and I served them salty blueberry pie! I cried and he felt terrible.

"I realized today that he taught me something powerful by his life and death. It is something I've always known but didn't fully understand until today. It explains our past and future. Simon lived the Jubilee. It was his passion, his joy. And for us it is the hope of life—life that is yet to be restored in full.

"When *Miigaadiwin* ended, the *Ogimaa* was crowned at the *Naawayi*—and on that very day, the Year of Jubilee began. It was a radical concept. All debts were cancelled. All land was returned to the original owners. All slaves were set free. The world became a different place overnight. The rules changed, setting something in motion that would transform the earth. Imagine… before the Jubilee many countries were enslaved by enormous debts, even trillions of dollars. Gone! And land that had been raped of its resources or paved under concrete for profit was parcelled out evenly among all people. Not everyone liked their allocation at first, but it wasn't long before useless land was fertile once more and even the most inexperienced farmer could create a decent life. And the slaves—thirty million men, women, and children—walked free, given homes and lands. Not to mention another thirty million refugees, who had been living as virtual prisoners in camps, were able to return home. And those who had thought they were free, but trapped by a lifetime of debt, working themselves into the grave for rich corporations, received forgiveness.

"Jubilee meant a fresh start for every living thing, for the earth itself. But the earth didn't instantly recover from millennia of abuse. This is where Simon comes in. He loved the lake—I mean, really loved it. I would wake up in the morning and he'd be gone. We would find him on the beach, skipping stones on the glassy water you only see at dawn. He swam every day it didn't snow. At least, it seemed like it. As soon as he could work with his hands, he was building a boat, and if he wasn't doing his chores or coaxing you into trouble, Abigail, he was out on the lake.

"Over the years, he began to know the lake's many faces: the flora it supported, weather patterns, tides and seiches, and the fish. Mostly the fish. He was fascinated by these beautiful creatures, because even centuries after *Miigaadiwin*, the fish population was still adapting slowly. Many species were thought to be lost completely due to pollution or fishing or dams, but as Simon watched the waters he began to recognize that they were not gone, only so rare in such a large body of water that they had gone unseen for hundreds of years. But Simon saw them.

"He wanted to help them fill the lake once more. He called himself the *wiidookaagewinini*, the helper, of the fish. He had a favourite, of course—the giant lake sturgeon. I personally thought they looked like some kind of dinosaur, and the first time Simon took me out on his boat to meet them, I nearly fell overboard with shock. What I saw was a giant, and I do mean giant, grey-green fellow. The two rows of spines down his back gave him a distinctly fierce appearance, and a pointed snout opened to reveal sharp teeth when Simon tossed him a bit of food. Several long, whisker-like organs dangled from his jowls—for searching the lake bottom, Simon said, but they made him look very, very old. Which apparently he was. He was at least four meters long and Simon figured he weighed around one hundred fifty kilograms. This fish was three times the size of me and well over a hundred years old!

"The lake sturgeon had once been plentiful in Lake Huron, but their eggs had become a delicacy and they were fished heavily. Later, when their spawning rivers were blocked by dams or silt, the population was decimated. Lake pollution seemed to be the final blow. Then Simon discovered a stream where they spawned, not too far from here. It took him a bit of work to identify them for sure. It was finally Jordan, across the channel on the great island, who pointed him in the right direction. Jordan was good friends with the island chief, an Immortal who had seen the lake sturgeon in their glory days.

"The problem for the lake sturgeon was that they always returned to spawn in the same river where they were born. So even though there was a small population, they were confined to this one river. As far as we know, there were no other spawning grounds on Lake Huron the sturgeon were using. But Simon and Jordan concocted a simple scheme—simple, but not easy. First they took a few seasons to scope out a new spawning site for the sturgeon: a stream that had just the right flow rate and depth and temperature. At spawning time, they waited at the rapids where the lake sturgeon always came. They observed the females laying their eggs amongst the males, and once the coast was clear they waded into the river to collect fertilized eggs from the rocky bottom. Easier said than done, Simon told me. They transferred the eggs to a hatchery they had built on Jordan's boat and then transported them to a new river. They had quite a system caring for those eggs, hatching them in river water from the new site. Once the fingerling fish were ready to thrive on their own, they released them. And they succeeded in getting a few of those eggs to hatch, survive, and stay in the area.

"But they figured they needed more eggs than they could gather off the river bottom, so after a few summers of observation they came up with a new plan. As spawning season approached, the adult fish once again gathered near the mouth of the stream. Simon and Jordan took two boats and waited for them. This time they recruited your father and Gizhaa to help, so when the sturgeon headed upstream to spawn they used a net between the boats to catch a good-sized female. With all four of them working together, they massaged her sides until they could collect her eggs. Then they had to repeat the process with a male to collect his milt. In the end, they came home bruised and tired, but with a few hundred thousand fertilized eggs to show for their efforts. Once more, the boys hatched those eggs and set them free in another river. They did this for ten years in ten rivers, but it can take twenty-five years for a female lake sturgeon to mature and spawn, so Simon never did see the next generation of his fish project.

"He spent so much time on the water, I guess he got too comfortable. He went out one afternoon to check the fish population as spawning season was approaching and didn't come back. When Simon didn't return home by evening, Jordan took your father and Gizhaa out to look for him. Thank God for Jordan. They did find Simon's boat, right about where he should have been, but no Simon. His clothes were there, as though he had stripped down to swim. They searched through the night, and for the next two days I went out with them while Inaa watched Abigail, Kris, and Solia at home. We kept hoping that by some miracle he had just gotten hurt and made it ashore somewhere. But he was gone…

"A couple of years ago, we began to see the young lake sturgeon Simon had hatched. They would swim right up to our beach, as though they knew this was their foster father's home. They gave us quite a show—jumping, spinning, and tail walking. They did that all summer. It was perhaps their way of saying thank you, or maybe the Creator's way of saying 'Well done.' Sometimes if you go out to the beach in the early morning, you catch a glimpse of a lake sturgeon leaping high out of the water with pure joy. Before Simon you would never have seen that.

"Simon's life demonstrated that Jubilee is something we live. Yes, the *Ogimaa* instituted it and at first it seemed to be economic and political—the land returned to its rightful owners, slaves set free, debts eliminated—but he intended for us to be its manifestation. When we work the land with wisdom, when we treat creatures with respect, when we discover the secrets of creation, we're living in Jubilee.

"Today Joshua told me something. He said that Simon has gone before us, that he's waiting to see us. I realized that Simon is even closer now to seeing the final fulfillment of Jubilee, the day when death is overcome forever. He worked on the lake because he had a vision for a world that was exactly the picture the Creator had painted on the first day.

"You see, Jubilee didn't just show us that society could be reset every fifty years. It foreshadowed that creation would be reset forever. It's a glimpse of the redemption of all things that are yet to come, when there will be no death and no separation between the Creator and humanity. When Simon was out there returning the lake sturgeon fingerlings to their ancient breeding grounds, he was, in a very small way, reversing the effect of the curse on creation. When the Creator redeems the earth, he will reverse the curse of death that lay hold of this planet from the beginning, and what was given first will be established last. Praise the Creator who restored us in the Jubilee!"

chapter fourteen

INDΔWEMΔΔ
"MY SIBLING"

Gizhaa shifted in his seat. The same bench that had felt like comfort fit for a king yesterday morning now seemed like a piece of granite. He wished he had volunteered to pay for a berth and wondered if he could stand up without disturbing his father. Then again, with both Inaa and that senseless Tom missing, it might be a good idea to alert him. His eyes scanned the car in the dim light, but the pair weren't there. It occurred to him that he felt strangely awake, although it was still pitch dark outside.

Everything in him wanted to search the train for his sister and give that would-be suitor of hers a reason to get lost for good, but the gift in his backpack nailed him to the bench. It was crazy to worry now, wasn't it? Ya Min had revealed that she was following them and she didn't seem much to fear. Tom might be a political nut case, but he was hardly a candidate for national sabotage.

Then why, Gizhaa reasoned, couldn't he get out of his seat and go find Inaa?

One thing still troubled him: the earthquake yesterday had been out of place. It shouldn't have happened. Nothing like it for a thousand years and then, by chance, just one tremor strikes a train full of diplomats headed for an important rendezvous? And no aftershocks? Even if they had been too small for others to feel, he wouldn't have missed them, even on a moving train.

And so he waited, wrestling as the kilometres slipped by, wanting to give his father the rest he needed for the long trip ahead, wanting to protect Inaa from herself. Finally, when he could wait no longer, he leaned forward, his feet pressed into the floor. At this moment, the car suddenly began to brighten—not the imperceptible brightening of a sunrise, but a light that seemed to rush toward them. Quite unexpectedly, they burst out of the tunnel and the train windows shimmered with the risen sun's rays.

Gizhaa wasted no time on the view of the Hudson Strait as passengers around him roused themselves and commented on the glorious morning. He grabbed the pack and slid past Rowan into the aisle.

"Good idea," his father mumbled, rubbing his eyes. "Beat the morning rush to the washroom."

Gizhaa turned toward the rear of the train, apologizing repeatedly as he bumped his way along. He passed through several cars, his anxiety increasing with each door he opened.

As he passed yet another row of seats without finding Inaa, a hand suddenly reached out and grabbed his sleeve. He looked down to find Ya Min looking up at him earnestly. She tugged lightly and slid over to make room for him.

"You are looking for something?" Even her whisper was music.

"I can't find my sister Inaa. I think she's with Tom." Gizhaa clenched his teeth, hearing the curtness of his voice.

Ya Min furrowed her brow. "You are concerned for her."

"I learned a lot yesterday. Perhaps it's stuff you know already, but it's news to me. I don't want Inaa getting involved." Gizhaa stood. "I'll catch up with you later."

Ya Min stood as well. "I will continue to the rear. You head back to the front." She turned and was gone. Gizhaa wondered if she could read minds.

As he passed his own seat, he saw that his father was gone now, too, hopefully to the washroom.

When there was nowhere else to look, he stood with his hand resting on the door marked Authorized Personnel Only. He made a fist to knock and the door swung open so that his fist nearly connected with Tom's nose. Both men stepped back in surprise. Inaa peered over Tom's shoulder as he bumped into her.

"Gizhaa? What are you doing here?" she sputtered.

His anxiety gave way to anger. "I've been looking all over for you is what I've been doing!"

"Whatever for? It's not like I could get off the train!"

"Not to worry, dear," a voice called cheerily from inside the cabin. A grey-haired woman stepped into view. "They were in good hands."

The woman smiled at Gizhaa and placed a wrinkled hand on Tom and Inaa's shoulders, giving them a tiny shove toward the door.

"But now I do need my command centre back, so on your way you go. Thank you for the company and enjoy the rest of your journey."

Gizhaa backed away, his cheeks flared with colour as Tom and Inaa stumbled toward him.

"And young lady," the conductor called merrily, "be sure to thank your suitors for their devoted attention."

Gizhaa and Inaa both opened their mouths to correct her, but the door shut and she was gone.

As they returned to their seats, Gizhaa and Inaa maintained an uneasy silence. Their father, having returned, rose soberly to greet them. He motioned for Inaa to take the seat beside him.

"It seems I'm the one who missed the tour this morning." Rowan raised his eyebrows but did not wait for a response. "The hostess just came by and said we are an hour away from Iqaluit. However, they will serve a full breakfast since yesterday's accident delayed our arrival."

Gizhaa was listening, but his eyes were fixed on the dome of smooth black hair visible in the seat directly opposite his father in the next booth. He was sure it was Ya Min. Apparently she had been concerned enough after their morning meeting to find herself a closer seat.

Gizhaa and Tom took the empty bench and Rowan proceeded to monopolize the conversation. This suited Inaa fine, as she was sulking over her brother's intervention in her affairs; it suited Gizhaa fine, too, as he worked to lower his heart rate after discovering Inaa and Tom together in the engineer's cabin.

Soon the delicious smell of warm maple syrup wafted through the cabin, and it wasn't long before the syrup was followed by heaping plates of hot cranberry pancakes. Gizhaa was surprised to hear his stomach growl. As he poured the thick amber liquid over his plate, the pat of butter oozing into the syrup, he felt the tension in his shoulders melt.

"Oh yes, *miigwech*," Ya min commented to the server behind them. "I like to call it 'Canadian gold.' It's quite a treat in China!"

The server moved along the aisle, but Ya Min continued to quietly chatter on. Her voice lowered as if for a nearby companion, but Gizhaa knew she had none.

Tom eagerly devoured his breakfast and occasionally interjected comments into Rowan's monologue. Inaa took small bites and stared blankly out the window.

Gizhaa leaned back against the bench as he slowly chewed his food, careful to focus his gaze on his father, as though catching every word even while he mentally tuned out.

"Of course, I would love to visit the port docks with you," Ya Min's voice lilted. "Let me know when it fits your schedule… Send a message to the Palais du

Nunavut… No, no, it will be no trouble at all… You must watch your step getting off the train, though. It can be a bit hazardous. And after the earthquake yesterday, I think you may feel some aftershocks… They say these earthquakes aren't what they used to be. Perhaps they will follow you… Yes, I will. *Miigwech*. And you, too… *Baamaapii* until then!"

In his mind's eye, Gizhaa saw her slide out of the booth and breeze away, but he forced himself not to turn his head.

After the breakfast dishes were cleared away, they gathered their things.

The train swooshed into the station dramatically and they jostled their way to the exit along with everyone else. Soon they found themselves outside, searching the crowd for Uncle Ben and Aunt Nancy. Gizhaa and Inaa, who hadn't seen them since their last visit to the alpaca farm, weren't sure what they were looking for, but they needn't have worried.

"Rowan! Gizhaa and Inaa!" a deep voice called from across the plaza.

Through the crowd, a trim, grey-haired man was taking long strides toward them. Behind him, a woman trotted to keep up.

Rowan set down his bag and threw his arms around the man.

"It's good to see you!" Rowan said. "How are you?"

Aunt Nancy wrapped her arms around Gizhaa and Inaa at the same time while Tom stood back awkwardly.

"Welcome, *boozhoo*, children!" Nancy said, greeting them.

"Children?" Uncle Ben boomed. "Not a bit—you have both changed so much! A real lady, Inaa. And Gizhaa, are you the same boy?"

They all laughed.

When the handshaking, shoulder-slapping, and hugging were done, Tom stepped forward to Inaa. "I have to go now. Where can I call for you?"

Nancy raised her eyebrows, smiling, and stuck out her hand. "*Boozhoo!* I'm sorry. We did not know Inaa had brought a friend. I'm Aunt Nancy."

"Tom. Thomas Waaban."

"Our guests will be staying with us at 43 Polar Street. You are welcome to call there," Nancy said.

Tom dropped his head in a quick thank you before disappearing into the crowd.

Inaa's dissenting hand had touched Aunt Nancy's arm a moment too late. She bit her lip. Would he call for her? Did she want him to? She sighed and bent to pick up two bags.

Yes to both questions, she thought grumpily. *Not that it matters what I want, apparently.*

The others were now hurrying to finish collecting the luggage. Uncle Ben had arranged a horse-drawn carriage to take them across the city. It waited patiently at the far corner of the plaza.

"Not our usual mode of transportation," he noted humbly, "but today is a special occasion. And you should be introduced to the capital in style!"

The horse was jet black, except for his white hooves, and the carriage behind was dark red with large wheels that reached as high as Inaa's chest. She swung the bags easily into the rear. She settled herself into a seat as Gizhaa stepped in front to rub the horse's nose and talk to it.

"Inaa, Gizhaa!" their father's voice called. He sounded upset, bordering on panic. "Did either of you grab that last pack from the plaza?"

Gizhaa came running back. "It's okay, dad! I've had it all along." He patted his shoulder straps.

"No, Gizhaa, not that one," Rowan said, lowering his voice but not his urgency. "The one with the tribute. It's not here!"

"It *is* here," Gizhaa tried again. "I rearranged the bags yesterday morning before we boarded the train." He shifted his weight on his feet and whispered, "I had a premonition of trouble, so I went ahead and moved the gift into my pack." He patted his shoulder strap once more.

Rowan breathed a sigh of relief. "Bless you, boy. You gave me a good start there. But now then, where is the other bag, even if it doesn't have the gift in it? I would like to have clothes to wear when I get to the *Naawayi*." He added in muttered frustration, "Can't appear naked, for land's sake!"

Gizhaa tried unsuccessfully to laugh at his father's angst. "No, no. It was my clothes I moved into that pack."

The five of them took careful stock of the luggage, then retraced their steps across the now-empty plaza. They were indeed short one pack.

"I know I had it when we got off the train," Rowan said. "I must have set it down when we were talking."

Nancy shook her head. "I can't imagine someone would take it on purpose. It might have been mistakenly picked up, or turned in to Lost and Found."

"Well, we had better check and report that it's missing," Uncle Ben decided. "Seems a little too suspicious for my liking, though. Let's get going." He cast a long glance around the empty plaza.

As Ben had predicted, the bag wasn't waiting at Lost and Found and the clerk seemed clueless as to what to do with the information of a missing bag.

"Really?" she said. "I've never dealt with a stolen luggage complaint. Perhaps you left it on the train?"

Eventually they did get themselves back into the beautiful, horse-drawn carriage, but a sombre mood had descended on the group. As they drove up the gentle slope away from the station toward the centre of the city, Gizhaa was forced to explain why he had taken the time to move the tribute from its original pack into his own backpack for safekeeping, though he was careful not to mention Tom or Ya Min. Then Rowan related how Elder Gichi-Baawiting had warned him of danger on the trip. Inaa chimed in to explain how the train had been delayed by an earthquake.

"I can't imagine what concern anyone would have for our journey," Rowan said. The anxiety he had felt in the plaza was given full vent in the relative privacy of the carriage. "The tribute has always been taken annually to the *Ogimaa* for the *Dagwaagin*[24] Festival!"

It was Uncle Ben, not Gizhaa, who glanced suspiciously at the driver of the cab and motioned to Rowan to lower his voice. "Your friend Gichi-Baawiting was right, and I think there is more to this story than we should discuss at the moment. Let's enjoy the view of the city."

Aunt Nancy had been planning for weeks all the places she wanted to point out to her guests, as well as the histories she wanted to relate, so this was all the encouragement she needed. Over the next half-hour, her quiet voice swept them over the swells and ebbs of the Arctic streetscape. Rowan, Gizhaa, and Inaa, only half-listening, learned that Iqaluit had once been an Arctic port city, isolated in a frozen wilderness. Her description was at odds with the lush gardens that adorned the streets and the fruit trees draped over their heads, some still heavy with the last apples of the season. They passed a tall ship and a small fleet of state-of-the-art commercial vessels at the docks—for making deliveries to the bio-miners, she said.

At the height of the ridge, they circled Parliament, called *Igalaaq*.[25] It towered above the modest proportions of the rest of the architecture with a grand red steel roof, but three of the walls were largely made of glass, and at the moment they were opened wide to the fresh air. Inside, a large courtyard could be seen overflowing with a storybook garden, complete with mown grass, plum trees, and birds that flew freely through the building. The birdsong wafted clearly to them, and for a moment Gizhaa thought he could recognize the tune to the rhythmic clatter of horses'

---

24 *Dagwaagin*: fall.

25 *Igalaaq*: window.

hooves. Parliament seemed to be more like an open terrace, albeit with a roof, than a fixture of bureaucracy.

Aunt Nancy proved to be the best tour guide imaginable as they rode down the picturesque streets. And although Rowan, Gizhaa and Inaa may have been consumed by their own thoughts, Nancy's charismatic storytelling proved no match for their private concerns.

chapter fifteen

NINGIDE
"MELT"

"A semi-ice age had imprisoned the Arctic for many centuries before *Miigaadiwin*, which made sense since the far north received little direct sunlight for half the year back then. Those were long winters, let me tell you! I remember our first winter here when Ben and I were newlyweds. We had arrived in September to work on a *National Geographic* piece about polar bears. In those days, it was the story of a lifetime, though you've never heard of the publication now. It was the kind of break every writer dreams of.

"I picked up a job as a nurse at the clinic. They were always short on nurses in those days. No one wanted to stay here longer than a year or two, it seemed. Anyway, that meant the pay was good and we figured we were tougher than the average white guys. We'd stick it out somehow. So we were slightly delusional. By the time the deepest days of winter hit, I had to head to work in the dark every morning, if you could call it morning. At noon, the clinic staff would step outside in the bitter cold to get some referred sunlight, as it at least warmed the sky a shade of dawn, but we didn't see the sun itself for weeks. About that time of day, Ben would be out polar bear hunting on his snow machine, with his camera and a gun for security—polar bears don't hibernate, of course. He'd do a little research in the field, then head back home to write and research some more. By the time my shift was done, dusk had passed and it was pitch black again."

Aunt Nancy shivered involuntarily. "I thought I would go crazy that winter, except for the northern lights. It was the best year on record. You don't see them like that anymore! The sky would light up all around and there wasn't much out here to block your view. Luminescent green fingers would reach up from the horizon. They danced—there's no other word for it. I could put up with the dark just to see those lights. Solar storms, apparently, is what we were watching. I don't know, I think it was the hand of God.

"At that time, Iqaluit was a mere village compared to now, a few hundred rectangular buildings on a barren landscape. Back in those days, nothing grew here—no trees, no gardens. Well, I shouldn't say *nothing*. There were the monster mosquitos, and lichen, and a few wildflowers managed to take hold in the short, dry summers. But fruit trees? Kiwi vines? Roses? Not a chance." Aunt Nancy laughed at the thought.

Finally Gizhaa was drawn into asking, "What changed?"

"What changed?" Nancy was clearly delighted to be asked. "Well, for starters, the earth had been warming for some decades before *Miigaadiwin*. No one was quite sure of the cause and people were pretty concerned about what would happen when the polar ice melted. I know it's hard for you to imagine, but the Arctic ice was over four kilometres deep in places! Imagine! The danger was that if enough of this ice melted, the pooled water would reflect less light, allowing the remaining ice to melt even faster. The melting could become exponential. Some scientists had estimated that if all the polar ice melted, the ocean would rise by seventy meters. And I suppose that's what would have happened, because the north was undoubtedly melting and warming. I think it had reached the tipping point.

"But before this environmental disaster came to be, our lives changed forever. Your Uncle Ben's journalistic work led him to an assignment in the Middle East. Both this and the new assignment involved rugged conditions, isolation, and guns. Maybe the feds figured he was a tough guy after surviving a year in the Arctic. He took the job. We weren't naive. We knew the war wasn't going away anytime soon. We knew that journalists were prime targets for jihadists. But Ben said to me, 'Innocent people are going to die and I might be able to make a difference.' Saying goodbye to him was the hardest thing I ever did. I thought I would never see him again.

"Within weeks, I couldn't stand the waiting, so I volunteered to go, too, rather than sit here in the dark waiting for whatever would come. North Africa was desperate for medical staff as a plague was sweeping across the region, moving from Africa to the Middle East—the virus of the millennium. I won't even tell you what it was like over there."

Nancy paused and bit her lip with the memory.

"It wasn't long after our change in circumstances that the world changed in a way no one could have anticipated. You say you felt an earthquake, but there's no comparison to this. This quake shook the very foundations of the earth and all the continental coasts were flooded. There wasn't a city on earth that didn't feel it. What no one could see at the time, but we discovered much later, was that millennia of tectonic pressure had finally succeeded in dislodging an entire plate. The tiny Scotia plate, off the southern tip of South America—are you familiar with it?—simply disappeared into the asthenosphere, the hotter, inner crust of the planet. That deeper, elastic skin flexed enough to accept the downward pressure, I suppose. It doesn't take much imagination to realize that a piece of the earth's mantle retreating underground means massive upheaval on the surface.

"For one thing, nearly every dormant volcano on earth erupted. The vast amount of ash released by those eruptions was incredibly destructive. Life everywhere immediately ground to a halt. Darkness prevented work and travel, making life miserable for some weeks. Wherever the ash settled, fresh water became undrinkable. The abrasive ash destroyed pumping equipment, and it was toxic to animals that fed off the grass, so wildlife and farm animals died in large numbers. The ashfall shorted out what was left of the electrical grid. Obviously, this was a catastrophe on many levels. That was the beginning of the change.

"The ash was so thick that the sun was blocked for many days, causing a sudden cooling of the earth. Water vapour that had been evaporating off those melting polar ice caps began to condense. Some of it came down as massive hailstones, some fell as acid rain, but the rest condensed as ice. The violence of the continuing eruptions spewed some of those ice-covered particles into the upper atmosphere—the ionosphere, to be exact. That's the scientist in me. In fact, you see those particles every day. Look up now and you can barely see *Didi* in the bright sunlight, but it's always there sweeping across the sky. *That* is the ashfall, now a thousand years old. Trapped in that ring is water—not much, mind you, or we'd all fry, but just enough to turn the earth into an all-round toasty greenhouse from the equator to the poles. Hot equatorial deserts cooled off and these frozen wastelands warmed right up.

"The second thing the ash gave us was fertile soil. The Arctic desert became covered with dust as the trade winds blew north from the equator, dumping a fine layer of fertilizer over everything. Of course, ashfall destroys the plants it rains on, but unlike the south, we didn't really have much to lose. And ash is a goldmine of minerals from deep inside the earth. It was exactly what the surface needed to become fruitful once again.

"By itself, that wasn't enough to make the Arctic bloom the way you see today, because we still only had a few months of long days, but a third thing began to happen. When the Scotia plate disappeared, the other plates rushed into its place. Well, *rush* is a relative term, but in a few centuries the Arctic had moved south enough that it was no longer abandoned to darkness half the year. The Scotia gap basically caused less resistance to the plates moving south and caused fresh layers of oceanic crust formation at the convergence of the Eurasian and Northern American plates. For us, that means longer, warmer summers. Are you following me?"

Gizhaa and Inaa nodded politely. Rowan was lost in thought.

"Here now we're passing the docks at Koojesse Inlet. Notice the colour of the water? That iridescent teal is the result of dissolved minerals, a gift from the glacial ice. Canada's most famous artists have painted here to capture that liquid spectrum." She gestured with great admiration. She couldn't have been prouder had she painted the hue in place herself.

"After *Miigaadiwin,* there was a massive migration away from the cities. There wasn't much left for the survivors there anyway. Although the polar ice continued to melt over the centuries, the coastal cities were relatively sparsely populated by then. The King allotted lands to everyone and most people were happy to start over on a parcel of their own.

"I don't suppose those who received a slice of the Arctic were thrilled at first. But when the King requested that Ben and I come back and work with the pioneers, we were elated. To be sure, that first decade was hard slugging, but even with the shortened days, the land responded so quickly we could hardly keep up. Every year, more land became viable to sow and the families worked side by side with us. Turned out, that frozen soil trapped under the ice for a few millennia was ripe for harvest, chock full of nutrients. We didn't need much land to feed ourselves since the population was still very small. And for those first years, we allowed the people to continue fishing and hunting to supplement what we could grow."

Inaa grimaced as though the idea had never occurred to her.

"Not only was the soil good for growing," Nancy assured her, "the food it produced contained micronutrients that had been previously undiscovered. Even today, the nutrient-rich foods we grow here are the best medicine this planet has seen since Eden. Our northern families grew quickly and soon children were running through the streets again. We're still very close to some of the generations who stayed in the city, but most have spread across Nunavut, some still breaking new ground in the far north. Make no mistake, it's hard work. In many places they have to build ditches to drain all that melted ice water from the soil, and dykes to hold back the ocean, but the results speak for themselves.

"That brings us to the nation's capital! It was only about a century after *Miigaadiwin* that the government recognized that the country's new centre really was here. Our strengths no longer lay in the wastelands of the polluted southern cities, but in the fresh, untouched north. Funny how the lowliest of Canadian capitals became the first, and so Iqaluit was chosen to be the Canadian capital. Of course, the offshore bio-mines certainly focused the world's attention here. That was a big part of the decision to move the capital.

"But here we are! Driver, please pull right up to the *Ma Tu*.[26] Yes, thank you. Notice the mountain range we've been climbing into the city? It creates a microclimate for our fruit trees. As you'll see, Ben and I have a bit of an obsession with fruit trees."

"Welcome Rowan, Gizhaadan, and Inaabam to our '*ma tu* with a view'!"

---

26 *Ma tu*: door.

chapter sixteen

MA TU
"DOOR"

Inaa didn't need to be told that *ma tu* meant "door" in Inuktitut, because that was all she could see of the house above them on the hillside. A forest of vines crept up the hill, forming into a seamless, vertical wall before spilling raucously down about a door. The *ma tu* seemed to be made of wood, though it may have been bamboo; it was hard to tell from below. It peered out from the vine wall, separating into two individual doors that together formed a delicate arch through the greenery. The doors met in a stained-glass pane, shaped like a pear. Light from within the house shone through the pane, scattering green and gold highlights across the wood. The carved leaves of a pear branch cascaded down the *ma tu*, coaxing guests to stroke the wood.

Inaa exhaled in awe. The long list of burning questions unearthed by Aunt Nancy's history evaporated from her mind.

Aunt Nancy laughed and patted her shoulder. "It has that effect on me, too, every day. I've always loved a good door."

Nancy jumped nimbly from the wagon. Ben was already collecting their luggage from the rear of the carriage, and soon they were climbing the stone-hewn stairs. The granite beneath her feet reminded her of the surety of the same Canadian Shield at home that occasionally raised its bare shoulders above the soil. Many days she pulled off her shoes to feel the steady warmth of the sun radiate into her legs from that granite. And here, after the weaving of the train and carriage, she instinctively stooped to place her hand on a sun-warmed stone step. It was secure.

"Welcome!" Aunt Nancy called as she swung open the double doors and swept out of view.

Inaa straightened and hurried up the last steps. The room before her filled with the golden sunshine of late harvest days. She instinctively breathed deeply, tasting the smell of fresh homemade bread. The floor beneath her feet continued in stone until it met the back wall, a wall of granite cut into the hillside; water trickled down the stone, blackening its surface, and disappeared into a trench at its base.

"I'm in the kitchen," Aunt Nancy called from a doorway to the left. "You'll be hungry for breakfast."

"You better run and tell her we ate on the train," Rowan spoke from the doorway behind Inaa. His voice sounded tired and strained.

Inaa followed her aunt into the kitchen, which faced back out to the road. From inside Inaa could see there were three windows from this room, but they had become so overgrown with vines that they'd been invisible from outside. The effect in the kitchen was a warm, green-lit room that seemed alive and safe.

"We ate breakfast on the train, Aunt Nancy," she said.

"Well, never mind then. We'll call it second breakfast. I'm half-hobbit, you know, living half-underground." Nancy laughed at her own joke.

Inaa wrinkled her brow. "You're half what?"

Nancy smiled. "You're too young for my humour, dear. I made fresh cinnamon buns and there's coffee and cider. I think it's time to hear more about your adventures."

The rest of that day passed very quickly. Stories were exchanged over many steaming beverages, and they spent the afternoon exploring the neighbourhood's extensive gardens and parks. Dinner at *Ma Tu* with a View was leisurely and dessert was hand-picked pears from the hillside orchard that threatened to overwhelm the burrow.

As they sat on the sun-warmed steps and sucked the sweet juice from their pears, Inaa marvelled at the sunset across the harbour.

Aunt Nancy slid down beside her and cosily tucked her hand through Inaa's arm. "We have some quality young people to introduce you to. And you, too, Gizhaa! A week in the capital isn't an opportunity to be wasted. But first you have an invitation to visit Parliament tomorrow morning with your father. I wouldn't be surprised if Prime Minister Waaban himself doesn't meet with you."

"And Tom," Inaa murmured.

"Hmm, what's that, dear? Tom?"

Inaa blushed. "Nothing." She shut her eyes. Why had she said that? Something was rattling in her mind. For a moment she had known something, but it was gone now.

"Is that the young man we met at the train station?" Nancy asked. "Will you see him tomorrow?"

Inaa shrugged. "Perhaps. He's working at the legislature." She shifted on the hard granite, then looked up, fixing her gaze across the harbour. "I would like to make time for a walk down by the waterfront this week. Is that big building the trace mineral refinery?"

Uncle Ben stood up farther down the stairs and pointed across the bay. "That refinery produces minerals used in many of the newest solar inventions. I can arrange a tour for us later this week if you're interested. What do you think, Gizhaa?"

Gizhaa startled from his own thoughts. "Tour the refinery? By the harbour? Ahhh… Sure, I would like to head down there sometime." He stood up and stretched. "I'm still wondering about that strange earthquake. What do you think?"

"I think we should go inside and chat before bed." His uncle nodded.

Gizhaa sent his pear core sailing across the hillside into a clump of trees with a quick flick of the wrist. "Excellent suggestion!"

As the fading light turned from gold to a red glow, the group moved through the *ma tu* into the waterfall room. Ben sat on a woollen couch and motioned for the others to do likewise.

"Your trip here represents a lot to our nation. But you are only a small part of a much bigger celebration. The train you came on yesterday carried many North American dignitaries: some destined for the Centre and others coming to celebrate the festival in the capital. I wasn't born yesterday, and I'm willing to bet there are people who would be very happy to see that train derailed. That earthquake wasn't an accident."

"But who would oppose a peaceful celebration?" Rowan burst out angrily. "What on earth would motivate such an act?"

"I don't know yet, but I promise you I will find out," Ben said grimly. Then he smiled. "I am still a journalist at heart!"

"And a good one," Nancy said, reaching over to pat his knee.

"The disappearance of your bag might be connected, Rowan," Ben continued. "You said that this bag originally contained the tribute?"

"Until yesterday morning when I moved it into my backpack," Gizhaa answered.

"Why did you do this?" Ben probed.

Gizhaa shifted his weight. "I had a sense that we may have been followed earlier, so I decided to play it safe."

"And you've learned to trust your instincts," Ben concluded.

Rowan grimaced. "We all have."

"Which makes me think that whoever wanted to stop that train may have been targeting you and the delivery of the tribute," Ben said.

Inaa shook her head. "What? We don't even know the earthquake wasn't a natural event. Now you're thinking that we were targeted? That's a huge leap!"

"It is, but it's a possibility that needs to be explored. And until we can rule it out we're going to have to be cautious," Uncle Ben replied. "But back to your original question, Rowan—what might motivate this? If the attack sought to stop you from delivering the tribute to the Centre, then a motive does present itself."

"I can't imagine one," Rowan said.

Inaa's eyes opened wide. "Stopping the tribute would release us from the Immortals' reign," she breathed.

Uncle Ben looked at her strangely. "Exactly. I've heard rumours that there are some who question the wisdom of Prime Minister Waaban's government remaining under the King. Preventing the tribute from reaching the King would send a clear message that Canadians favour moving away from his authority."

Aunt Nancy blew out a loud sigh. "As if the fools didn't know that Waaban is immortal himself!"

Inaa caught her breath. "The prime minister is an Immortal?"

Nancy laughed. "Goodness, of course he is! How else could he rule the country for nine hundred years?"

Inaa blushed. "I don't know. I don't pay attention to politics."

"I suppose that's understandable," Uncle Ben said, nodding. "But I'm not sure ignorance is the excuse of these troublemakers."

"Inaa is right, though," Nancy said. "If the tribute were not to arrive at the Centre for the Festival, it could be seen as an act of rebellion against the King's reign."

"More than that," Ben continued. "It could be the impetus to springboard our country into civil conflict. If this rumour is true, if dissent against the King is turning into organized rebellion, then a reckless move like this makes perfect sense: stop the tribute, highlight the cause of the rebellion, and lure us into civil war."

Inaa bit her lip. The dream, so real in her mind just this morning, now made sense in light of Ben's convictions. Had the man in her dream not announced the Revival's intention to throw off the Immortals' bonds? Surely the Creator had given her this dream, but why? She must enter into the dream, whatever the outcome. She was called to go.

"How do we know that the *Ogimaa* wants the Immortals to reign?" Inaa asked tentatively.

Uncle Ben smiled. "After Miigaadiwin, the Ogimaa gave the 'Immortals,' as you say, leadership over the nations. It was a responsibility earned by their sacrifice."

"Sacrifice?" Gizhaa asked.

Uncle Ben and Aunt Nancy gave each other a knowing look. "That is not bedtime story material, I'm afraid," Ben said with a sigh.

"But Uncle Ben," Gizhaa pressed, "you're right about the opposition to the government. There is something organized."

Inaa's stomach knotted. Did Gizhaa know her secret? Or was he making assumptions from Tom's rant last night?

Uncle Ben held up a hand. "Gizhaa, we must talk more on this, but if we don't get you folks to bed before morning we will endanger the entire tribute mission. No conspiracy theory required!"

Everyone smiled and chuckled and the cloud of foreboding ebbed.

"All is well tonight and we will pray sweet rest for each of you," Aunt Nancy called to them as they disappeared into cool, lavender-scented rooms.

Inaa was sure she would never sleep, her mind full of puzzles and questions. But she remembered nothing from the moment her head touched the pillow and she dreamt no dreams that night.

chapter seventeen

MIZHAKWAD
"CLEAR"

"Transparency. That was what they wanted people to see here."

"Well, they got that right," Gizhaa said with a touch of awe. "No place to hide, is there?"

Uncle Ben chuckled. "They wanted the people to know that there would be no secrets in our government. All has been revealed."

Inaa was only half-listening as she marvelled at the glass building in which they stood. The morning sunlight streamed through the walls of Parliament, filtering through the ambrosia vines. Some of the walls had even been slid open, allowing the cool fall breeze to flow through from the Hudson Channel.

"What has been revealed, Uncle Ben?" she asked. A small white bird circled her head before alighting on the stone pavement between them.

"A ptarmigan, the official bird of the North." Uncle Ben stooped down and reached his hand toward it. The little bird hopped forward and pecked at his fingers. "Before *Miigaadiwin*, Inaa, a mystery had been hidden until the fullness of time had come. It was the mystery of God's plan."

Inaa wrinkled her brow. She had heard that phrase recently. Wasn't that what Tom had said, that many things were about to be revealed in the fullness of time?

"But now we no longer have any mystery," Ben said. "Although we cannot yet see all that God has in store for us—the complete restoration of creation, the restoration of his relationship to it—the mystery is revealed."

The little bird hopped up onto Ben's hand and looked at him expectantly. He slowly stood and reached his other hand into his pocket, bringing out a seed for the bird.

Rowan walked up behind Ben and clapped his hand on his back, startling the bird into flight. "Ben, Prime Minister Waaban is ready to meet with us."

An aide stood politely to the side, ready to escort them to the Prime Minister's office.

Gizhaa and Inaa looked at each other, disappointed.

"We'll just hang around here until you're done," Gizhaa volunteered, holding out the backpack which still contained their precious tribute.

Rowan took the pack with ceremonial care, though it had bounced across a thousand kilometres already, and turned to follow Ben and the aide.

Inaa watched as they passed through a pair of wrought-iron gates that opened silently into the Hall of Windows, the invitation-only area. Words had been engraved into the gold above the door. As the gate swung shut behind her father, she approached it and read the inscription:

One road will be green and lush and very inviting.
The other road will be black and charred, and walking it will cut their feet.
Take neither road, but instead turn back, remember
and reclaim the wisdom of those who came before.[27]

"I wonder what it means," she said to Gizhaa as he came up behind her.

"I don't know," he admitted. "But I wonder if there's a washroom in this place? I'm going to see if I can find one—preferably without glass walls."

Gizhaa walked on through the atrium, disappearing around a grove of magnolia trees just as a group of tourists came through the lobby. The tour guide was chattering on about the building's architect.

Inaa slid into the group as it passed. When the guide took a breath, Inaa waved her hand.

"What is the meaning of the *mazinikojigan*[28] engraved above the gate?" she asked.

"Excellent question!" the guide enthused, clearly delighted to have a curious student. "I'm glad you drew our attention to this insightful piece of history! This is the last warning of the Seven Fires that was passed down through generations of our brothers, centuries before *Miigaadiwin*. The speaker saw mere shadows of the mystery that was to be revealed. And yet he pointed ahead to the days in which the truth

---

27 *Wikipedia*, "Seven fires prophecy." Accessed: October 19, 2017. Excerpted and edited by the author from the Anishinaabeg oral tradition.

28 *Mazinikojigan*: carving.

would be available to all—even to this great period of history! The words you see here warn the settlers of Canada to seek the road of life. The engraving does not elaborate, but the speaker also pointed to a time when a New People would retrace their steps to the teachings of the elders. With the Fall Festival less than a week away, it is appropriate to remember this ancient declaration. Indeed, the Creator has established a New People over us and among us."

Inaa opened her mouth. Who were the New People? What were the two roads? What wisdom were they to reclaim?

But before the words came out, a voice whispered in Inaa's ear, "Excellent question, Inaa!"

The tour guide pointed to a group of birds winging overhead. Everyone moved on through the magnolia trees as Inaa stepped away and came to face Tom.

He frowned dramatically. "Why didn't you tell me you were taking a tour of Parliament this morning? I would have set you up with a private tour." His playful grin broke out. "There's still time! Come on."

Inaa followed Tom through a set of wide glass doors into a hallway. She was vaguely aware that Gizhaa would soon return to the lobby and wonder where she had gone. His disdain for Tom was more than evident, but this seemed like her only opportunity to warn Tom about his affiliation with the Revival. Maybe if he could be made to see where this was taking him, he could be saved from what she had seen in the dream. Surely if he understood what the Revival was becoming, he would change his mind.

"It's only my first day on the job, but let me show you the best part of the building," Tom said.

He took a quick turn and began up a flight of stairs while Inaa ran to keep up. Breathless, she walked through a door that Tom swung wide and held open for her. A gust of wind from the harbour caught her braid and blew it across her face. As she swept it away, an expanse opened before her. They stood on a transparent balcony off the great red roof. The land fell away behind Parliament, leaving them to hover over a glass building. Tom watched her expression eagerly.

Inaa gulped. "It's beautiful." She looked out over the water and bit her lip. "How did you land such a great job, Tom?"

Tom stood at the glass railing and leaned out. For a moment, he hesitated. "You know, I'm not exactly sure. I didn't even apply actually." He tilted his head to one side. "I figure they sent head-hunters to check my school for prospects."

"Oh, sure," Inaa said, nodding. She wished she had sounded convinced. She drew a breath and decided to just say it. "Do you think any of your Revival friends might have pulled some strings for you?"

He frowned. "Of course not. It's a grassroots organization. It's not like we have people in every political office getting appointments for all their friends." His offense was undisguised.

Inaa was in too far to turn back now. "Tom, I think you should be careful about your connection to the Revival. I… I know about the Revival."

Tom's eyes lit up. "You do?"

"They aren't just trying to rebuild the great civilizations of the past. It's much bigger than that."

"Yeah, that's the amazing part. It's really about putting power back in the hands of the people. Supporting their rights to land ownership and self-governance. Ultimately, it's a revolution of ideals."

Tom put his hands in his pockets and rolled against the railing, his back to the harbour now, studying her.

Inaa's heart pounded in her chest. She felt sweat trickling down her sides. She had to say this just right. She had to use all her diplomacy.

"I can see you are passionate about helping people, Tom. I understand that you want to make a difference, but the Revival leaders aren't going where you think they are."

He opened his mouth to interrupt, then closed it, listening.

Encouraged, she continued. "They are forming an alliance. They want to revive more than just the culture."

Tom exhaled loudly. "So, you know about that? Look, I figured you were in, but I didn't know you were this deep. Maybe I did say too much the other night, but I really wanted to know where you stood with all this."

Inaa's head spun.

"The alliance is still top secret," he reprimanded her. "Grassroots aside, our guys at the top have worked hard getting that deal lined up. You need to be careful who you're talking to."

Inaa's confusion turned to irritation. "Clearly I'm talking to you!" she sputtered.

"All right, all right. I'm safe." He blew out his breath. "The alliance between the Revival and China is far from ready to be disclosed, that's all. It's a necessary piece of the puzzle to give people back the power to control their future. See, before the Immortals arrived, the planet's water supply was bankrupt: polluted, frozen, expensive, or dried up. People everywhere were desperate for clean water. Everywhere except

Canada, it seemed. So the Canadian government wisely decided to share their resources with other good-willed nations. In particular, the Chinese won the bid to
purchase Canadian freshwater. This arrangement brought money into Canada and
supported China's burgeoning population. Today, there's no shortage of drinking
water, but Canada obviously inherited more than its fair share of the bio-mining
industry, more than we know what to do with. The Revival is simply working to
re-establish the trade alliance these nations once enjoyed. Such a relationship would
clearly benefit both nations economically, providing the Chinese with the trace
minerals necessary to develop their own technologies and putting money into the
hands of every Canadian."

Inaa couldn't breathe. The alliance he spoke of wasn't with *Ohsh* at all. Everything he said sounded so simple and logical. No conspiracy, no revolution. No attempt to hide his political ambitions. But the dream was real. And now that Tom had
revealed the plans of the Revival, she needed to play along.

She attempted to shrug nonchalantly. "Of course, I understand about the water
situation. We all know that whoever controls the water wields the power." As little as
she understood about the Revival's goals, she had figured out enough to know that
power was an important one. "Putting power back in the hands of the people could
revolutionize our culture… However, it seems to me that the Revival," she choked
on the words, "that *we* might be in danger of being infiltrated."

She tried to slow her breathing, tried to sound like this was a normal discussion
she had every day with other progressive thinkers.

Tom's eyes narrowed. "How so?"

"I'm not at liberty to reveal my sources." She flipped her braid arrogantly and
turned away from him. "However, I am privy to information which reveals that
Ohshkagoonjing Giizis wants a piece of the pie," she finished firmly. It was her best
acting job ever.

Tom began to laugh behind her. She whirled to face him. He rolled his eyes.

"You can't be serious! The *Ohsh* were eradicated a millennium ago. In fact,
I'm not even sure they ever existed at all. There's nothing left but legends: no foundations, no culture, no writings. Do you think an entire civilization could have
simply vanished?"

Inaa wanted to cry. She bit her lip.

He went on. "Look, I don't know what they're working on at your local Revival chapter. Hey, if dropping hints about *Ohsh* gets you guys fired up and brings in
new members, that's fine. We all need a reason to get on board, right?"

Inaa stared at him. She moved her mouth but couldn't think of anything to say.

"I'm not crazy." It wasn't exactly the most un-crazy thing to say, she thought. "I know more than you think I do." Like what? What did she really know? She closed her eyes and remembered the face in her dream. "I know who the leader of the Revival is."

For the first time, Tom honestly seemed caught off-guard. "How could you know that?"

"I've seen him." It wasn't a lie. She hadn't said she had seen him *in person*. She hadn't said she knew his name.

Now it was Tom's turn to be confused. "Nobody has met him. Not the head of my chapter, not even the head of the whole New York Revival."

Inaa straightened her shoulders. "I know who he is and I've seen him," she declared boldly. "And he told me that *Ohsh* will join us."

At this moment, the door to the stairwell opened wide and a smartly dressed woman with short blonde hair strode onto the deck, followed by an entourage of a dozen politicians. Among them Inaa recognized the ambassador from Mexico who had invited her father to dinner. Her eyes briefly locked with a young Chinese diplomat who seemed familiar. But then the group flowed past to the railing overlooking the waterfront.

Tom straightened, his skin turning a shade darker. Inaa didn't have the blessing of brown skin to hide her reddening cheeks.

The first woman smiled with surprise when she saw them. "Tom, I'm glad you've arrived early for our al fresco lunch meeting." She raised her eyebrows and turned toward Inaa.

Tom seemed shaken and fumbled his words. "Ah, yes, of course. I was just taking in some air before we get down to work. Um, I ran into a friend who was touring Parliament today. We've just been catching up. Inaa, this is the Minister of Foreign Affairs... ah, my new boss. Minister, this is Inaa Selah."

The Minister's eyes lit up. "Selah? You must be travelling with the tribute!"

Inaa bowed slightly. "Nice to meet you, Minister. Yes, my father is carrying it to the Centre."

Inaa sensed Tom turning toward her, his mouth slightly agape, but she didn't glance at him.

The woman beamed. "Are you travelling all the way with him?"

"No, my journey takes a different direction."

Tom's chest lifted slightly. Inaa realized ruefully that he was proud of her, proud of the "different direction" she was choosing.

The entourage began to spread out around the balcony; some sat on wicker furniture, others leaned against the railing. Each had arrived with a linen-enfolded lunch which they began to unwrap as conversations wafted on the wind.

"Oh, my dear, that is a shame. It is the journey of a lifetime! To stand in the court of the King is a moment that changes you forever." The woman turned toward the harbour and Inaa felt that the Minister had let herself float somewhere far away. "The smell of the incense is heavenly." She shook herself and smiled at Inaa once more. "I hope someday you are able to go yourself."

"Thank you, Minister. I will excuse myself now. I'm sure my family will be looking for me."

Tom walked Inaa to the door. He seemed to be studying their shoes as they moved in step with each other across the clear surface. He opened the door for her.

As she stepped past him, he whispered in her ear, "I trust your mission will go well then, sister. It seems you have been chosen for such a time as this."

Inaa was quite sure he meant something entirely different than she intended, but her answer was honest and clear. "I have."

chapter eighteen

THE SEVENTH FIRE

Ben led them along the streets, always heading slightly uphill, back toward *Ma Tu* with a View. The afternoon sun was no longer warm and they walked quickly.

They had made several stops at historic points of interest since their morning at Parliament. Gizhaa had insisted on seeing the Palais du Nunavut, shaped like an enormous igloo, the traditional hunting shelter of the Inuit people. Although hard-packed snow was no longer available from which to cut the blocks, the builders had fashioned it from bales of straw, coated in white plaster—a simple structure on a grandiose scale.

While Inaa and Rowan were delighted to tour the serene, domed interior with its crystal chandeliers and deep oriental carpets, Gizhaa's only interest seemed to be in leaving a message at the desk.

With the city centre behind them and the gentle slope of the suburbs rising ahead, Inaa spoke. "Uncle Ben, what is the meaning of the inscription above the gate into the parliamentary chambers? Something about two roads: 'One road will be green and lush, the other road will be black and charred. Take neither road.' Something like that."

Uncle Ben was silent for some time, and Inaa began to wonder if he hadn't heard her. Then he began to tell a story with the deep, humble voice that could only mean a *gikinoo'amaagoowin* teaching. His words came with a measured flow and careful enunciation, so that his voice resonated.

△   △   △

"Before your ancestors set foot on this continent, the Ancient Peoples—the *Nisay-enh*, you say—did not have the Word. They had only the oral traditions passed down from generation to generation, as we pass our wisdom down to you. Nevertheless, the Creator had not left them without a witness to Himself. He gave them the great expanse of the sky, the call of the lark, and the ripples in the water. And across the generations came speakers to point some on a path to the Jubilee, the redemption of all things. The Creator was always calling them to the knowledge of his plan, but it took many generations for them to find it.

"The Seven Fires guided the Anishinaabeg peoples to migrate many times. Each time the Creator drew them closer to his heart, to Jubilee. The last warning to the Ancient Peoples, which you read above the gate, opened, 'In the time of the Seventh Fire, New People will emerge.'[29] This occurred in the days of *Miigaadiwin*, for a New People did emerge on the earth… I was there to see it.

"Nancy told you yesterday that I travelled east to expose the conflict there. At that time, most people still thought it was a regional war in danger of spilling over into other parts of the world. There had been isolated acts of violence even here in Canada with roots in *Ohsh*, but our government feared that casting these in light of the larger conflict would create an environment of fear and hatred. To their credit, most Canadians remained a determinedly optimistic people.

"I, however, did not have the luxury of optimism. Leading up to my placement as a journalist with *Ohsh*, I gradually got myself noticed in the wrong circles. Not by chance, by choice. *Ohsh* had chapters in every city. My work gave me all kinds of connections, so it wasn't hard for me to 'volunteer' as a recruiter for a new Iqaluit chapter. The isolation of the far north had thankfully protected the people here and gave me enough freedom to allegedly continue my work as a recruiter without any real accountability, except for what I invented on my own with multiple aliases. Basically, no one from *Ohsh* checked my work and I drummed it up big-time, supposedly recruiting a small northern army. Meanwhile I collected bucketloads of hard data on *Ohsh*: names, addresses, meeting places, plans, dates.

"Of course, the inevitable did eventually happen. The feds caught up with me, which was exactly what I had been expecting all along. After a couple days in prison, I was able to convince the investigators that I was legit and had information they badly needed. Fortunately, I'd had the foresight to keep strict records of all my

---

29 *Wikipedia*, "Seven fires prophecy." Accessed: October 19, 2017. Excerpted and edited by the author from the Anishinaabeg oral tradition.

aliases, so proving my duplicity was easy. And it was much faster and easier to get taken seriously by the feds as a would-be terrorist recruiter than as a polar bear researcher. That was the way the world turned in those days.

"My assignment from the feds was to get behind *Ohsh*'s lines and feed information back. I signed up to go to war with *Ohsh*, leaving Canada under the guise of journalism. The feds got me out of the country since border officials weren't letting many people travel to the conflict zone any longer—too many recruits.

"Once I arrived, my assignment from *Ohsh* was to work as their journalist. Propaganda producer would have been a more suitable title. Now that *Ohsh* controlled the entire east and had ambitions around the globe, they seemed a bit more interested in giving themselves a shiny new image.

"Under the guise of a journalist, I was given safe passage with *Ohsh* to the very Centre. They believed that their supreme leader's establishment on his throne ensured that all their prophecies had been fulfilled. The days of their conquest had indeed been completed, as had been foretold.

"The Centre was eerie. Peacekeepers stood watch, emptyhanded, as throngs of worshipers cascaded around, jubilant music filling the air. The peacekeepers did nothing. They had no will to stand against the conquest. *Ohsh* wasn't afraid of them, wasn't afraid of anybody anymore. Made blindly confident by weapons and prophecies, they had nothing left to do but fulfill their destiny. Peace to the entire earth, they proclaimed, when all people would bow to them, when every voice of dissent would be silenced.

"My undercover mission was to support the effort to control *Ohsh*'s nuclear weapons by hacking their codes, taking control of their flight paths, and sending them into the ocean after deployment. We had the brightest hackers on the planet working night and day to get into the network. And the deal was, not one of them was paid. Plenty of kids wanted to make big money hacking in those days, but they could all be bought. If they were doing it for the money, they could always turn us over to *Ohsh* for more than we could match. My job was to dig up any clues that might speed up the hacking. Anything to gain us hours could save millions of lives. We were getting very close. It might have even worked.

"The day everything came down, I took my biggest risk ever. I had crept into the high security area around the Centre by hiding in a military vehicle to cross into the restricted zone. It wasn't that I couldn't have simply walked into the Centre. If fact, I had done so many times. *Ohsh* was obsessed with sending photos of their supreme leader on his throne to every newsfeed around the globe. But on this day, I wasn't taking photos; I had decided to risk it all and try getting into one of the security computers. I knew that if I was discovered, I would lose my head. I had made it into one of the underground chambers using the false security pass that had been smuggled to me just the day before. It was a dimly lit stone archway that led under the ancient walls of the Centre.

"From there, I heard the commotion start: an explosion first, then gunfire and shouting. People were running everywhere. The security guards in the tunnel raced out into the plaza. After my initial instinct to hide, I realized that God had handed me a miracle. The tunnel was empty. Whatever was happening above, I had the only opportunity I was going to get. While the blasts and gunfire rang out overhead, I had fifteen minutes alone with a computer. Fifteen minutes before anyone returned to the tunnel. I used every second I had.

"I wasn't sure how much information I had successfully uploaded to our hackers. I prayed it would be enough. When the security guard returned, I didn't even try to run. I played my part. I straight off berated him for leaving his station unattended. I told him he was a worthless soldier who should be shot for his crime. I told him I would let it go this time, since he had served us well by defending the supreme leader. Well, he locked me up. Apparently they kept a cave farther down the tunnel for such traitors just like myself.

"I later learned that the commotion which had bought me time had been caused by a local rebel force attacking the Gagi's cloister. It was an act of rebellion that *Ohsh* couldn't resist making a spectacle out of. It was exactly the excuse they needed to prove their power and total intolerance to resistance.

"They responded with six nukes. Fortunately, five out of six were the smallest, portable weapons—the kind that can be moved around on the back of a jeep and tossed a few kilometres. An hour after the violence erupted, the weapons were on their way. Six strategic urban areas were chosen for their show. Five of these weapons were capable of killing everyone in a half-kilometre range.

"Miraculously, five of the six never made it to their targets. One jeep was rolled over by a band of rebels who lost their lives but succeeded in destroying the launcher. One was accidentally detonated en route through the desert. One misfired and destroyed the entire area where it was launched. One was fired but detonated in flight and rained down radioactive dust. One jeep missed a corner and drove into the sea.

"But the last weapon, the sixth, was different. Launched as a missile from the east, it was far more powerful and aimed at the heart of the capital city on the coast. The missile flew directly over the most populous cities so everyone could see the power of *Ohshkagoonjing Giizis*. The display was meant to strike fear into the hearts of all who wouldn't bow to their system. Four hundred thousand people were going to die in a split second.

"But the *Nitamoozhaan* had been preparing for this very moment for decades. Billions of dollars had been spent developing the most advanced shield the earth had ever known. They launched the anti-ballistic Arrow. As the seconds ticked by, air horns sounded all over the country. The explosion could not be stopped, but where would it occur?

"With a piercing whistle, two streaks of lightning converged in the sky, joining in a bright flash. But the explosion did not come. Instead the light fell straight down. It gained speed. Faster and faster it descended under the incredible thrust of jet engine fuel until it screamed into its target—not into the nation's capital, but directly into Gagi's throne. The two missiles plunged over a kilometre into the earth, levelling Gagi's complex. And finally, deep in the heart of the mountain, the explosion came. The ground split in two. Every window in the city broke. Every foundation in the country shook.

"I wish I could tell you what I saw at that moment, but there are no words for it. When my prison melted away from me, I could see for the first time. The nuclear explosion had sent a hot yellow cloud straight into space, but I saw it was not a cloud. The sky itself was rolling back to reveal an unearthly brightness. I knew I could not survive the light, but I couldn't pull my eyes away. I could smell the light. It was the smell of rain. I could taste the rain as though I had never had a drink in my life. The light, the rain, entered my body, my soul.

"And he was there in the very centre of the light—the King. Terrifying and more real than anything I had ever seen before. And with him was our army, dressed in white. This is where the Seventh Fire began, as the New People emerged from the light. In that moment when earth and sky ripped open, I realized I was one of them. The Seventh Fire is the story of my people, my home, my King.

"Remember: 'In the time of the Seventh Fire, New People will emerge.' Today some call us the Immortals. I have heard you say it yourselves. Our brothers of the Ancient Peoples recognize us as the *Wabunukeeg*,[30] the keepers of the eastern fire to lead the people back to the trail. Yet I am none of these. I am simply and forever a servant of the King.

---

30 *Wabunukeeg*: daybreak people.

"As the prophecy reads, 'In the time of the Seventh Fire, New People will emerge. They will retrace their steps to find what was left by the trail. Their steps will take them to the Elders who they will ask to guide them on their journey.'[31]

"And so I awakened into a new life. The King gave me a new position, to retrace my steps here and find what was left after *Miigaadiwin.*

"Indeed, the Ancient Peoples were among the first to recognize the King. Some of them hadn't followed the path of materialism. The true seekers had been yearning for redemption for so long that they immediately recognized the rightful King when he arrived. In fact, they were among the first to arrive at the Centre with tribute in the days after *Miigaadiwin,* though it cost them everything and they had so little to bring. You are honoured to follow in their steps tomorrow, Rowan.

"I returned to Iqaluit to begin rebuilding the community, the land, and the nation. We turned to our elders for guidance. Those who had reawakened taught us the way to govern our people justly. But we also turned to the Great Elders of the *Nitamoozhaan,* and they taught us the most ancient way: the way of Jubilee.

"But there is more to the Seventh Fire. You see, the warning is for you, too, Inaa and Gizhaa: 'Now, the light-skinned race will be given a choice between roads. One road will be green and lush and very inviting. The other road will be black and charred and walking it will cut their feet. The people decide to take neither road, but instead to turn back, to remember and reclaim the wisdom of those who came before.

"'If they choose the right road, the Seventh Fire will light the Eighth and final Fire, an eternal fire of peace, love, brotherhood, and sisterhood. If the light-skinned race makes the wrong choice, the destruction which they brought to this country will return to them and cause much suffering and death to all the Earth's peoples.'"

Silence held for some minutes and a bird trilled wistfully. Finally, Gizhaa spoke very quietly. "Uncle Ben—the war, the explosion—how did you survive?"

Ben stopped in his tracks and looked at Gizhaa, astonished at the question. "But don't you understand? I didn't."

---

31 *Wikipedia,* "Seven fires prophecy." Accessed: October 19, 2017. Excerpted and edited by the author from the Anishinaabeg oral tradition.

chapter nineteen

GAAGIGE-BIMAADIZIWIN
"EVERLASTING LIFE"

izhaa vaulted up the granite steps three at a time. After his adventure at the boardwalk that morning, his heart was pounding and it felt good to burn off some energy.

The rich odour of roasting coffee hit him as he swung open the front door. His extraordinary sense of smell was nearly overwhelmed. After a week with his aunt and uncle, he had grown to appreciate their obsession with coffee, though he still didn't understand why, after a millennium, they had yet to switch to locally grown beverages.

Aunt Nancy's voice, ever cheery, called from the kitchen, "Gizhaa, welcome back. Come into the kitchen and I'll pour you a cup of coffee. You missed Corrine. And before her, it was Shaza." She appeared in the doorway and put her hands on her hips in a scolding fashion. "Really, Gizhaa, if you are serious about playing suitor, you need to make yourself available."

Inaa looked up from the book she was reading on the couch in time to see Gizhaa drop his eyes. She raised her eyebrows at Nancy in mock surprise.

"Are you sure they were coming to see Gizhaa?" Inaa asked. "I thought Corrine came for the bag she forgot here after dinner last night. And Shaza said she wanted a copy of your recipe for gingered pear crumble. That's a legitimate excuse to visit if I've ever heard one."

Aunt Nancy rolled her eyes at them both. "And I thought from your letters that you two were serious about socializing with other young people."

It was Gizhaa's turn to raise his eyebrows. "Letters?"

"You and Inaa both sounded quite eager to meet someone special. I thought you'd be pleased that I invited over every nice young person I know."

Despite the thoughts weighing on Gizhaa's mind, he couldn't help grinning at Inaa.

Inaa bristled. "All right, all right. I may or may not have also sent a letter ahead to Aunt Nancy." She softened, smiling at Gizhaa. "Don't be so hard on him, Aunt Nancy. Maybe he's already secretly found someone."

Aunt Nancy's face brightened. "Well, then we need to hear all about it! Come and sit down while I whip up our lunch."

Gizhaa shifted the weight on his feet. "Um, I need a few minutes to get cleaned up. I did a bit of running this morning."

Nancy suddenly sniffed the air and jumped. "Oh, my coffee beans!" She ran back into the kitchen and Gizhaa gratefully slipped away to the guest room.

Alone in the bedroom, Gizhaa stripped off his sweaty shirt and threw it across the bed. He took a washcloth and dipped it into a basin of water that had been gathered from the household waterfall. Cool water evaporated his anxiety as he swept the cloth over his face, shoulders, and arms. He held the cloth against his ear and let a bit of dried blood dissolve so he could wipe it away, grimacing.

He rinsed the cloth and folded it neatly, then closed his eyes, letting his chest rise and fall slowly.

He envisioned once more the long wooden boardwalk that wove along the harbour. He saw Ya Min's petite figure hurrying in his direction, her quick steps almost skipping along to meet him. It was a familiar sight after a week of these surreptitious dawn meetings. He thought of his little alpaca Tristen tripping along toward him in the early morning, then smiled and wondered if any woman would like to be compared to an alpaca.

In his daydream, Ya Min stopped and browsed a jewellery stand whose vendor, an early riser, was sitting quietly to await the tourist rush. Gizhaa watched her meander on more slowly then, the sun rising over the water, until she arrived at the light pole where he leaned. She fell into step beside him as they walked along.

Sounds filled his thoughts: the water slapping the boardwalk, the sweet voice floating on the waves, the disturbing words.

"It's clear that the Revival is becoming radicalized more quickly than even I feared," Ya Min had said. "I now have firm evidence that they were indeed behind the earthquake we experienced on the train."

Gizhaa's mind replayed the questions he had asked. Why would the Revival want to derail a train? Why had his father's travel bag disappeared?

Ya Min's answers had made his stomach knot: "From time out of mind, the ancient prophecies have foretold that one last deception is yet to come. The kingdom will face one final insurrection. *Ohshkagoonjing Giizis* will arise once more and seek to overthrow the throne. They will even conspire to lead entire nations out of the commonwealth. You see, the Revival is simply a new name for an old idea. Replace the King with *Ohshkagoonjing Giizis*. If they succeed, the consequences will be severe, for the prophets wrote, 'If any of the peoples of the earth do not go up to worship the King, they will have no rain… He will bring on them the plague he inflicts on the nations that do not go up to celebrate the Feast.'"[32]

Gizhaa felt Ya Min's hand on his arm and the shudder that filled her.

"There is no doubt now that they have their sights set on removing Canada from the commonwealth," she'd said. "The easiest way to do that is to prevent your tribute, your representative, from reaching the Festival."

Gizhaa's heart twisted as he remembered her next words: "Do you understand the grave danger your father is in?" Gizhaa had not understood, but he was beginning to. "*Ohshkagoonjing Giizis* has now established a contact here. I didn't want to tell you earlier, Gizhaa, but your sister has been compromised. I do not believe she can be trusted. I overheard her with Tom at Parliament the day after you arrived and I believe they are conspiring in the plot."

Even now, Gizhaa wanted to tell Ya Min she was wrong, but there wasn't time.

Gizhaa began to sweat once more as the memory of what had happened next flooded his mind. He saw Ya Min turn toward him, the rising sun reflecting off the water and lighting her eyes, pleading with him to believe her. He heard the boat on the water: a power boat with an engine that roared unlike anything he'd ever heard. He smelled its dirty diesel fumes. And then he heard a pop, a sound that might have been a branch breaking in the forest, but it travelled across the water. He felt Ya Min pushing him with a mighty shove, unnatural to her tiny frame, so that he fell hard onto the boardwalk. Pain flooded his hands, his skin tearing on the rough wood. He rolled into the planks, hitting his head and scraping his ear across a board. Fear tore through him.

He had tried to block Ya Min's fall, and she'd bounced hard off his leg.

He opened his eyes and looked around the dim guest room, but he could still see Ya Min rolling across the boardwalk and jumping up like she had just woken from a good night's rest. She raced ahead of him down the boardwalk, trying to get a better look at the boat that was speeding away. Gizhaa sprung up after her. He felt his chest constricting with his shouts for her to stop, to get down! He heard again popping sounds and then silence as the boat sped away. Ya Min had turned and walked calmly back to him.

---

32 Zechariah 14:17–18.

All the years of learning history had never prepared Gizhaa for a real gun.

△ △ △

As Gizhaa emerged, freshly washed and wearing the only good shirt he'd brought, he almost looked presentable. He paused in the doorway and apologetically tucked the shirt into his pants.

Inaa set her book down and stood up. She took a deep breath and nodded solemnly at him.

"Making it up to Aunt Nancy? Good idea. She will approve." Inaa patted Gizhaa's shoulder encouragingly as he headed past her to the kitchen.

Inaa had been acting strange on this trip, and if everything else on this trip hadn't already been strange, he might have paid more attention. But for a moment, he did notice. He paused beside her.

"What are you reading these days?" he asked.

She waved away the book that lay on the couch. "It's just a history of the Seven Fires. I picked it up at the legislature when Father left for the *Naawayi* last week."

"At the gift shop? I didn't notice it there," he mused, reaching past Inaa for the cover.

"It was given to me."

For the briefest moment, Gizhaa smelled her fear as he leaned past her. He turned to see her face, but she had already ended the conversation, moving toward the kitchen.

He was astonished. Not since the earthquake had he smelled such a distinct fear. Not even on Ya Min today when they'd been fired at. Fear was the rarest of smells.

He touched the book, tracing the map on its cover lightly before turning it open against the couch. Nothing unusual: migration maps of the Ancient Peoples, drawings of traditional dresses, pictures of shells and lakes, copies of historic treaties.

What caused her fear? he asked himself.

The kitchen was brightly lit as the late morning sun beamed directly through a sun tunnel in the ceiling. Uncle Ben had appeared, summoned by the smell of roasting coffee, French toast, and warm pear sauce. He pulled out chairs for Inaa and Gizhaa. The party of four settled down around the table of food.

Uncle Ben reached for their hands. "Good Father, we are grateful for this food. We ask you to bless my nephew Rowan as he travels to bring tribute to your King. Amen."

Gizhaa gladly heaped several slices of toast on his plate when Aunt Nancy passed them to him. The adrenaline from the morning had hit his appetite. He swallowed several bites before pausing to ask, "Uncle Ben, I've been wondering about this. How can Father be your nephew if you are an Immortal?"

Uncle Ben chuckled, though it wasn't clear if it was at Gizhaa's appetite or his question.

"First of all, please don't call me an Immortal." He turned the question around. "What is immortality?"

Gizhaa's forehead wrinkled. "To live forever. To never grow old or die."

"Then there is only one who is immortal—the King." He paused. "My immortality is only a product of existing in connection to the source of immortality."

"The King." Gizhaa sounded dubious. "The Immortals—I mean the New People, as you say, remain immortal by staying connected to the King. How do they do that? Is there a ceremony? A secret ingredient?"

"He told us once, 'Remain in me, as I also remain in you.'"[33] Uncle Ben seemed satisfied by his own answer.

Gizhaa set his fork down, silent for a moment. "Then it was the *Ogimaa* who gave you life at *Miigaadiwin*."

Uncle Ben's voice was low and sober. "He is my life. The Word was fulfilled: 'When he, who is your life, appears, then you also will appear with him...'"[34]

"Then how can we know who the Immortals are?" Inaa's voice was edged with awe, or perhaps it was fear. Gizhaa wasn't near enough to tell the difference.

Uncle Ben's eyes crinkled a little. "Can't you tell? Why do you need to know anyway? We're all human."

Gizhaa pressed on, his curiosity overwhelming his sense of respect. "Wait a second. If the Immortals are human, born into this world, why would they conquer us?"

For the first time, the siblings saw anger flash in the man's eyes. "I prefer the term 'rescue.'" His tone softened. "These ones you refer to as the Immortals are no different than you. The King summoned the New People to return as his servants and restore the Kingdom. And although we daily recount our stories, in a few short generations some have chosen to forget this!" He smiled reassuringly then. "In answer to your original question, Gizhaa, your ninth grandfather Howard was my brother. I suppose that makes your father, Rowan, my eighth great-nephew-in-law? But I like to call him my nephew."

---

33 John 15:4.

34 Colossians 3:4.

"Then…" Gizhaa's thoughts raced. "Could I be one of the New People?"

Ben sighed contentedly as though he felt they were finally making progress. He nodded, but his words were slow and cautious. "I can't read men's hearts. It is not something you receive through your parents' blood. But you could be. You might become."

Inaa pushed a piece of toast through a pool of sauce. She looked shyly at Aunt Nancy. "What about you, Aunt Nancy? Are you one of the New People?"

Nancy sipped her coffee. "I came to know the King when I was a little girl. Yes, I am one of them."

Inaa swallowed hard. "Did you die?"

Nancy didn't seem offended by the question. "Yes, my dear. At the time of *Miigaadiwin*, you remember that I was fighting the plague in North Africa?" She sighed. "There were many who survived and many who did not. I kept on until the end. Eventually it was my turn, too. And when the King came, I went to him—just that simple."

"Did you regret it? Was all your work in vain? Uncle Ben, you left your wife and home and risked everything. You… died." The word stuck in Inaa's throat.

Aunt Nancy's smile rivalled the sunlight pouring into the tiny room. "Regret dying? For a life like this? Never!"

Uncle Ben laughed. "Never mind that. Best moment of my life. Ah, and there was a detail I didn't mention before. Remember the five jeeps, the five explosives that didn't hit their targets? The information I was able to upload in those fifteen minutes contained the Gagi's retaliation plans: the jeeps' license plate numbers, targets, routes, weapons. It gave the *Nitamoozhaan* enough data to thwart the attacks. I think my sacrifice was more than worth it." He sighed. "But even if I had failed in every way, it would have been worth it to hear the King say, 'Well done.' I simply did what I was called to do. Nothing could have taken that away from me."

Gizhaa poured himself a cup of coffee and drowned it in maple syrup. "I find it incredible that Gagi was killed by his own weapon!"

"Not quite," Ben corrected. "Gagi's base and much of his army was destroyed when that bomb fell on the Centre, but Gagi himself had been whisked away by his security when the initial violence broke out earlier that day, so he was still alive and well when the King captured him."

Inaa swallowed her last bite of toast. "Uncle Ben, you said that the Seventh Fire is for us, too. That we must choose between the roads: green and lush, or blackened and charred. Is the charred road the way of *Miigaadiwin*, the path of Gagi?"

Uncle Ben looked surprised at this question. "It is exactly that."

"Then the green road is the path of the *Ogimaa*?"

Ben tilted his head to one side thoughtfully. "Is it?"

"Then what is the way that turns back, to remember and reclaim the wisdom of those who came before them?" she asked earnestly—almost desperately, it seemed.

Aunt Nancy reached out and took Inaa's hand.

Ben paused. "The answer to that is right in front of you."

The wall clock ticked unfamiliarly in the silence. They'd had no need of one back home.

"Your father should be nearing the Centre by now," Aunt Nancy said as she stood and cleared away the dishes. "And your mother is expecting you home in time for the Fall Festival in three days, isn't she? Your trip home begins tomorrow. Of course, there's still dinner tonight and there are guests coming again." She turned back to the table. "So no running away tonight!"

When the table had been cleared and the dishes washed, Inaa disappeared outside. Gizhaa watched through the pear-shaped glass as she sank wearily onto the granite steps in the afternoon sunshine. She wound her long, woollen cardigan tightly around herself and slipped her feet out of her shoes, tucking them up into her cocoon.

Gizhaa hesitated and then pulled the door open. Inaa didn't move.

"Ready for our trip tomorrow?" Gizhaa asked as he sat down beside her.

Inaa nodded. "I guess as ready as I'll ever be. How about you?"

Gizhaa was silent a moment. He wanted to trust Inaa. "I wish I could stay a little longer."

Inaa glanced at him sideways. He remained fixated on the harbour below.

"You were right earlier," he said. "I did find someone. Or maybe she found me." He looked at Inaa and she nodded encouragingly. "But it's complicated. She isn't exactly the farm girl type, and I think she could use my help here a while."

Inaa put her chin on her knees. "You want to stay longer? Maybe you should. You could wait until Dad comes back and travel home with him." Her voice sounded resigned.

"No way. I'm not sending you home alone. There's been too much…" He searched for the right word and couldn't find it. "…stuff on this trip."

Inaa drew herself up resolutely. "Not home yet. I have to make another trip."

Gizhaa smelled it, the fear. Was she afraid of him?

"I don't understand," he said slowly.

"Do you remember the day Simon went away?" Of course he did. "That day… that day, Jordan came to see me. He didn't go with Simon, because he stayed with me." Her voice broke. "I couldn't convince him to go. I tried to tell him that Simon needed him. He didn't believe me, but I knew. I knew…"

Gizhaa didn't move. He wanted to put his arm around her, to tell her that it wasn't her fault, but he was sure she would push him away.

She gained control of her voice. "Sometimes I know what's going to happen, but I can't change the future. I have to make a trip. I don't know why, I just know it must happen."

Gizhaa spoke matter-of-factly, though his heart was pounding. "Where will you go?"

"To New York. With Tom."

Gizhaa couldn't stop the rush of air that filled his lungs, the blood that pounded in his ears. "Inaa, you can't do that!" he exploded.

She stood up and thrust her feet back into her shoes. "I must."

He jumped to his feet, trying desperately to keep his voice level, but it rose in exasperation. "Tom is insane. Don't you know what he's into?"

"I know more than you do!" she spat out angrily. "I couldn't save Simon. I couldn't keep Jordan. But I must follow Tom."

"Inaa, please listen to me. What happened to Simon, it's not your fault! And if things didn't work out with Jordan, he's not good enough for you. But you've got to believe there's someone better for you than Tom. Don't settle for this!"

"I'm not settling for Tom. I'm saving him," she whispered with such fierce determination that Gizhaa couldn't respond.

Inaa shoved her hands through her hair and pushed past him into the house.

Gizhaa stared blankly at the horizon. "Not Tom," he groaned. "Tom? Thomas Waaban… Prime Minister Waaban?" He groaned again. "What is the connection? Is the Prime Minister wrapped up in this too?"

chapter twenty

BAAMAAPII
"UNTIL LATER"

G izhaa slipped quietly out the front door, the sun not yet visible above the horizon but the low-slung clouds creeping along in shifting shades of raspberry. As Gizhaa had hoped, the streets were clear at this hour of the morning; his errand would be undetected.

He retraced his steps from the day before, back to the boardwalk where a solitary jewellery vendor had once again beat the tourist rush. As Gizhaa approached the booth, the weathered man inside sat hunched over a little workbench covered in tiny glass dishes, each containing even tinier bits of precious metals or stones or fittings. His long braid ran down his back, his head bent over a ring held between his fingers. He was examining it with a magnifier.

Gizhaa coughed awkwardly and the man jumped. He pushed aside his magnifying glass and rose with eagerness that crinkled the skin around his bronze eyes.

"A friend of mine came by here yesterday morning," Gizhaa said with a smile. He gestured. "A young woman about so tall with black hair?"

The vendor's smile seemed to freeze and Gizhaa wanted to slap himself. Of course this man remembered her. No doubt he had heard the gunshots and now associated it with Ya Min.

The man nodded slowly. "Yes, yes, I 'member this lady."

Gizhaa forced himself to keep going. "I am looking for a gift. For my friend. I thought maybe..." he said hopefully, "...maybe she had looked at something here yesterday that she liked?"

The vendor's eyes brightened and his hesitation evaporated. He nodded and moved to the showcase of necklaces. "Here." He tapped his finger on the glass. "She says this is beautiful."

He pointed to a necklace on which hung a silver-plated leaf. In the heart of the maple leaf was embedded a tiny ruby.

"May I see it, please?" Gizhaa asked.

The man handed it to him and Gizhaa turned it over carefully in his hands. The leaf was too fragile to be engraved. He would send it as it was.

Gizhaa nodded to the man. "I'll take it. Could you box it and send it to…" He paused, unsure of where to send it. He had intended to say Palais du Nunavut, but if Ya Min was in danger, he shouldn't reveal where she was staying. "Could you send it to Parliament, please, to the Chinese ambassador?"

The man's eyebrows went up, but he simply nodded. "Sure, be happy to send it for you, mister."

Gizhaa was certain this man hadn't known Ya Min's position. He decided to press ahead with his plan. "I wonder if you had ever seen that boat before yesterday?"

Clearly he didn't need to elaborate further as the man immediately scowled. "I never seen or heard a thing like that before! Noisy beast! It's not our way to travel like that."

"No, I'm sure it's not. You don't know where it may have come from? Or who was driving it?" The man shook his head. Gizhaa sighed. "Well, if you happen to see the boat again, would you please send word to the ambassador?"

"I would be happy to, so long as you keep our waters clear of that kind of aggravation," the man agreed heartily. "Seems like the world is getting crazier all the time."

Gizhaa paused. "Was there something else? Crazier?"

"Well, couple days ago, when all those ambassadors from all over are coming 'long here for a tour, I see a group of people marching 'long behind them waving signs, like they couldn't just as easy say that nice and polite. But no, they go waving their signs like it's a big new idea. And then just yesterday, after I see that noisy boat you're asking after, then I see one of those great big bio-miner ships. It just turns 'round and leaves the harbour. They never do that." His eyes narrowed and he leaned toward Gizhaa. "You're not from 'round these parts, but I've been putting up shop here for decades, and every day I see the same ships sleeping in the same place every morning in this here harbour. Then that one," he pointed to a space of glassy water, "just pulls down its flag like it's packin' up ship. Just slides away. Harbour looks empty without it."

The man shook his head disapprovingly.

Gizhaa gazed out at the harbour. Now that he was looking, the harbour seemed emptier than it had yesterday morning. Although it wouldn't have occurred to him that this change was unusual. In light of the other activity around the harbour, it was unlikely to be coincidence.

"That happened yesterday?"

The man nodded solemnly. "Yesterday morning, right after that boat you're asking after went skimming through."

Something clicked in Gizhaa's mind. He knew from Ya Min that the Revivalists wanted Canada out of the Commonwealth. He knew that they wanted to prevent the Canadian tribute from reaching the *Nawaayi*. And if they succeeded, the prophecies foretold that there would be no rain. Was it possible the Revivalists were so sure of their success that they were already preparing for drought by hijacking a bio-miner? But a single state-of-the-art ship would never be enough, even if it was capable of filtering trillions of litres of water!

Gizhaa shook his head in disbelief. Everywhere he looked there was water, as clean and clear as the day it was created. The idea that Canada could ever run dry of its greatest resource seemed inconceivable. What other reason could there be for the miner's disappearance?

"Could you do me another favour?" Gizhaa asked the vendor. "Will you please write a message to the Chinese ambassador telling her what you've just told me about the ship leaving harbour right after the power boat passed? I believe the two events are related. Will you please send the message today? Seal it up and hide it in the box under the necklace."

"Sure thing, mister. I've been 'round long enough to know that something just isn't right about this whole thing."

Gizhaa paid the man as generously as he could afford, and noted that the circle of the sun, though invisible behind the clouds, had certainly risen above the horizon now. He decided he had better jog back to the house.

Δ   Δ   Δ

Inaa stood at the couch buckling up her pack as Gizhaa stepped through the door. Her hair was swept up again in the fashion she had taken to on this trip. She shoved her new book into a side pocket of the pack and buttoned it shut. She swung the pack onto her shoulders.

"I thought you might miss saying *baamaapii* to me, Gizhaa," she teased. Gizhaa was always gone first thing in the morning and he never missed anything.

"*Baamaapii*? Not a chance! I'm just grabbing my stuff."

Inaa looked at him quickly. "Gizhaa, you should stay! Mother will manage without you. Stay and see what happens with this girl." She sounded genuinely concerned.

Gizhaa shook his head resolutely. "You know, she's not really my type. I need to get back to the farm. The alpacas will be missing me."

"What if this is it? Don't throw it away," Inaa pleaded, rubbing her hands together hard as though she were cold.

Gizhaa wondered if Inaa was just trying to get rid of him so she could follow her heart straight to New York. Or was she honestly worried he was going to blow his one-time chance at love?

He cocked his head to one side and smiled ruefully. "Inaa, you know what they say, blood is thicker than water. I'm going home with you."

Gizhaa was certain that tears spilled down Inaa's cheeks as she turned away, but she spoke harshly a few seconds later. "You can't change what's going to happen, Gizhaa. I'm going to New York."

△　△　△

By the time they arrived at the train station, the sun was at high noon. Gizhaa had never seen so many people in one place before. Arriving trains from north and south had just ejected their passengers into the plaza; Uncle Ben had linked his arm to Inaa to prevent losing her in the crowd as they pressed toward the train platform. Gizhaa took that cue and offered his arm to Aunt Nancy as they jostled along.

The Canadian Arctic train, in its red glory, stood before them and the porter waited to take their tickets. They hugged and cried and said "*Baamaapii*" until the whistle blew. With a final squeeze of their hands, Uncle Ben and Aunt Nancy stepped away, letting Gizhaa and Inaa dash into the train door before it sighed shut.

The train was eerily empty. The masses of tourists were going to celebrate the Fall Festival at the capital where the festivities would be bright and noisy. It seemed no one was interested in leaving the capital to spend the holidays at a gentler pace further south.

Inaa looked around the empty car. "I guess we have our pick of the place! Let's check out some of the other cabins."

As Inaa had discovered on their first trip, each car represented a nation of the earth, and for twenty minutes they tried to see who could figure out which country they were in first. It wasn't until they hit the Australian outback, at the very end of the train, that a friendly voice called out, "Imagine meeting you here!"

Gizhaa and Inaa both turned at the same time.

"Tom?" Inaa gasped.

Gizhaa looked in shock from one to the other, until he saw a mischievous grin get the better of Tom's expression. "I'm on my first official trip for the Minister of Foreign Affairs. I'm going to be preparing facilities in New York for our continental meetings after the holidays." He ducked his head and chuckled. "And it was easy enough to find room on the same train as you."

Inaa's expression flattened. "Of course, of course…"

Tom slid into a booth and patted the seat beside him. Inaa complacently took it.

"I knew you would be heading to New York," she said, "I just didn't realize it would be so soon." Her voice sounded hollow.

Gizhaa sat across from them. He couldn't think clearly. If Inaa hadn't known that Tom was going to New York, why had she been so adamant about going with him?

"You picked up the book I left for you at the legislature?" Tom asked Inaa. "How did you like it?"

Inaa nodded thoughtfully. "There's a lot of think about," she admitted. "The Seven Fires cover many hundreds of years. I'm not sure I understand yet how it will be completed."

Tom's eyes lit up with childlike eagerness, and for a moment Gizhaa saw the passion that Inaa seemed to find attractive.

"Don't you see?" Tom said. "That's the best part of all. *We* get to bring about its completion!"

Gizhaa stretched his long legs into the aisle and leaned back. There was no way off this train now, so he had better make the best of it. "How can we complete it?" he asked with as lazy an air as he could manage.

Tom rifled through a messenger bag he had been carrying across his chest and pulled out an identical book to the one Gizhaa had seen Inaa reading earlier, except that the cover of this copy had been folded back and the pages dog-eared and stained. Tom flipped to a page near the end of the book, and read,

"In the time of the Seventh Fire, New People will emerge. They will retrace their steps to find what was left by the trail. Their steps will take them to the Elders, who they will ask to guide them on their journey. Now, the light-skinned race will be given a choice between roads. One road will be green and lush and very inviting. The other road will be black and charred and walking it will cut their feet. The people decide to take neither road, but instead to turn back, to remember and reclaim the wisdom of those who came before."[35]

---

35 *Wikipedia*, "Seven fires prophecy." Accessed: October 19, 2017. Excerpted and edited by the author from the Anishinaabeg oral tradition.

Tom grinned, but said seriously, "Maybe I'm not technically 'light-skinned,' but I hope I will be given an opportunity to lead those who are. We need to choose the right road, to turn back and remember and reclaim the wisdom of those who came before us. Great civilizations came before us: technological integration, architectural advancement, vast wealth! We must remember these great civilizations and reclaim their greatness, their power."

Gizhaa tried to think of some way to disprove Tom's conclusion, but his brain seemed clouded by such a sense of doom that he couldn't form a complete thought.

Inaa, too, seemed to be lost in contemplation.

"Turn back," she murmured. "The way back… he said the answer is right in front of me." She looked at Gizhaa with wide eyes. "What did Uncle Ben mean?"

Gizhaa struggled to switch gears. What had Uncle Ben said to them just yesterday about "the way back"? He could picture his aunt and uncle leaning in, hope written across their honest faces.

The cabin door swung open. "There you are, my dears!"

It was the brightly dressed engineer, blazing a trail through the car straight to their booth.

"You decided to sit as far away from me as possible this trip, did you?" She shook each of their hands perfunctorily. As she pumped Tom's hand enthusiastically, she added, "Thomas Waaban, congratulations on your new appointment to the Minister's office! I'm sure your uncle must be very happy to see you following in his footsteps."

Tom looked bewildered. "You must have me confused with someone else. I don't have an uncle in politics."

"I make it my business to know who's riding my train and you, Tom dear, have an uncle. Besides, Prime Minister Waaban is a very old friend of mine. He expressly told me that he was concerned about you following along on the right path."

Tom pressed his lips together and raised his eyebrows. "We do share a last name—that's true. But I'm afraid I'm not related to Prime Minister Waaban at all. It's merely a coincidence."

The engineer tipped her chin to one side and tapped her fingers on the table near Inaa. Finally, she clicked her tongue.

"They don't teach as much history in university as they should." She smiled her all-encompassing smile again. "When you're ready for a walk about the train, be sure to come sit in my cabin for a few minutes, Tom. I will set your story straight for you."

Then she sauntered out of the car, muttering cheerfully to herself on her way back to work.

The three passengers stared after her for a minute, then silently shifted their attention to the window.

Finally Tom spoke. "I can't be related to Prime Minister Waaban." He rolled his eyes. "He's an Immortal!"

Tom rubbed his forehead, pressing his eyes shut in concentration.

Gizhaa watched as Inaa took a breath to speak. He knew she was going to tell him of their own recent discovery of Immortal relatives. Gizhaa pressed his finger to his lips, looking intently at Inaa. She closed her mouth and they waited in silence.

Tom clenched his teeth. "You guys seem like you come from a pretty easy family—probably a neat line of grandpas and grandmas, uncles and aunts." He sighed. "Not me. My ancestors didn't get played the 'neat' hand. It's been a messy road. When my seventh grandfather was five years old, he was taken away from his parents by government workers and forced to attend a residential school. He lived a day's journey away from his village and family. He cried himself to sleep for a week, and then he never cried again. The food was strange: no fish, no moose, few squash. The language was strange. He couldn't speak to his cousins and friends, even though he saw them daily.

"As soon as he was old enough, he quit school and went to work in the lumber camps. He was suddenly making money and had a sweet wife and two children who made life perfect. But he was haunted by nightmares that left him sweating with fear night after night. His pay was enough to keep food on the table, and keep the nightmares at bay with strong drink, but that was all. Life spiralled into a vicious cycle: work, eat, get drunk, sleep it off, start over.

"One night, there was a terrible fire at the mill where he worked. It was somewhere close to where your family lives now, I guess. He wasn't home that night—out drinking again. His wife struggled to carry both their children by herself. Although she escaped before the flames consumed their rental house, their daughter was already very sick with pneumonia. The smoke was more than she could handle, and she later died of her illness. His wife never forgave him for not being there that night. Or maybe he never forgave himself. Either way, she took their baby boy and left him."

Tom paused a long while.

"We have heard this story from our father," Inaa said quietly. "The story of the fire and the death. It is very tragic."

"My seventh grandfather then gave himself entirely over to strong drink night and day," Tom continued. "I suppose it would have eventually killed him. But something happened. They say the Creator gave him a vision. He saw himself back in that awful school, in a bathroom, and there was blood on his hands. He washed and washed, but the blood couldn't be washed away. Suddenly, another man stood in the bathroom, or someone in the form of a man. He took my grandfather's bloody hands in his and told my grandfather that he was forgiven. When the man said this, my grandfather looked and saw that his own hands were completely clean, but the man's hands were scarred.

"From that day on, my grandfather never touched strong drink. He never again saw the nightmares. And although he was always known as a quiet man who had many private thoughts, he was well-respected among his people as a man of peace. He married again. Together with my seventh grandmother, he had another son, of which I am descended."

"After *Miigaadiwin*, my ancestors chose to go back to their traditional ways, avoiding the new system of politics. While I have no relatives in government, I am convinced we need a new direction. A millennium ago, our simple ways left my people at the mercy of a government who took their children away from them. I prefer to think we will do better to position ourselves in power than wait for someone else to make decisions for us."

Δ   Δ   Δ

Later that evening, after a satisfying dinner and a hot beverage, a porter delivered a message from the engineer. As her special guests on this trip, they might choose any berths they liked. Gizhaa noted that Inaa seemed visibly relieved at this suggestion and she quickly excused herself for the night. Gizhaa and Tom sat a few minutes longer and watched the dying light. The red glow in the distant valley seemed to light the feathery tops of massive tamarack trees.

Gizhaa rose leisurely and stretched his long arms and legs. "I believe I'm ready to try out one of these fancy berths myself. You, however, might be interested in hearing the engineer's tale of your history this evening."

Tom shrugged and rose as well. "I need to look over my notes for these upcoming meetings. There's a lot to get up to speed on. And I can't afford to arrive overtired and underprepared for my first major assignment."

As Tom disappeared, Gizhaa couldn't help but wonder if the engineer's history lesson might be more preparation than Tom gave it credit for.

chapter twenty-one

BAWAAJIGAN
"DREAM"

It seemed Inaa had barely drawn the heavy velvet curtain across her berth and let herself fall onto the soft feather bed when the dream began.

She saw the hills of home, not covered by the majestic pines she knew, but overgrown with scraggly trees fighting for a place on the hillside of the channel. Though dark, the moon threw an unusually clear light onto the ramshackle village at the edge of the water. Inaa watched as a man crept in the shadows past the dark houses, pushing through the overgrown trees toward a group of larger buildings, not houses, surrounded by piles of woodchips and sawdust. Though Inaa had never seen this before, she instantly knew this was the infamous mill of Cook's Mills.

She fixated on this shadow man and his mission. He rested against the side of a building, crouched and waiting for something. She waited, too. She heard the waves gently slap against the dock. Then the clouds shifted, sliding across the moon. The man ran forward and she saw that he carried a can, liquid sloshing from it onto the ground. She realized he was throwing the liquid, heaving it onto the woodpile.

He muttered to himself as he worked, and she could hear him as though he was whispering in her own ear: "One night's work, one year's wages. Just clean up their mess for them. One night's work, one year's wages."

Then, dropping the can, he paused and a flame suddenly sprang from a tiny match between his fingers. He dropped the match and ran.

Something happened that Inaa had never seen. A match fell into the wet sawdust and a blaze leapt up. It raced wildly into the woodpile and, within minutes, red fingers of fire curled against the night sky, greedily reaching for more to consume. It grasped at the piles and lashed out toward the mill's buildings.

Inaa looked for the man. He stood in the shadows again, watching the fire grow.

And then she felt the wind, screaming in delight as it flew across the lake and bore down on the village. It raged at the fire and the flames turned away from the wood and the mill, spying the hill of shacks beyond the scraggly bush line.

Inaa saw the man's face closely now, wearing an expression that was entirely new to her. It was terror. He turned and ran again, this time not away from the fire, but past it. He ran into a shed and Inaa saw him pulling madly on a rope. The heavy iron bell in the shed swayed, pounding out an alarm that rang "Fire! Fire!" into the night air.

Once again the man ran, this time toward the houses. He pounded on doors and walls as he went, shouting for people to get out. The smoke was thick as he entered a door and staggered through a room, grasping at a little crib, rifling through the beds. The house was empty.

The man emerged from the house relieved, but he continued running. A woman ahead was moving slowly through the growing smoke. She carried an infant in her arms and dragged a small girl by the hand. The girl struggled for breath and coughed heavily. Seeing them, the man caught the girl up in his arms.

"Why didn't you get out faster?" he demanded of the woman.

She began to cry as she ran to keep up with him. "The children... the children."

Inaa saw the man turn for a moment and stare in horror as the flames captured the first of the village homes. She looked clearly into his face, and this time she recognized it. It was a face she had seen just days before at Parliament—in a portrait. It was the face of Prime Minister Waaban.

Δ   Δ   Δ

When Inaa awoke, her face was wet with tears. She reached out into the darkness and whispered, "Good Father, please take this away! I don't want to see this sadness anymore!"

She covered her face with her hands and cried bitterly. But after some time, her breathing slowed and her mind returned to sleep.

Δ   Δ   Δ

Inaa dreamed she was in a beautiful park on deep, green grass surrounded by hundreds of people—many with brown skin, brown hair, and brown eyes were colourfully dressed in beaded tunics, some even wearing the headdress of a chief. Around her waved placards reading "Strong Peace." Some carried drums.

Silence settled over the crowd as a man stepped up to a podium. Inaa gasped as she recognized the man, Prime Minister Waaban, though a much younger version than the one she'd seen in the portrait.

"My people and my friends. I stand before you today as your brother. We are here to call on our government to stand with our brothers and sisters in the Middle East during their time of distress. In this time of war, we reject our government's account of peace. As Canadians, we have learned the hard lessons of forgiveness and true peace that we must share with the world.

"Let me remind you of our own history, which has brought us to a place of healing in Canada. Here our nations have walked side by side for many generations. Today we live as brothers in this great land, but it has not always been so!

"Let me tell you one story of peace. It is my father's story. Like many of his generation, he was taken from his family to live in a residential school where he lost his language and his culture. As a young man, he left the reserve to begin a new life. Although he was a hard worker and got a job at a lumber mill, his pain led him into alcoholism. His alcoholism eventually drove him to become an arsonist. When our village was destroyed by the fire he set, my mother rescued my sister and I from the fire, but the smoke was thick already and a month later my sister died of pneumonia. The grief destroyed my parents' marriage."

Waaban's voice faltered a moment. "This pain which began with two nations living without peace would have continued to destroy lives—to destroy my life without a father. But my father found peace with God. He discovered that when we are forgiven, we are free to forgive others. Before my father died, he found me and asked for my forgiveness. I share his story today so that you may understand the power of forgiveness to change lives.

"Today I come to you, my people, because these terrible tragedies have etched in the hearts of our First Nations people a lesson many Canadians have forgotten: peace between nations does not come by weak treaties. True peace cannot be bought by either political will or violent coercion. Today we have peace because our people have turned to the source of all peace. Our people became peacemakers by choosing the grace our Creator gave us in his Son! This is my father's story. After many years of trying to punish himself for his mistakes, the Creator showed him that justice had already been paid. The Creator showed him the path of repentance. And when my father found forgiveness, he was healed."

Waaban's voice strengthened. "Peace can only come when there is justice, repentance, and forgiveness. Today we stand with our brothers and sisters who are oppressed in the Middle East. The government of Canada has stood idly by while this war escalated from regional conflict into global violence. The government of Canada has seen the violence of the Alliance. We have seen the news reports of burnings, crucifixions, and beheadings. The Alliance chooses violent coercion, chooses to oppress free nations. And yet our government now claims they have made peace with this group. We call on our government to renounce the weak treaty with the Middle East Alliance and stand against oppression and violence!"

The energy of the crowd grew as Waaban declared passionately, "True peace is not found in treaties! There is no peace without justice through the Creator. There is no peace without repentance. There is no peace without forgiveness. Today the First Nations of North America stand against the Alliance!"

The crowd began to cheer, but at this moment a man with a backpack ran straight toward Waaban. Inaa heard the explosion; she saw the podium crumble and Waaban fall as chaos erupted.

Through the noise, somewhere a headset microphone still amplified Waaban's dying words: "He is our peace."[36]

---

36 Ephesians 2:14.

chapter twenty-two

MIIGIWEWIN
"GIFT"

When Inaa awoke and drew back the velvet curtain, the sun streamed in through the overhead glass. "He is our peace," sang in her mind. It was a tune she hadn't known before, the melody simple, the harmonies complex. She remembered the dream as clearly as if she were reliving it, but unlike the bitter tears of the night, her heart was at rest.

"He is our peace."

She imagined the birds sang in the trees beyond the train's rushing path. She dropped her legs over the side of the feather bed and gathered her new insights.

Prime Minister Waaban was the son of the Cook's Mills arsonist. He was the baby boy who had survived the fire, and Tom was the ancestor of this same arsonist, though he didn't know the full story. That made Tom and Prime Minister Waaban nephew and uncle, by some degrees.

Inaa rubbed her cheeks as her thoughts tumbled over one another. So the Prime Minister *was* an Immortal—one of the New People, she corrected herself—who had died at a peace rally during the days of *Miigaadiwin.*

Inaa took her time getting changed and washed for the day. For once, she didn't feel anxious about the coming adventure. The new tune hummed through her mind as she wriggled her toes back into soft, felted boots.

She sat once more on the bedside, stretching her hands, palms up, in her lap as she listened to the last intricate harmonies. She opened her eyes, glistening with tears of wonder.

Gizhaa stepped into the corridor. He was carrying two steaming, frothy mugs.

Inaa smiled at him. "Sleep well, brother?"

He handed her a mug and nodded. "I hate to admit it, but those mattresses might actually beat an alpaca wool mat. Don't tell Mom." He laughed.

She was relieved that he didn't ask how she had slept. She wasn't sure she had an answer yet.

Gizhaa seemed contemplative as they settled into a booth. He scooped up some froth with a spoon. "It's only two days until the Festival. Mother will be cooking up a storm. Nanda will be decorating the yurts with branches. Kris and Solia are probably busy keeping up with guests. I wonder if Abigail is planning to make us do one of her crazy skits again for the final night? It won't be the same without Father this year."

Inaa smiled to herself. "Remember the year Abigail cast Father as the prince disguised as a beast? I thought Mother was going to die laughing."

By the time Tom joined them and the three had feasted on breakfast, they were content to simply absorb the ever-changing view. First, cascading rapids spilled from a crystal smooth river, where willows paused with their branches dipping to drink as the train passed. Then there was a climb up to a steep cliff where the trees fell away to reveal a valley of poplars touched with the gold of autumn. Quite suddenly, a lake appeared on the horizon, reflecting the blue sky and peppered with billowing sails. Ever-present *Didi*, the frosty gas halo, swept through the clouds and danced on the waves.

The train plunged back into valleys of dense pines, so old and wise that their deep beds of brown needles might silence even a train rushing past. Then the porter announced their arrival at their own station.

Inaa squirmed uncomfortably as Gizhaa stood and began to gather his backpack. He raised his eyebrows at her. "Ready, Inaa?"

"Can I talk with you a moment, Gizhaa?" She tried to smile but faltered under his glare.

Gizhaa led the way into the next car and closed the door. He folded his arms across his chest.

"Stop looking like that! I want to tell you something." She paused and tried again. Her voice came out barely above a whisper. "Sometimes I learn things through dreams."

His expression softened a little.

She took a deep breath and continued. "Last night I saw who Tom is… who Prime Minister Waaban is."

Gizhaa looked irritated. "Inaa, just because you dream about a guy doesn't mean you know who he is."

Colour flared into Inaa's face, and she growled. "Not like that, Gizhaa! I was shown their relationship. Tom really is a nephew of the Prime Minister."

Gizhaa pressed his lips together and waited for more. They were running out of time.

"I had another dream before we came to Iqaluit. I saw myself with Tom at a meeting in New York, and I saw the leader of the Revival." She saw that Gizhaa was going to argue again, so she hurried on. "This must take place. I must go to New York and do what I can."

Gizhaa face paled. He leaned closer, his voice a harsh whisper. "Inaa, you cannot join the Revival! These guys are in way deep." Desperation entered his voice. "They are conspiring against the *Ogimaa*!"

The door handle at the far end of the car turned and Inaa realized the train had already begun to slow.

"I know, but I must help," she pleaded.

Gizhaa's face had a look of complete astonishment as the porter entered.

"We are pulling up to the station now," the porter announced pleasantly.

Inna turned to him with a false smile. "I've decided to extend my trip. I will be staying on the train."

"Of course, miss. As you can see, we have plenty of room! I will be around later to collect the fare."

The train glided to a perfect stop and the doors hissed open. Tom was standing on the other side of the door between cars, holding Inaa's pack for her. She took it silently and stepped onto the platform behind Gizhaa.

"I guess this really is *baamaapii*, brother," she said to Gizhaa.

Tom looked bewildered, turning from one to the other.

"Inaa, I beg you to reconsider," Gizhaa pressed.

She shook her head, turning suddenly back toward the open train door. At that moment, she collided hard with a man who was crossing the platform. She stumbled and he caught her arms to steady her. The curly haired stranger's eyes seemed to laugh.

"I am so sorry!" she burst out.

"No harm done," the stranger replied. "Are you all right, Inaa?"

Inaa tried to smile and straightened her backpack. "Fine, thanks." Then she blinked. "Have we met?"

"I had the pleasure of visiting your family farm last week. What a gift you have there! Your mother and sisters are well. Now I'm off to the capital to celebrate the Festival with my old friend, Prime Minister Waaban." He stuck out his hand to her. "I'm Joshua."

Inaa shook it. "I'm Inaa." Then she remembered that he must know that.

A bell sounded, warning of the train's departure.

"I have to go," she said. "*Baamaapii.*"

"You have an important job to do," Joshua said seriously, the laughter gone from his eyes.

Inaa started to correct him, to tell him that their work of delivering the tribute was already complete, but Gizhaa stepped forward and wrapped his arms around her.

"*Baamaapii*, little sister," he whispered into her hair.

She wished she could stay, enveloped in wool and the strength of his heart-beat, but she pushed him away and hurried through the doorway before he could see her tears.

Tom reached out his hand to Joshua. "Goodbye," he said.

Joshua shook it heartily and held on a moment longer than necessary, looking steadily into his eyes. "You look remarkably like your seventh grandfather. A great man."

Tom pulled his hand away. "You knew my seventh grandfather?"

"Know," Joshua corrected. "A great man. He began a fire that you must put out."

Tom stared at Joshua and then shook his head.

"I can't miss my train," Tom said, hurrying away. He didn't remember to shake Gizhaa's hand.

Gizhaa shifted his backpack heavily and turned away. Joshua touched his shoulder. In that moment, Gizhaa smelled his mother, instantly feeling himself wrapped in one of her blankets as she rocked him to sleep.

Gizhaa looked down at Joshua's arm. "You're wearing one of my mother's creations!"

Joshua's face lit up with appreciation. "A very special gift." He leaned closer. "Your sister has not yet learned how to use her gift. She will need your help."

Gizhaa was confused for only a moment, but how could this man know about Inaa's dreams?

"I will send word to your mother of your change in plans," Joshua assured him.

The second warning bell sounded from the train.

Gizhaa shrugged. "Thanks anyway, but my sister is going on alone."

"Alone?" Joshua looked into the train door past Gizhaa's shoulder.

"With Tom, really," Gizhaa said, his shoulders slumped in defeat. "She won't listen to me. She says she has to go to New York."

Joshua's voice was sad. "Yes, she does." He paused until Gizhaa met his eyes. "But she doesn't have to go alone. You know what they say—blood is thicker than water."

Gizhaa opened his mouth, but Joshua was motioning to the train door and Gizhaa could hear the last bell ringing.

"You were given a gift for such a time as this, Gizhaa. Get back on the train."

In years to come, Gizhaa never could remember turning or putting his feet over the train's threshold. He couldn't remember the sound of the door sighing shut in his face. He couldn't remember the rush as the train accelerated away from the platform. All he could remember of that moment were two things: the eyes that compelled him to obey without question and the sound of the voice that had spoken his name.

chapter twenty-three

DΛSOOZO
"TRΛPPED"

T he porter didn't appear even slightly surprised when he saw Gizhaa seated alone at a booth. "Welcome back. I'll let the kitchen know to prepare lunch for you, sir."

"Thank you. I'm sorry to be so impromptu. My plans were changed."

Gizhaa reached for his backpack and began rifling through it. With a sinking heart, he realized that he didn't have nearly enough money to pay the fare. He ruefully remembered the generous gift he'd sent to Ya Min.

The porter smiled graciously. "If you are looking for your fare, sir, there's no need. A man paid for you at the last station. Shall I let your friends know you are here?"

"Was it Joshua?" Gizhaa asked, incredulously.

"He didn't leave his name, sir."

Gizhaa paused. "Don't let my friends know I'm here yet, perhaps. I need some time to think. I'll find them when I'm ready."

Inaa and Tom had apparently moved to another car. Explaining himself to them was going to be an awkward conversation. "I decided to tag along and chaperone you two." Inaa was going to love that. Or "I hear New York is beautiful this time of year. And look who's here? Tom! Inaa!" What about the truth? "This guy I've never seen before told me to come." That was the strangest one of all.

Gizhaa closed his eyes and remembered Joshua's voice. He didn't hear it with his ears; he felt it in his chest, like a heartbeat stronger and louder than any voice: "You were given a gift for such a time as this, Gizhaa."

Someone else had said that to him not long ago. Who was it?

Ya Min. The first time he had met her. But what was his gift? Sure, he could hear and smell things other people couldn't. Was that it?

Gizhaa looked out the window. *Didi* seemed to float above the trees. He imagined himself there, circling the Earth as a tiny speck of volcanic ash. That's exactly how he felt, like a trapped, imperceptible speck of dust. He let his mind float. The smell of his mother, caught from Joshua's coat, took him back to his childhood. He let himself be wrapped in her blanket. She rubbed his back, settling him down for the night.

Her remembered voice: "Gizhaadan,[37] never forget who you are. Your name means to guard, to watch. We live in peace, but it was not always so. Every generation must choose again. Guard your heart, so that you love only what the Creator has made pure and lovely. Guard your family so that they choose the path of the *Ogimaa*. Guard your country so that we remember the ancient ways."

Gizhaa looked at the gas ring. Together, these billions-strong particles of dust and ice had altered Earth's climate. Was this his gift? To be one speck standing guard against a plot to overthrow the entire planet's balance?

He shook his head in frustration. But what was he supposed to do? His father should already be at the *Naawayi* to deliver the tribute. Ya Min had said he was in great danger. The Revival didn't want the tribute to reach the *Ogimaa*, but Gizhaa couldn't do anything about it, could he? Ya Min was back in Iqaluit trying to find out what the Revival was up to there, and she was clearly getting too close for someone's liking. Why else had someone tried to shoot her? Inaa and Tom were wrapped up in a madcap scheme to bring about the completion of the Seventh Fire and return the earth to some supposed golden age of prosperity and advancement!

Gizhaa's heart raced and he felt it hard to breathe.

Voices spoke on the other side of the car door: Inaa and Tom. Gizhaa made a hasty and, he thought later, foolish decision. The washroom was open nearby. He dove in, pulling the door shut behind him, and hid.

"When will we arrive in New York?" Inaa asked, her voice drawing near to Gizhaa's hideout.

"We will transfer to another train at Toronto, in a couple of hours. Then it's only a few more hours to New York. We should be there by evening."

Gizhaa could hear the hesitation in Inaa's voice: "Where will I stay?"

"No worries," Tom said. "I have friends we can stay with. I was going to take a hotel, but I'd like you to meet some people." Tom laughed. "Don't look so worried, Inaa. Separate rooms! I'm a gentleman."

Gizhaa felt like charging out of the bathroom and knocking Tom down for treating his sister's honour lightly, but that certainly wasn't a great way to announce to Inaa that he was following her.

---

37 Gizhaadan—guard, watch over it

"My friends are Revivalists, too," Tom continued. "They can show you around while I'm doing business. There's a big Revival gathering tomorrow night we won't want to miss. Apparently some major announcements are coming down."

A door opened and Gizhaa heard a porter's voice announce, "Lunch will be served."

"We'll take ours here then," Tom decided, and Gizhaa heard him slide into a booth nearby.

If Gizhaa hadn't been focusing on staying perfectly silent, he would have groaned. He wasn't to get out of this bathroom any time soon. Not only that, he was about to miss a mouth-watering meal while trapped just two meters away.

As the dishes were served, he settled on the floor, his knees drawn up to fit in the space.

△   △   △

Inaa unfolded her napkin and laid it across her lap. She bowed her head and silently thanked the Creator for his gifts. As she raised her head, she found Tom watching her, his fork in one hand, knife in the other. He chewed slowly.

"You actually do that when no one is around?" he asked.

"I am grateful, so I pray," she answered simply. "You're not so much a praying person, are you?"

He shrugged. "Gratitude is a good thing. I'm just not sure the Creator is really interested in hearing what I have to say, you know?"

Inaa felt like it was hard to swallow the tender, butter-soaked vegetables. "The story you told us last night about your ancestor who lost his daughter after the fire … I've heard some of that story often in our traditions, but let me tell you more that I've learned."

Tom paused with his fork halfway to his mouth. "Go on."

Inaa prayed for words. "The man who started the fire was paid a year's wages to rid the mill owners of the buildings, presumably so they could collect the insurance money. He paid dearly for that one night of work, for his own daughter died after the fire. Then his wife left him and took their infant son. That man was your seventh grandfather."

Tom swallowed hard, but said nothing.

"But your seventh grandfather found forgiveness in the Creator." Inaa set her fork down and leaned forward.

Tom looked outside, and Inaa followed his troubled gaze. A very light snow had begun to fall, but the speed of the train made it look like the windows were being pelted.

"The man on the platform said something to me," Tom said, seeming to speak to the window. "Something… A fire was started that I need to put out?" He turned his face back to Inaa. "Who told you about my seventh grandfather starting the fire?"

Inaa took a deep breath. "The Creator told me. In a dream."

Tom didn't laugh or roll his eyes. "What else did he tell you?"

"The son of your seventh grandfather is Prime Minister Waaban. The one who escaped the fire."

This time, Tom couldn't contain his disbelief. "That's impossible. He would be a thousand years old!"

"You said yourself, he's an Immortal."

"Well, he can't be my great-whatever-uncle and be an Immortal!"

"Of course he can," Inaa replied simply, as though she had known this from infancy. "My Uncle Ben and Aunt Nancy are Immortals, though they prefer to be called New People."

Tom and Inaa ate silently for several minutes. Finally, Tom asked, "How did they supposedly become Immortals?"

"They died."

Tom did laugh now. "So, we were actually invaded by a zombie apocalypse? That's an interesting idea."

Inaa didn't rise to the bait. She quoted her Uncle Ben: "Immortality is only a product of existing in connection to the source of immortality."

"And the source is?"

"The Creator, of course."

"So, you're telling me that my ancestor, Prime Minister Waaban, died and yet lives as an Immortal because of his connection to the Creator?"

Inaa couldn't tell if Tom's voice was sarcastic or awestruck.

"And he got this connection by…?" Tom opened his hands.

She paused, not knowing how to answer. She spoke slowly, trying to recount young Waaban's words in her dream. "He said that peace came through justice, repentance, and forgiveness through the Creator. The Creator showed his father that justice had been paid through the Creator's Son. When his father found forgiveness, he was healed."

"He told you this," Tom pressed.

"No, he said it at the peace rally, in my dream," Inaa admitted. She didn't expect him to believe her.

Tom stared at the snowy window again and didn't speak for a long time. The porter brought plates of fruit and a pot of tea, then cleared away their dishes.

"It doesn't make sense," Tom said. "But you knew about the fire, and that man on the platform knew. The rest of it, I don't see…"

Inaa poured the tea, adding milk to hers. "I've been thinking a lot about that Seventh Fire. I know you think the prophecy says that we're supposed to choose the way back, back to the way to the world was a millennium ago when these great societies existed: prosperity, advancement, power." She stirred her tea before taking a tentative sip. It was still too hot. "I don't think that's what it means."

Tom sighed. "No, I don't suppose you do."

Inaa smiled and went on. "When I visited my aunt and uncle in Iqaluit, I asked them this question. What was the way back, the way that the Seventh Fire referred to? My uncle told me the answer was right in front of me." She laughed to herself. "Leave it to him to give me a riddle. Do you know what was right in front of me?"

Tom looked curious, but shrugged.

"*They* were," she answered. "My aunt and uncle—they were right in front of me! The way back is to follow the New People." She leaned across the table, her eyes lit with the excitement of solving the puzzle.

Tom fell back incredulously. "The path back is to follow the Immortals? Inaa, have you lost your mind? That is exactly what we're fighting against!"

chapter twenty-four

BIMINIZHA'AN
"FOLLOW ALONG"

Gizhaa gratefully extended his legs and shook them out as he stood. Opening the door of his cramped closet, he stepped into the light and stretched his arms, rolling his shoulders back. After two hours in that bathroom, he'd had to make a clandestine train connection in which Inaa had only looked his direction once, forcing him to dart behind a baggage cart. This had been followed by, certainly worst of all, five hours in a dark closet with mops, rags, and cleaning supplies for travel companions. He was grateful there had been a sink with water to drink, but he was famished.

At last, the train had arrived in New York and Gizhaa knew he needed to spot Inaa quickly or lose her completely in this crazy place. The train door stood open to the platform and Gizhaa sucked in his breath. Even in the darkness, he could see that the gentle snow that had begun north of Toronto covered the ground thickly here. In all his life, Gizhaa had never experienced a snowfall this early in the year, before the Festival even! Where were the gentle fall rains?

He didn't have time to contemplate this mystery. Stepping into the wet snow, he ducked his head against the wind and scanned the area left and right. Passengers were boarding for overnight trips south, no doubt to celebrate the beginning of the Festival tomorrow with family and friends.

Further down the platform, Gizhaa spotted a couple hurrying through the snow toward the station, which glowed dimly through the storm.

Gizhaa followed more slowly, grateful that the wind meant that Tom and Inaa kept their heads down. He watched as they entered the building and approached a large, glossy wooden counter. A woman stood behind it, dressed in a crisp blue suit, shaking her head several times and gesturing to the weather outside.

Gizhaa shifted his backpack and shuffled his feet to stay warm outside. The temperature was dropping quickly.

Tom's shoulders slumped and he led Inaa to a bench under a window. They dropped their packs heavily and sat side by side.

Gizhaa realized that he needed to hear what they were saying if he had any hope of keeping up with them. The darkness and snow provided excellent coverage as he slid up to the window where they sat. He leaned against the wall as though waiting for someone on this cold, wet night, and listened intently. He could barely make out their voices through the brushing of snowfall against the glass.

"If the ferries aren't running tonight, we won't be able to make it to my friends' place. The government has reserved a room for me here in the hotel, and since they're booked solid..."

Gizhaa forced himself not to turn his head and look at Tom through the window.

"...why don't you take the room, and I'll sleep here in the lobby tonight?"

Gizhaa sighed with relief as Tom finished.

"Thank you, Tom. I would appreciate that very much," Inaa said. It was almost too low for Gizhaa to hear.

"Surely this freak storm will clear tomorrow and you can tour around with me while I'm doing business anyway." Tom sounded hopeful. "Hey, why don't we see if they serve a bedtime snack?"

Inaa laughed, but Gizhaa's stomach growled at the suggestion. "Really? After *all* that food on the train? All right, let's ask."

Gizhaa heard the sound of their backpacks being scraped across the bench. After a minute, he dared to look through the window and confirmed that Tom and Inaa had indeed headed back to the counter, Tom's hand resting lightly on Inaa's shoulder strap. They conversed once more with the attendant before disappearing down a hallway.

Grabbing the opportunity, Gizhaa pulled his collar as high as it would go and headed into the lobby, watching carefully for any sign of Tom or Inaa.

The attendant at the counter looked at Gizhaa with curiosity. "Can I help you, sir?"

He lowered his gaze, having been ready to bypass the desk. Fumbling for words, Gizhaa shook his head. "No, I'm just passing through."

"I'm sorry, sir, but you do need to check in for the night before heading up-stairs. Do you have a reservation? I'm afraid all of our rooms are booked. It's a very busy season."

Gizhaa swallowed. He knew he had very little money left and the lobby was already taken for the night, apparently. He couldn't very well sleep on the street in this weather.

The attendant patiently checked a room list while Gizhaa stood, awkwardly sorting through his thoughts.

"The only guest left to check in is… Mr. Selah?" She looked at Gizhaa hopefully. Gizhaa nodded, dumbfounded.

"Well then, Mr. Selah, welcome. Is this your first time staying with us?" Gizhaa continued to nod. "Wonderful! You will find the restaurant behind me here on the first floor…"

There followed a long list of other features and instructions, of which Gizhaa heard none.

"You will find your room on the third floor, last door on the right. Enjoy your stay!"

Climbing the stairs felt exhausting with his cold, cramped legs. But a single day of being locked in a tight space was far tougher than a day of hard work on the farm.

He wondered how long it would take Tom and Inaa to get their bedtime snack. Was there a back way to the restaurant that wouldn't take him through the lobby? He desperately hoped so.

His room was located at the farthest corner of the hall. He wondered how far away Inaa's room would be. How early would they get up in the morning? How would he follow them without being seen?

He sighed as the door opened. The room was simply furnished, less luxuriously than their earlier room at the Canadian Arctic Hotel. Crisp white walls and navy blue linens lent the space an old-fashioned appeal.

He shoved his backpack under the desk. At least he didn't need to worry about Tom and Inaa leaving the hotel tonight. For now, they were all stuck here.

Δ   Δ   Δ

As morning light filtered into her room, Inaa rolled over and sat up. Someone was knocking on her door. She stumbled to grab her wool sweater, wrapping it tightly around her before cracking the door ajar.

"Good morning, sleepyhead!" Tom grinned from the other side. "We need to get a move on. The snow has let up some, and apparently the ferries are running again."

Inaa stifled a yawn. "Is it late?"

"I need to be at the legislature in a couple hours, but that gives us enough time to hit the waterfront and catch a quick ride around."

"Okay, I'll be right down."

"Meet you in the restaurant," Tom called as the door shut.

Inaa hurried to dress. She pulled her hair up on top of her head, then hesitated. She pulled it down again, created a familiar braid, and squared her shoulders. She would certainly meet important people in this city as Tom's guest, but she would meet them as she was.

The room didn't have a private washroom, so she headed for the one a few doors up. The door beside hers, at the end of the hall, clicked shut just as she went out, but she didn't notice.

It wasn't long before Inaa and Tom were stepping out of the hotel lobby into a winter wonderland. The soggy snow of the night had wrapped itself around every branch, draping them heavily toward the ground. Inaa mused that the trees reminded her of the weeping birch at home, along the path past the beach. She briefly ached to brush those branches, to walk the trail toward home and wrap herself in security: home, parents, stories.

She shook herself and walked beside Tom.

The snow still fell, steady and gentle. She hadn't packed for winter, so she wore several layers under her light coat this morning. Her travelling boots weren't warm, but they were waterproof and that was enough for now.

As they walked toward the waterfront, Tom pointed out features of interest: a favourite deli, a museum of local history, a library. After Tom's passionate description of this great place, Inaa had somehow expected a spectacular metropolis. Yet she was surprised at how common it was. There were no grand towers the height of six trees. No bridges weaving from island to island. No brilliant scientists proclaiming new discoveries in the streets. Just tiny white flakes drifting down.

"Does it always snow like this in New York?" Inaa asked.

Tom shook his head. "Just for you, Inaa."

The waterfront wasn't far from the hotel and Inaa was relieved to discover the ferry was enclosed, offering some protection from the weather. There were comfortable benches to sit on. Inaa marvelled how unlike Simon's sturgeon-chasing dory this was; his tippy, sandy-bottomed boat with oars was a far cry from this windowed, cushioned luxury vessel.

Tom chose a spot for them near the driver. "They tell great stories," he whispered to Inaa as the ferry bell chimed and they pulled away from the dock.

The boat accelerated and the driver tipped his hat, calling back in an exaggerated accent, "Welcome aboard the New York Puddle Jumper. We're casting off from our beautiful gateway city of Sunshine Metropolis, soon to be arriving at Destination Ice Age in twenty minutes!"

There were fewer than fifteen people on the boat, but their collective laughter relaxed Inaa. Perhaps the dark waters weren't menacing after all.

If she had been sitting farther back, she would certainly have noticed a man who didn't laugh, a man who wore a wool jacket, much like her own, and a low-brimmed hat purchased at a store along the street with his last precious bit of spending money.

chapter twenty-five

FESTIVAL

The hair around Inaa's temples curled into her face as the wet snow melted off the strands. She shivered and pushed the hair away with her shoulder without pulling her cold fingers from her pockets. Tom had been gone for over three hours in the legislature and she had walked the lobby of that building at least a dozen times, reading and rereading every plaque, studying every piece of art and history in detail, before finally deciding to do a little exploring on her own. After leaving a note at the information desk, she ventured back out into the snow.

Great windmills churned endlessly along the harbour; the ocean breeze never seemed to let up in this place. She wondered if that wind alone wasn't enough to harden these spirited people, as Tom described them. A sudden gust caught her coat and pulled it open. She wrapped it tighter around herself and decided it was time to head back inside to warm up.

Something about this city made her skin prickle. Was it the sensation that people moved surreptitiously everywhere she turned? Was it the events of that foreboding dream? Was it the bizarre autumn snowstorm? Or was it simply the fact that she felt lost for the first time in her life, being a thousand kilometres from home as the Festival was about to begin.

Approaching the legislature entrance, she blinked back unwanted tears and bent her head against the wind.

The door opened and Tom exited, smiling as he saw her. "Enjoy your walk?"

She subdued a shiver and nodded.

He lowered his voice. "Ready for our big meeting?"

"Actually, I need to warm up inside for a few minutes before we go any further."

"No problem. That will give me time to drop in on a friend who works here in the legislature. Let's go back inside."

Tom led the way through the legislature's winding hallways until they approached a door in what seemed to be the farthest corner of the building. Tom knocked smartly.

"We will see Regent tonight at our meeting as well, but this will give me a chance to ask him some questions alone," he whispered.

Tom opened the door to a tiny office as a voice welcomed from inside.

A tall man with red hair stood behind the cluttered desk. "Tom, back so soon from Canada?" he asked, grabbing Tom's outstretched hand in a hearty handshake.

"They put me to work right off the bat setting up the intercontinental meetings here for after the Festival," Tom acknowledged. He stepped aside and shut the office door behind them, giving Inaa room to come forward. "This is my friend, Inaa Selah. She's a northern Revivalist."

The man behind the desk stepped out, his eyebrows rising. "I wasn't aware we had such an attractive northern chapter. I'm Regent. Nice to meet you, Inaa."

"You too," Inaa responded automatically.

Tom shrugged and nodded. "I guess the northerners have a little different perspective on some of the Revival's goals, but they're moving along."

Inaa shifted her weight from one foot to the other uncomfortably. This conversation wasn't going where she had expected.

Regent sat on the desk, smiling. But his eyes fixed on Tom, who leaned easily against the door.

"That's interesting. I'd like to hear more about your chapter's ideas," Regent said to Inaa, shifting his intense gaze back to her, lowering his voice slightly.

Inaa returned his steady gaze, but said nothing.

Tom spoke up. "Inaa has some upper connections. She's good, Regent." He crossed his arms decisively. "I just want to find out where our chapter is at right now. Apparently, there's some concern that the *Ohsh* might be finding new members, maybe even wanting to join up with us. Any word at your level about that?"

Inaa couldn't breathe. Regent's smile hardened; his gaze didn't leave her face. "Where would you get an idea like that, Tom? You know the powers-that-be don't release information on their connections to the members."

"Okay, I'll take that as a yes," Tom replied nonchalantly. "So will there an opportunity to vote on this merger? Or is it a done deal?"

Regent stood. "Tom, the Revival leaders have built this grassroots movement on basic principles of individual rights and empowerment. Clearly whatever plans are in the works are for the common good." His voice was smooth and reassuring.

"That's exactly what I was thinking to myself, Regent," Tom levelled a serious gaze across the room, "which is why I fully expect there *will* be a vote tonight." He moved his hand to the doorknob.

Inaa stared at Tom. Was he pressuring Regent to comply?

A slight flush rose in Regent's neck and he cleared his throat. "You would be mistaken if you think that 'grassroots' means you have veto power, Tom. The Revival has taken great pains to place you strategically. It may take great pain to remove you as well."

Inaa shivered. The word *pain*, coming from Regent, had been spoken with deep intention.

Tom nodded toward the snow-caked window, unfazed as always. "Well, there isn't much grass growing around here anymore. Perhaps the Revival's roots are dying as well?"

As Tom opened the door to the hallway, Regent hissed quietly to Inaa, "You may not find your northern ideas as welcome as you hope."

Inaa raised her chin and stepped into the hall ahead of Tom. She momentarily caught sight of a coat and hat disappearing around the corner. Her skin prickled.

Δ   Δ   Δ

Outside, Tom and Inaa trudged through the soggy streets. Inaa struggled to slow her racing heart.

"Tom," she finally gasped, "I thought you said you didn't even think *Ohsh* existed."

Without glancing her way, he spoke dryly. "I didn't. But then I didn't think my uncle was an Immortal yesterday either."

She stopped walking to catch her breath. "So you believe me that Prime Minister Waaban is your uncle, the son of the arsonist?"

Tom turned back toward her, but his eyes focused on something behind her. She turned to follow his gaze, but he took her arm and forced her to continue walking beside him.

"Yes, I believe you," he whispered. "At least, that much I believe. But I think someone might be following us, so let's keep it down. Although I'm not a fan of where the Immortal invasion has left us today, I'm not convinced I'm ready to throw my lot in with a resurrected *Ohsh* yet either."

They walked on in silence.

"Then do you see the way back? Do you understand the Seventh Fire?" Inaa asked.

Tom didn't answer for a long time. The blue light of the snowy day had begun to fade to grey. Tom stopped and faced her, glancing around quickly.

"No," he said simply. "I don't see the way back, if by that you mean following the Immortals… But if the two roads forward, green or black, are the Revival or the *Ohsh*, then I'm sticking with the Revival."

They were standing in front of an old building. The tall, dead grasses around them were overlaid with snow, the windows were missing, and a hulking wooden door stood slightly ajar.

Tom waved his hand toward the door. "Well, let's find out what's going on, shall we?"

He bowed to Inaa, took her hand, and led her through the door.

Δ   Δ   Δ

Gizhaa skirted the building perimeter, his hat pulled as low as it would go. He was cold, miserably wet, and hungry. He had caught enough of the conversation in the legislature office to know that Tom was walking into dangerous territory.

"And taking my sister with him!" Gizhaa fumed. "Either the guy is completely unaware of the danger, or he's a fool who thinks he's an Immortal."

Gizhaa remembered the sound of the gun that had been aimed at Ya Min and pushed himself faster through the snow. There had to be another way into this place.

On the far side of the building, Gizhaa found a row of windows near the ground. All were cracked, but one had shattered. He pulled off his coat and draped it over the broken edge of glass. Working slowly, he squatted low and eased his shoulders under the shards hanging from the upper frame. He couldn't fit his legs through and was forced to sit and slide across the lower frame. He felt the coat dragging against the sharp points. To save the fabric, he lifted himself over it, but pain shot through his hand.

He dropped heavily into the basement of the building, grasping his hand. His foot caught a large pail under the window and he crashed awkwardly to the floor. Gritting his teeth, he lay panting in a pile of shattered glass. He rolled upright and held his hand in the bit of daylight coming from the window. He succeeded in dislodging a large glass shard, gasping as he did so. Blood flowed freely and pooled in his palm.

Pressing his back against the wall, Gizhaa used his good hand to rescue his coat from the windowsill. Even in the dim light, he could see that it had been shredded in several places. He grabbed the lining and tore a piece free, wrapping it tightly around his wound. The bandage was bulky and awkward, but at least he wouldn't have to watch his blood drip on the floor.

He allowed his eyes to adjust to the dark room. It had been a kitchen at one time. A row of sinks ran along one wall and cupboards ran around the other sides of the room. Sadly, his entry point had missed the counters, which might have saved his hand and his coat.

The dismal space looked as though it had been long abandoned. Gizhaa moved stealthily toward the door. He hoped that, despite his clumsy arrival, his bush survival skills would keep his presence unannounced.

Pausing in the doorway, he listened carefully. The small room before him wasn't completely dark; light filtered through two small, dirty windows set into double doors. Beyond, Gizhaa heard voices speaking in hushed tones. Though Gizhaa's experience with fine dining was limited, he assumed this may have been a staging area for a restaurant at one time. If so, he suspected a dining room would be on the other side of those doors. He moved quietly to the doors and peered through the gap between them.

The room was larger than he had anticipated, well-lit and crowded. Yellowed paintings hung askew on the walls; threadbare carpet covered the floor. Gizhaa tried to see if Inaa and Tom were there, but more and more people entered from a stairwell on the far side of the room and his view was soon completely blocked.

Gizhaa found a stool toppled on its side in the back corner of his hideout. He quietly placed it behind the doors and stood on it. Now he could see over the heads of the crowd. There had to be at least two hundred people packed into that room. He couldn't make out Tom or Inaa anywhere.

The crowd hushed and Gizhaa saw a man with red hair climb above the crowd, presumably standing on a box or chair of some kind. He raised his arms and total silence fell. Gizhaa tried to silence his own breathing and remind himself that most people couldn't hear as well as he could.

"It is my inestimable honour to introduce to you tonight, for the first time at any New York Revival meeting, the very distinguished Dr. Sybil Magog, international leader of the Revival! Please welcome him to New York."

The crowd erupted into applause and the red-haired man jumped down from his perch. Another man mounted in his place and turned slowly before the hushing crowd. Even from his poor vantage, Gizhaa could see that this man's shoulders were broad and muscled, his dark features strikingly handsome. He was neither young nor old; in fact, if Gizhaa had ever imagined what an Immortal ought to look like, this was it. Despite the man's appearance, Gizhaa immediately smelled the unmistakable scent of fear. It wafted through the gap in the door so strongly that it must have represented the reactions of not one, but many people.

"My brave Revivalists, we have much to celebrate tonight." He articulated each word carefully as by one who has learned a new language. His voice was rich and deep. "While the world begins tonight to cower once more in mock celebration of the invading army, we will stand tall. Tonight, we will display the strength of our rebellion. Many years of hard work by local groups such as this, faithfully growing our numbers around the world, have paid off! Now we are ready to show the world that we need not cower any longer before a cru... cruel king."

This leader choked on the words, Gizhaa realized in amazement. Or had the man meant to say something else?

"Let me tell you of our great achievements around the world. Makkah Revival has laid the foundation for the rebuilding of a great tower, rising from the desert rubble. Already it can be seen from kilometres away. This unsurpassed achievement of culture and architecture will serve as the rallying cry to Revivalists across the globe!

"But that is just the beginning. In every government on earth, we have now planted Revivalist politicians. Together we are striving to free the nations from Immortal laws, laws which decimate wealth and opportunity, enslaving you in an ancient colonial system. In some places, these politicians have begun to effect real change: introducing legislation that affirms individual rights to personal prosperity, to religious diversity, and to land transfer. We have even succeeded in delivering a nation into the first democratic system since the War. I am proud to announce that Egypt will soon be voting for its first president in nearly a millennium!

"I could go on. We are winning this battle in Tokyo, Amsterdam, Mumbai. But I want you to understand clearly, these key successes would never be possible without a partner you have not yet heard of. Tonight you will be the first to know that the Revival can never be stopped. We have forged an alliance that has proven unshakeable. While the Revival has sought to restore economic prosperity and freedom, another group has been working in secret to restore a great system, once nearly lost to our world. You have known it as *Ohshkagoonjing Giizis*, but now it will be known as the glorious way. It has returned to take its place of glory on the earth."

The man paused dramatically and drew himself up.

"Tonight I am here to tell you that *Ohsh* has elected me as their first leader in a millennium," he said, starting low but his volume escalating with each word. "We now have the strength to overthrow the Immortals once and for all!"

The crowd seemed stunned for a moment, and then hands began to clap, until a thunderous applause filled the room.

The leader raised his arms for silence. "Not everyone has yet seen the wisdom of our new system. We must now show them that we will be taken seriously. A recent trade agreement between the Canadian and Chinese Revival chapters ended in a setback due to an information leak."

Gizhaa caught his breath. Had Ya Min succeeded?

The man's voice took on a menacing tone. "The Chinese chapter has not accepted our new leadership and has declined the investment of a Canadian bio-miner we confiscated on their behalf." He smiled and the sight made Gizhaa's skin crawl. "But tomorrow we will set the record straight. Our power will be revealed to the world."

Once more, applause began slowly, reaching a crescendo.

The leader shouted above the noise. "Last night we made our most recent victory! Canada has overthrown the bonds of tribute to the King. The Canadian tribute was confiscated and destroyed by the Revival before it reached its destination! Our message was clearly heard: 'There will never again be Canadian tribute paid at the Centre!'"

The crowd continued to cheer wildly, hands raised as they clapped and yelled.

Gizhaa's heart stopped. What had become of his father?

He barely had time to consider the impact of these words. A thud sounded nearby and the door Gizhaa was pressing his face against suddenly smashed into his forehead. The stool teetered beneath his feet and Gizhaa jumped backward to avoid crashing down. He stumbled through the darkness into the kitchen, diving behind the counter as the door into his hideout swung open, scraping the fallen stool out of its way. Someone bumped through the door, grunting as though moving a weight.

As the door swung shut again, the leader's voice rang out loud and angry. "We have bowed to the King long enough! The Immortals have taken our great nations and made them pasture for goats and pheasants. They demand tribute, but what do they give in return? Nothing. The time has come to throw off their bonds. We will have no king but ourselves. We will resurrect the great culture that once ruled the earth! Let us return to *Ohsh!* We will join our forces and overthrow the Immortals!

"To the legislature! We protest the Festival!"

chapter twenty-six

OGIMΔΔ
"KING"

Inaa's heart pounded so loud that she was amazed she could hear anything being said by the man who had just declared himself the new leader of *Ohsh*. Her throat threatened to close with fear. She pressed her trembling hands against her thighs, rubbing the sweat from her palms. Beside her, Tom leaned against a wall, his arms crossed in defiance, his eyes dark with unrest. Clearly, there would be no grassroots process, no vote.

As the applause receded briefly, the leader drove home his final triumphant announcement: "Canada has overthrown the bonds of tribute to the King. The Canadian tribute was confiscated and destroyed by the Revival before it reached its destination!"

The sound rushed into Inaa's ears. She could still see the leader, but the room around her narrowed rapidly. His voice, the echoing applause, began to fade. The world spun. She grasped for the wall and felt it against her hand, but it seemed to slide away from her.

Through the disappearing roar of the crowd, she faintly heard Tom's voice. "Inaa? Inaa, it's okay. Hold on to me."

She felt his arm wrap around her waist. The room was gone from her vision entirely now and she knew she would hit the floor any second. But Tom pulled her backward, through a door she couldn't see, and eased her onto a cold, hard floor where she let consciousness slip away entirely.

A couple of minutes later, Inaa became aware again of her surroundings. She was slumped against a block wall in a dark room. She was vaguely aware of Tom standing at a door, looking through a dirty pane of glass. The sound of many feet shuffled nearby.

"Where are we?" she managed to ask. Her words sounded garbled; her tongue felt thick.

"In the kitchen," he whispered. "The meeting is over. Everyone is leaving now."

Inaa thought she was nodding, but she wasn't sure. Her mind felt as soggy as the snow. Then she remembered: the snow, the tribute, her father. She groaned. "Did he say what they did to my father?"

Tom motioned her to be quiet, then took a step in the darkness. The sounds from the dining room had ceased, but somewhere deeper in the kitchen they heard the distinct sound of breaking glass. Tom felt around in the darkness and took hold of the stool he had pushed out of the way as he'd dragged Inaa in here. He raised the stool above his head and proceeded toward the rear of the kitchen.

Inaa heard him bump into counters and kick a pail in the thick darkness. The stool seemed to bang against a cupboard door. Finally, she heard the sound of broken glass underfoot.

Tom sighed. "Whoever it was is gone. This window is out."

Inaa shivered and realized she was cold. She pushed herself to her feet, keeping her back against the wall to prevent swaying. "We need to get out of here, Tom," she urged.

He came back and stood beside her. "You think you're ready to move already? You went down pretty hard." He sounded genuinely concerned. "I gather from your reaction that you weren't part of the operation to confiscate the Canadian tribute."

She couldn't see his face, but Inaa could hear the irony in his voice. She groaned again. "Tom, for all I know my dad is dead, or worse!"

He sighed. "I'm sorry, Inaa. I honestly had no idea the Revival was planning that manoeuvre." He squared his shoulders. "But if we want to find out if your father is… *where* your father is, the best thing to do is to play along with this merger."

Inaa closed her eyes and rested her head against the wall. She wanted to go home. She wanted to wrap her fingers around a mug of her mother's sweet tea. She wanted to sleep for a very long time.

Tom laughed sourly. "Merger. What a joke! The two have always been one and the same, haven't they?"

Inaa rubbed her forehead.

Tom shook his head. "Two roads: one green, one black. Is that what it is, Inaa? The Revival and the *Ohsh* have always been the two roads going the same direction." His voice sounded tired.

Inaa didn't answer him. She didn't need to. "All right, how do we 'play along,' as you suggest?" Inaa asked, her tone harder than she intended.

Tom studied her, as though appraising her condition in the dingy light coming through the door. "We head back to the legislature."

"At this hour?" Inaa asked. "Why?"

"Because that's where the party is tonight, and we need to be seen protesting the Festival if we want to… to find your father."

Inaa wondered if he had been about to say "if we want to live." May she had just imagined it.

Δ   Δ   Δ

Gizhaa ran through the snowy streets, heading back in the direction they had come earlier that day. His lungs dragged in the cold air, but he couldn't stop. Fear consumed his thoughts. At least the exercise kept him warm, despite his torn coat, and the snow had finally stopped falling.

Though he hadn't been able to spot Tom and Inaa through the door gap, they must have been in that room. The last thing he'd heard before scrambling back through the broken window had been the leader urging everyone to form a protest at the legislature. Although he desperately hoped that Tom and Inaa would finally escape this crazy mess, he was half-afraid he wouldn't find them at the protest and lose track of them completely.

Gizhaa forced himself to slow to a walk as he approached the legislature. The clouds had miraculously parted and a full moon shone over the cityscape. The New York legislature was entirely unlike Parliament. This compound was very old, perhaps as old as *Miigaadiwin*—a collection of brick buildings surrounded by what were no doubt grassy lawns in summer.

Silhouetted by the moonlight, a large group could be seen gathered around the main building, waving bright purple flags and singing. At first Gizhaa thought it was the Revival protest, but as the song reached him, he recognized it.

"He rules the world with truth and grace,
And makes the nations prove
The glories of his righteousness
And wonders of his love."

The voices swelled in triumph and broke into cheers as fireworks lit the sky overhead.

Under different circumstances, Gizhaa would have loved to have been here, celebrating with these jubilant merrymakers, waving a flag in the wind, enjoying the light show. But now every bang of fireworks, every spasm of colour, made his heart contract with fear. He studied the crowd anxiously for any sign of Inaa or Tom. It was the tall, red-haired man he was able to identify first, standing on the highest step of the legislature. Gizhaa scanned the crowd below the steps and began to pick out a group that focused their attention away from the fireworks toward a darkly cloaked figure who ascended the stairs—Dr. Magog, no doubt.

Over the sounds of whizzing and popping fireworks, a chant penetrated the night. "We have no king!" came in loud, defiant tones.

Gizhaa moved toward the sound quickly as the festive crowd hushed and turned toward the commotion. He shouldered his way through the protestors to gain a spot at the base of the stairs, hopeful that he might spy Inaa if he could get a little higher.

A curious crowd had begun to gather around the protestors. The last of the fireworks crackled brightly overhead, and in the moments of silence that followed the chanting rang clearer.

The *Ohsh* leader signalled for the crowd's attention, raising his arms high above his head.

"New Yorkers, you are a strong people who have watched your city eaten away by the ocean, forcing many to flee inland, displaced and impoverished. You are a proud people who have sought diligently to renew your city. You are a longsuffering people who have waited a millennium to be rewarded for your labours! What has the King done for you? While the Immortals have sequestered your resources, exploited your ideas, and collected your tribute, you have been nearly pushed into the ocean. It is time for you to take the justice you are due. Tonight we are here to demand that your leaders throw off your bondage to the Immortal king. We demand freedom for New York! Freedom for the world!"

Gizhaa faced the crowd, his back turned to the speaker, as the protestors erupted in wild cheering, pressing forward. Gizhaa felt he would trip backward on the stairs and was forced to stumble up several steps to avoid falling. He stood straight, studying the faces below.

They began to raise their fists, pounding them into the air. "We… have… no… king! We… have… no… king!"

Gizhaa could see no sign of Inaa or Tom. A strange relief flooded him, for the faces in the crowd were contorted with inhuman rage. Gizhaa stared at them in sudden comprehension. This protest had nothing to do with power or tribute or resources. This was pure, unadulterated hatred of the *Ogimaa*.

He stumbled back two more steps as the rabid crowd moved closer.

"Speech!" someone cried out very near him. A man's hands reached forward and pushed Gizhaa encouragingly. "Speech!"

Gizhaa's mind stilled. He felt rather than heard the voice in his chest whisper, "...for such a time as this, Gizhaa." Standing on these steps, facing this angry crowd, he realized he looked very much like a perpetrator of this heinous event!

So be it, he decided.

He turned and vaulted the last three steps to the top, where the red-haired man and Dr. Magog were intent on driving the crowd's venom. They didn't recognize Gizhaa's own intent until it was too late.

Gizhaa raised his arms high as he had seen the leader do. Even in this moment, he continued to scan the crowd for two familiar faces.

"New Yorkers!" he yelled. Digging deeper into his lungs, he tried again: "New Yorkers!" The crowd stilled, waiting expectantly. "I have travelled four thousand kilometres to be here. Where I come from, we have been telling stories of the days before the great war for a thousand years. We remember that our ancestors were held captive by a harsh and demanding climate. We remember that disease was everyone's lot and that life ended before it hardly began. We remember that our ancestors drove themselves to the grave in hard labour that could never satisfy their heart's desires. Most of all, we remember that our King restored us and our planet!"

He drew from the depths of his lungs and shouted, "We remember that we have a good King!"

From the corner of his eye, Gizhaa saw the two leaders reaching for him, fire in their eyes.

"I have a king!" he shouted in desperation as enraged hands dragged him down the steps. "I have a king!"

chapter twenty-seven

ISHKODE
"FIRE"

I naa's hand flew to her mouth. Arriving moments before, she had been shocked at the crowd here at the legislature, far bigger than the one at the meeting. That chanting had been terrible to hear, but this was far more terrible.

"That's Gizhaa!" she gasped, pointing at a man shouting from the steps of the legislature. She moved into the crowd as Tom ran to catch up.

"No way," he called after her. He caught sight of the man's face as he was dragged heavily down the steps. It was none other than Gizhaa.

Tom sprinted past Inaa and disappeared into the mass of people.

The angry protestors, at first stunned by the rebuke from what they had assumed to be one of their own, screamed with indistinct outrage. Inaa worked her way forward, pressing her shoulders into those around her, using her hands to force an opening through the crowd. She became wedged between two men and could see nothing of her brother or Tom.

"Let me through!" she pleaded, but no one seemed to hear. "Please let me through!"

No one seemed able to move at all.

The roar of the crowd gained momentum, reaching a fever pitch. Someone screamed from the top of the steps, "We… have… no… king!"

But before the chant began once more, a deep voice beside Inaa shouted, "I have a king!" Immediately the declaration was taken up by others nearby. A new chant began as the original Festival crowd found their voices. All around Inaa, they lifted up their avowal proudly, "I have a king! I have a king!"

Inaa began to weep, tears running freely down her face.

The man beside her who had first echoed the affirmation now began to sing in a great bass voice that carried clear over the crowd, the ancient song of the Feast:

"No more let sins or sorrows grow,
Nor thorns infest the ground…"

The festive crowd caught the melody and it swelled around Inaa like a rising ocean crest. She lifted her voice, though she couldn't hear herself:

"He comes to make his blessings flow
Far as the curse is found."

The song was more than the protestors could stand. As one body, they turned and rushed upon the celebrators. The entire field became a mass of clashes. Fists, teeth, flags all became weapons.

Δ   Δ   Δ

Tom dove between people, elbowing his way to the front of the protest. The closer he got to the legislature steps, the angrier the crowd became.

"Get him! Teach him a lesson!" he heard someone cheer.

With one final burst of energy, he threw himself into the circle that surrounded Gizhaa. He arrived in time to see a man kick Gizhaa in the ribs as he lay curled in the snow. Tom sprang forward and grabbed Gizhaa by his torn collar, dragging him to his feet and waving the others back.

"All right, everyone. That will do. I'll make sure this troublemaker is taken care of properly." Tom's voice dripped with menace. He didn't flinch as he took in Gizhaa's bleeding lip and swollen eye. "Come with me," he growled.

Gizhaa reached out to throttle Tom, wrapping his uninjured hand around Tom's neck. As the two men became paralyzed in conflict, a voice nearby spoke harshly.

"Not with you, Tom. This was all part of your plan, wasn't it?" the red-haired leader sneered. He turned to two of the men who had been beating Gizhaa. "Put them inside and get it lit. It's time to show them we mean business."

The enforcers wrestled Tom and Gizhaa up the stairs and through the thrown-open legislature doors.

"This is ludicrous!" Tom shouted. "I'm one of your best men, Regent. I demand an explanation for this treatment!"

Nevertheless, the two were violently shoved into an office. The door locked behind them.

Gizhaa collapsed to his knees, holding his side. He seemed to be struggling for air.

Tom knelt beside him. "Man, I'm sorry! I was trying to get you out of there."

Gizhaa coughed and lifted his head to look at Tom. "Right. That sounds convenient about now, doesn't it?"

"What are you doing here anyway?" Tom cried in exasperation.

Gizhaa glowered at him. "What do you think?"

"Look, whatever you think of me is probably fair, but the fact is that we need to get back to Inaa before they pick her up, too."

Gizhaa grabbed hold of a desk and pulled himself up slowly. He cocked his head to one side. "Oh no," he whispered.

"What?"

Gizhaa clenched his fists. "I smell fire."

Δ   Δ   Δ

A man beside Inaa had stumbled heavily into the snow when the closely packed crowd tried to shift away from the attacking mob. She barely managed to avoid falling on him. She was nearer to the edge than she had thought, having not made much progress. When she spied a gap in the row of bodies surrounding her, she ran through, escaping into the open plaza. Without pausing to view the clash behind her, she raced in a wide arc around the building complex. There had to be another way to reach Tom and Gizhaa.

Moving to the rear of the main legislature building, she stopped short as two silhouettes emerged from a door on the west side. For a moment Inaa wondered if it wasn't Tom and Gizhaa, but her hope proved unfounded when the two shadows moved to the front of the building and began lobbing fireworks into the crowd.

Inaa cast a glance behind her before dashing across the lawn to the door the two men had just emerged from. It was unlocked. Slipping inside, she reasoned she might be able to find her way back to the front steps where she'd last seen Gizhaa and Tom.

The interior was darker than she had anticipated. The building had seemed bright and welcoming that morning; now it felt like a dungeon. She slid her hand along the wall, moving cautiously. As she came to the end of the corridor, she realized that somewhere far away she could hear the sound of pounding. Her heart contracted and she considered turning back. Instead she spun around, gasping in terror. The ceiling suddenly collapsed with a roar, engulfing the door behind her in flames. There would be no going back that way!

Inaa turned a corner and moved forward faster than before, the inky blackness lit by an eerie glow. The terrible pounding drew closer, she realized, but at least she was moving farther from the flames. When the space in front of her opened up, she saw that she had made it to the front foyer. The heavy oak doors to the front steps were only a few meters away. Moonlight flooded through the windows.

Suddenly the pounding, which seemed quite close now, paused. A great splintering sound ripped through the foyer as a door on the far side of the room tore from its hinges. Inaa stifled a cry and pressed herself against the shadowy wall while two silhouetted men rushed through the broken doorframe. The air between her and them seemed to hang with clouds. She held her breath while they bolted down a hallway in the opposite direction from Inaa.

She would have sighed with relief, but a large piece of the ceiling collapsed directly between her and the oak doors. This time she did scream as a piece of falling plaster caught her shoulder, knocking her to the ground. Stunned, she struggled to push herself to her feet, but found that the heavy plaster lay over her legs. Not only that, but the way out had been completely blocked. The ancient doors had caught fire and the hallway she'd come through glowed red with greedy flames.

Δ   Δ   Δ

Tom led the way to Regent's office. "Hurry!" he called back to Gizhaa. "We'll grab some evidence and escape by the window!"

But Gizhaa had stopped running. "Go on, Tom! I heard someone back there. They need help!"

"Gizhaa! We've got to move or we're not going to make it out!"

Gizhaa was gone already. Tom hesitated and then sprinted toward the office. Within seconds he was tearing open drawers, grabbing armfuls of papers and shoving them into a garbage pail he'd picked up from beside the door. Finally satisfied, he slammed a lid on the pail.

He unlatched the window and threw it open. Smoky night air rushed in. Tom hoisted the pail through the window frame and let it drop to the ground below, then turned and raced back the way he had come.

Smoke poured down the hallway leading to the foyer and within seconds Tom's eyes smarted with tears. He stumbled toward a figure hunched over in the hazy darkness. It was Gizhaa! Grabbing his shoulder, he tried to pull him back.

Gizhaa wrestled away, unwrapping a piece of fabric from his hand and then tying it around his face. "Inaa's in here," Gizhaa gasped hoarsely. "On the other side of the fire. Have to…"

Tom could see nothing but smoke and flames ahead, the only light coming from the fire. He pulled his shirt up over his face as the air became harder to breathe. How Gizhaa could possibly know Inaa was in this building was unfathomable, but given that Gizhaa had somehow traced Tom this far made it insanely logical at the moment.

Tom pulled on Gizhaa's shoulder again, this time with greater urgency. "There's another way! Follow…"

Staying low and keeping one hand on Gizhaa, Tom pushed open a door that led into a hall leading toward the back of the building. The two men stumbled through and shut the door behind them. This hall was utterly black without windows or fire, but they moved rapidly.

Tom talked nonstop in a raspy voice, leading Gizhaa by sound where sight was not available.

"This protest was a setup all along. The Revival has been overtaken by the old *Ohsh*. Inaa knew it. I thought she was crazy." Tom coughed, then continued, his voice hoarser. "Turn right. A door and then stairs to your right… They kidnapped your father. We thought, Inaa and I, that we could play along, try to find out what happened to your father."

Tom stumbled while climbing the last step. They then started down another hall, this one ending at a glass-panelled door. Red light glowed menacingly through the door pane.

They ran to the door and Gizhaa pushed past Tom to see through the glass. The frame was hot and they both pulled their hands away. This door led onto a narrow balcony above the vaulted foyer. Through the door, they could see that the ceiling, once an ornately decorated piece of art, had brought the flames from the upper floor down upon the front entrance. Beams lay strewn throughout the foyer, burning like tinder, the bulk of the fire blocking the front entrance.

"I'll see if I can spot her!" Gizhaa shouted over the muffled roar.

Gizhaa opened the door and stepped onto the balcony gingerly. It held under his weight.

He held his arm to his forehead as the heat roared upward. Gizhaa scanned the foyer floor from underneath the protection of his arm. At first he was sure she wasn't there, but then he took a step forward into the heat and spotted a pile of plaster almost directly beneath the balcony. The plaster wasn't burning and a leg could be seen extending from under one corner.

Gizhaa jumped back through the door, slamming it shut behind him. "She's below us, trapped under plaster. I'll climb down—"

"No, I know the way out," Tom said. "Lift me down and I'll get her free. There's a hall below us out the back. Inaa and I can escape that way. You go back down the stairs. Door out at the bottom. Meet there. Now! Quick!"

He didn't wait for Gizhaa to agree to this plan. He opened the door and the heat blasted through. Tom stepped onto the balcony, instinctively turning his face away.

"I can't see anything," Tom moaned.

Gizhaa was beside him, motioning. "She's right below."

There was no time to question. Tom grabbed the hot railing and swung his legs over it.

"Sit!" Tom yelled as he grabbed two balusters and let his legs swing free of the balcony.

Gizhaa slid his legs under the railing as Tom's body lurched to one side. Tom released a hand to transfer his grip to Gizhaa's leg. Then he released the other hand, and for a moment his grip on Gizhaa slipped.

Gizhaa reached through the balusters, grabbing Tom's shoulders with rough, farm-worn hands, and grimaced with pain as his grip tightened over the wound in his palm. With Tom's hands grasping Gizhaa's knees, he let his own body lean against the railing, praying desperately that it wouldn't collapse under their combined weight.

Gravity slowly pulled Tom downward until he dangled between the balcony and the floor below.

"Go, Gizhaa!"

Tom dropped. As he hit the ground, he rolled painfully across the broken ceiling debris. The heat immediately felt less intense than above, but the smoke began to blind him once more. It only took a second to orient himself to the pile of plaster where Inaa was trapped. He crawled toward it, using his shirt as a shield against the smoke.

"Inaa! It's me, Tom!" he shouted as he tore the first piece of plaster off the pile. He was afraid she was already dead, lying motionless beneath three pieces of ceiling.

She cried out suddenly, rousing in pain, and looked at him in bewilderment.

"I can't move! It's too late. We're trapped!" She shook her head at him as though the sight of him was tragic.

He could barely see the rubble that had fallen, but there was no time to be careful. He grabbed another piece and began to lift. It was larger than the first and heavier.

"Inaa, push while I lift," he ordered.

She pushed briefly and then cried out in pain.

"Inaa," Tom yelled. "You *must* push!"

They tried again and this time the heavy piece yielded a few inches. Inaa pulled one leg free.

Somewhere up above, they heard the shattering of glass as heat had finally broke the front windows. With a burst of adrenaline, Tom hoisted the last piece of plaster and Inaa scurried backward. Miraculously, she rolled over and crawled toward the rear of the foyer. Tom dropped down beside her and nudged her toward a doorway under the balcony.

"Back entrance," he shouted. "Don't stop!"

Inaa pushed the door open and crawled through. Smoke poured in behind her and her eyes burned with tears. She kept her head down and scurried blindly on, ignoring the pain shooting through her knees and ankles. Through the roar of the fire, she heard more glass breaking and a great crash from the foyer.

The hallway became darker, but she pressed forward until she banged her head into a solid wooden door. She reached up and struggled with the handle until finally it turned and cold night air swept around her. She fell forward as the door yielded under the weight of her shoulder. Inaa rolled down two steps into the snow.

"We're out! We made it! Tom, we're alive!" she cried.

But turning back, she saw no one behind her in the black hallway.

chapter twenty-eight

BIMAAJI
"SAVED"

"**G**o, Gizhaa!" Tom cried.

Gizhaa closed his eyes as Tom released his ankles. Pain seared through his hand as he released his intense grip on the railing. Gasping from the pain and heat, he stumbled to his feet. His head spun with the uprush of hot air. He staggered away from the railing and fell back through the open door. Instinct forced him to slam the door behind him, sealing the fire away.

Orienting himself to the semi-darkness, he turned and ran. His lungs burned as he raced down the hallway he and Tom had followed just a minute earlier. Eerie flickers lit the stairs from the door pane behind him. He pounded down the stairs until two doors met him. One he knew led back to the burning foyer, back to the wall of fire separating him from Inaa, back to Tom's frantic efforts to set her free. The other led to fresh air and life. He hesitated, torn between his desperate need to help and the plan to meet outside.

An enormous crashing sound filled the hallway and Gizhaa felt the floor tremble. He tore open the outside door and ran into the moonlit snow. He backed away from the building, heart pounding, head spinning, chest aching in the fresh air. His gaze flew from one end of the building to the other, searching for movement, a sign of life, a silhouette.

Suddenly, a dramatic spray of light erupted from the roof above the front entrance. Gizhaa's stomach contracted. Fire shot into the sky above the foyer, the roof now completely gone.

Inaa! Tom! He saw no sign of either at the rear of the building. The door they should have exited had no tracks in the snow coming or going.

He ran farther along the wall as the rioting crowd broke up, people staring in awe or horror, depending on their convictions, at the flaming structure.

Panic rose in Gizhaa's throat. He noticed a door farther along the west side of the building, the moonlight illuminating footsteps. Hope rose in Gizhaa as he rushed toward it. Perhaps Inaa and Tom had escaped after all!

The footsteps clearly led toward the front of the building. Gizhaa followed them until they were lost in the crushed snow left by the dispersing crowd. He searched through the onlookers, keeping a low profile; the jubilant Revivalists might recognize the stranger who had waylaid their triumphant protest.

The night wore on and the fire continued to burn into the wee hours of the morning. Gizhaa scoured every inch of the legislature complex and found no sign of Tom or Inaa, except perhaps for a garbage pail. He stumbled across it by accident, the wind having rolled it across the lawns until it became wedged under the steps of an adjacent building. When he opened the pail, he discovered a bevy of papers covered with names and places of the New York Revival's people.

Tom succeeded in saving the evidence then, Gizhaa thought wearily. He breathed a prayer of thanks as he crawled under the steps, pulling the pail behind him to block the entrance somewhat. Then he sat and let his head fall back against the brick wall, darkness descending over his mind.

△ △ △

Inaa rose shakily to her feet, keeping her weight on her left foot. Pain shot through her right ankle as she tried to balance. She felt as though her chest would explode. Her mind was dull.

Where was Tom? Where was she? She was vaguely aware that onlookers were beginning to gather around her. She felt herself swaying and realized her legs wouldn't hold her weight much longer. Someone grasped her arm, pulling Inaa's gaze. She stared at the stranger's hand in confusion.

"You just barely escaped," a woman gasped, her face clouded in motherly concern. "Let me help you."

Inaa couldn't answer. She grabbed the woman's hand, her knees buckling.

"Adil! Adil! Quick! This girl needs help!" The woman knelt in the snow, her black hands holding Inaa's white ones. "Look at me. Everything is going to be okay. We're going to take care of you. Just hold on now."

Strong arms lifted Inaa from the snow and she clung to the broad neck with her last bit of strength. As she was carried away, she glimpsed fire arching over the legislature.

△ △ △

When Gizhaa awoke, it was to the sound of heavy feet stamping overhead, as though banging snow off boots.

"What did you find?" a man's voice asked matter-of-factly. Gizhaa instantly recognized it as the voice from behind the office door the day before when he had tracked Tom and Inaa.

"There's not much left. The entire building is gutted," another male voice replied.

"Bodies?"

"Yeah, we found one, but the ceiling had caved. The other guy's probably buried there, too."

There was silence. "Let's hope so," the first man conceded. "What about my office? Everything destroyed?"

"The fire didn't finish the job, so we cleared out the drawers at dawn. Everything is destroyed now."

Gizhaa heard the sound of a door opening above his head. He didn't move.

"Perfect." The first man sounded confident. "Last night's spectacle would have been a total success without that traitor Tom and his fool orator. Nevertheless, we'll send a clear message to Canada—the Revival will not be dismissed!" His voice faded as he entered the building Gizhaa leaned against. "With those troublemakers out of the way, phase two should move ahead smoothly now." The door banged shut, but Gizhaa's sharp hearing caught the final phrase. "If those obstinate Chinese don't want to pay the price for our resources, no one will have them!"

Gizhaa waited a long time in the darkness. He thumped his legs and beat his arms on his chest. His hideout was relatively sealed, keeping the snow at bay. The temperature had risen overnight, but the cold coming through the ground still made it difficult to move.

While he waited, he wrestled with several numbing conclusions. The men had been looking for two bodies: Tom's and Gizhaa's. They had found one. Tom? Inaa? Gizhaa pressed his fists to his eyes, stifling the sob that rose. The other body was probably buried in the rubble.

Gizhaa knew he could wait no longer or he wouldn't have the strength to crawl out of this cave. He pulled the garbage pail to safety under the stairs and then wiggled past it.

Listening carefully, he dared to raise his head from his hiding place. The early morning sun shone brightly through the trees as though it didn't know that tragedy had struck. The twittering birds alit on the melting branches. A few people still looked at the burning husk of the legislature, but their backs were turned to him.

He dragged himself upright, shoved his hands in his pockets, and sauntered away—as though hours before he had not screamed protest to an angry mob, risking his life to save another and escaping from a fiery furnace. H had lost a sibling and a friend, but he just kept walking.

△   △   △

When the harbour came into view, Gizhaa stared at it blankly. It was a different place than he had seen the day before. Every boat was moored to the docks. No ferries chimed their departure. The busy storefronts were vacant, yet the paths were full of pedestrians.

Gizhaa remembered suddenly that the Festival had begun during the night. Happy couples walked together on the frosty boardwalk. A group had ceremonially gathered, waving the flag of the *Ogimaa* as they proceeded. A pack of children on bicycles wove their way cheerfully around and through pedestrians, calling to one another as they went. Bells began to ring, some deep and melancholy, others clanging and bright. It was the moment that the Statue of Liberty had sunk, centuries ago. The city remembered once again.

Gizhaa stared at the scene, his mind dulled by grief. Something else was out of place. And then his eyes locked on it—the Canadian bio-miner ship standing in the harbour, as out of place as Gizhaa himself. Its bright red and white paint against the navy ocean seemed torn from a child's storybook. The modern apparatus rising from its deck seemed to mock the charming ferries along the wharf. The ancient tolling bells seemed to declare their disapproval of this contraption in their harbour.

Gizhaa cocked his head, studying the ship. It was certainly the same ship from the Iqaluit harbour. The flag of the *Ogimaa* flew from its deck, a Canadian flag below it. But the Iqaluit jewellery merchant had said the flag had been taken down from the stolen ship.

The last remembrance bell rang out across the water, low and long. Its vibrations hadn't yet ceased when a massive blast rocked the bio-miner. A second blast reverberated through the air as the Canadian flag caught fire. Gizhaa ran forward along with everyone else, forming a wall of people along the water's edge, all anxiously searching for signs of where this attack had come from. The ship quickly began to burn; the explosions had come from onboard.

"The Revival is sinking the Canadian bio-miner!" Gizhaa groaned. "This is their message…"

A third explosion rocked the boat and it flipped heavily to one side, water surging onto its low deck. The crowd murmured in fear.

The person beside Gizhaa grabbed his hand. It was an elderly man with white hair and glasses. He also held the hand of the woman beside him, and she held the hand of the woman beside her. All along the boardwalk, a chain of solidarity formed. Gizhaa awkwardly reached for the next person in line, a boy whose bicycle lay on the slope behind him. As he did, the boy whispered, "I have a king," his gaze fixed on the sinking ship. Gizhaa stared at him. The group of biking children grasped each other's hands as they stood side by side, now solemn, and whispered the fervent chant.

These young ones had been at the legislature last night! His heart still ached for Inaa, but it burst with longing for his little sisters, Nanda, Solia, Kris, and Abby. He heard them whisper, "I have a king," and he whispered it, too.

One by one, the onlookers took each other's hands. One by one they caught the phrase until the line stretched as far as Gizhaa could see and their voices, not loud and defensive like they had been last night, but gentle and swelling, rose to a great anthem of worship. Without music, the cries of gulls and crashing of waves accompanied them. The sound became so sweet that it may have been a melody in some foreign liturgical style—"I … have … a king."

As Gizhaa watched the last of the bio-miner disappear forever, he thought that Tom had been only half-right that the Immortals had come for resources. Gizhaa saw as clearly as the sun in his eyes that the *Ogimaa*, the one Immortal, had come for only one resource; he had come for the people, the people who needed a king.

chapter twenty-nine

GIIWE
"RETURN"

The windmills churned endlessly in the November wind that tore across the lake. Gizhaa had been sitting on the hard sand for an hour already, wrapped in his mother's blanket, watching the whitecaps crest and fall. In the full moon that had passed since he'd found his way home, he had taken to coming here every afternoon to sit and pray after the alpacas were watered, fed, and cleaned. Sometimes he cried, but more often he simply watched the sky.

He heard a footstep behind him and startled. He wasn't accustomed to being surprised. Jumping to his feet, he turned. Ya Min's black hair flew wildly behind her in the stiff wind, but her smile was all sunshine as she stood respectfully some feet away.

Gizhaa gasped. "Ya Min?"

She laughed and then pulled her long hair around, tucking it into the shoulder of her sweater to tame it.

"Your mother told me where to find you." Her eyes twinkled as she gestured to the ground. "You won't mind if I have a seat?"

Gizhaa shook his head. "The beach is cold already. Winter is coming early this year. We'll stay warmer if we walk."

Gizhaa led the way and Ya Min fell into step beside him, wrapping her coat tighter around herself.

"Your sisters are sweet," she cooed. "I had a hard time convincing them I should be able to find you here by myself. They are so eager to help."

He dared to smile at her. "So how *did* you end up here? Shouldn't you be on your way back to China by now?"

"I believe I need to say thank you for the beautiful gift you sent me." She reached inside the neck of her coat and drew out the delicate leaf necklace. "I love it! But I'm also on business for the *Ogimaa*."

Gizhaa nodded. Of course she hadn't come just to see him!

"He sent me here to thank you and to ask for your help," she continued.

Gizhaa laughed incredulously. "Thank me? Why would the *Ogimaa* want to thank me?"

Ya Min seemed oblivious to his disenchantment. "But of course! You were the voice that brought the rallying cry to the people. And when I received word from you of the files Tom had rescued, we were able to retrieve them before any further evidence could be destroyed. Tom's contribution was invaluable. The New York Revival's backroom deals have been brought to light and the leaders will be prosecuted."

Gizhaa remained silent for some time. "But Ya Min, I failed! I lost my sister. I lost my father." He choked on the words.

She stopped and looked at him compassionately. "You don't know the end of the story yet, Gizhaa. I bring word that we have evidence that your father lives! Don't lose hope." Her voice softened. "And Inaa's sacrifice was not wasted. She was undoubtedly the one who convinced Tom of the Revival's dark motives. Without each of you, who knows what may have come of the New York Revival protests?"

Gizhaa pondered this for a moment. "Joshua told Tom that he needed to put out the fire his ancestor had started. Tom didn't put out the fire of the New York legislature, but he did put an end to the New York Revival. Was that the fire his ancestor started?"

Ya Min contemplated this silently as the waves broke on the shore. "The Revival fire is more ancient than even Tom's ancestors' trials. I don't know Tom's story. Maybe the fire was the deep animosity between the two peoples. Tom's sacrifice for you and Inaa was significant, perhaps as an ending to an old wound between two nations, a wound that has been healed." She reached into the deep pocket of her coat and brought out a letter. "This is for you."

As she handed it to him, the wind off the lake caught the envelope, curling it up.

Gizhaa nodded toward the path under the weeping birch's bridal bower. "Come this way," he said, crossing the sand and ducking into the shelter of the tree. He crouched down on a bed of fallen leaves and Ya Min crept in after him. He tore open the envelope, his chilled, rough hands fumbling.

The plain letterhead announced it was from the Prime Minister's office. He scanned the page and stared at the handwritten signature at the bottom of the page.

He began again, carefully reading the text of the letter.

Dear Gizhaa Selah,

I am writing to you personally to thank you for your invaluable service to our country and our king. In these troubled times, you have proven yourself a courageous citizen. The information you gathered about the hijacking of our bio-miner by the New York and the Chinese Revival allowed us to circumvent the completion of that operation.

You acted courageously, proudly taking a stand for truth during the New York protests, thereby consolidating those noble citizens against that violent outbreak. In addition, the information you found will allow us to continue to respond to these events in New York and around the world.

Nevertheless, we are only entering these dangerous days. Since this opposition began, our tribute has been destroyed and Canada's place in the commonwealth is under assault. We have already begun to see the effects on our nation. As the Word foretold, "If any of the peoples of the earth do not go up to worship the King, they will have no rain." Therefore, we must act quickly to reverse the momentum of the Revival in Canada.

We are, of course, immediately seeking to locate your father. We have some information on his whereabouts and I assure you that everything will be done to bring him home soon.

However, I am asking you, on behalf of the King, for assistance in responding to the new threats we face. You will be given details shortly on your assignment.

My people once said, "Decide to take neither road, but instead turn back, remember, and reclaim the wisdom of those who came before."

Gizhaa, you have chosen well in reclaiming the wisdom of us who came before you.

In His Service,

Prime Minister Waaban

Gizhaa folded the letter slowly and put it back in the envelope. Ya Min crouched before him, studying his face.

He cleared his throat uncertainly without looking at her. "I suppose then you are bringing my assignment?"

"You need not say yes, Gizhaa. It is an invitation, not an order."

"I'm not sure I have a choice. My father is lost. Inaa is gone." He shook his head, frowning. "But I still have a family here. My mother—the baby is due in less than two moons—and my sisters. They need me. But I want to help my country, and you." He did look up now, his brow furrowed.

She stood. "Then we must ask your family."

Gizhaa stretched his legs, too. "What would we do?"

"If you accept?" she asked. "We go west, to the coast. The movement there is very large, with strong ties to the global work, especially to Asia, my specialty." Her answer wasn't dismissive, but her tone was all-business.

Gizhaa sighed heavily and lifted the branches of the tree so Ya Min could pass under them. The wind wrestled around them as they returned to the beach.

"I had hoped that someday our partnership might be less platonic," he announced with resignation.

Ya Min stopped and looked at the water intently. "Gizhaa, what is that?" she asked, pointing into the blue expanse.

He squinted. The November light was yellow, the sun bright, and there seemed to be no line between sky and water.

"It's coming this way," she said.

Gizhaa had never met someone who could see something he couldn't. He stared harder.

"Ah, I see now," she said. "It's a sail. A white sail." She turned toward Gizhaa as he continued to search the horizon for a glimpse of the sail. "Gizhaa, my allegiance is entirely to the king, to the *Ogimaa*."

He smiled at her, a little sadly. "It's okay, Ya Min. You don't have to explain. Your world is very different from mine. I am a farmer. You are a …" He glanced at the horizon. "A government agent. With superpowers, no less."

Ya Min laughed and Gizhaa joined her. "No, Gizhaa, we aren't different because you are a farmer and I'm a government agent." She sat on the hard sand. "But we are different."

Gizhaa noticed that he had left his mother's blanket lying on the beach earlier. He retrieved it and offered it to Ya Min. She drew it around her shoulders and watched the lake as she spoke while Gizhaa settled beside her.

"You are from one world, a world in which people live and grow old and die, although much slower than they did a millennium ago," she said. "It's a good world now that the *Ogimaa* rules. But there is another world, a world I have tasted. In this world, there is no death or disease, no sorrow or tears. And although I am privileged to serve the *Ogimaa* here, it is not my home. These two worlds are still held apart for a time."

Gizhaa watched Ya Min. "I have no idea what you're talking about," he admitted.

She tilted her head to one side and sighed. "I began my life before the War—*Miigaadiwin*, you say. I was still a young child when the war began. There was a great famine in our country. To conserve food, lots were drawn of the children who had siblings. I was chosen to be eliminated. My father feared God. He risked his life to hide me, but we were caught and executed."

Gizhaa's stomach turned, his head spinning. "How awful!"

Ya Min reached out and put her hand on his arm. "Gizhaa, I am as human as you, no superpowers required. Can a fish become a dog?" She laughed at this idea. "But I'm now of both worlds. The day will come soon when the King will bring the two together forever. But first there are difficult times ahead."

Gizhaa placed his hand over hers. "Ya Min, you are the most amazing woman I have ever met, Immortal or New Person or whatever you call yourself! Even if your first allegiance is to the *Ogimaa*, even if there are difficult times ahead, can you not care for someone who is just human? If the two worlds are coming together soon, can we not be together, too?"

"There is so much more than your eyes see. Can you see the stars? No, it's broad daylight and they are hidden by the sun's light. In the same way, there is a spirit world you cannot yet see. But when the sun goes dark, it will become light for you."

Gizhaa scowled a little. "Ya Min, you are talking in riddles."

"Because you lack the language for me to speak clearly. How can there be words for things which are unknown to you?" She smiled. "I'm sorry. Look, now you can see the sail, yes?" She pointed to the water.

A white sail could be clearly seen moving through the water. An old excitement awakened in him. "Why, I think that's Jordan's old boat!" he cried.

Ya Min picked up where she had left off. "The days of trouble have begun. The prison has been opened and the spirits are flooding this world once more. What once was, will be again." She wrapped her arms more tightly around her knees. "But we still have work to do, as the final redemption is coming. Then we will celebrate, celebrate like never before, and the two worlds will be one forever."

Gizhaa watched the sailboat draw nearer in silence for a long time. Suddenly, on the water between them and the boat, a school of lake sturgeon rose to the surface, the spines on their backs breaking the water again and again.

"These fish are my brother Simon's project!" he explained. "They were all but extinct before *Miigaadiwin*. Simon and Jordan worked for their return in great numbers this last century. See that?" A massive sturgeon sprang out of the water and flagged its tail back and forth as though walking on the water. "It's called tail-walking! I've only seen it once before."

The school of fish seemed to understand that they had an audience. Whether for those on shore or in the boat, they leapt and tail-walked in a display that had never before been recorded. Ya Min and Gizhaa clapped and cheered for a full hour while the show went on. Finally, no doubt exhausted from their effort, the school swam on.

Gizhaa flopped back on the ground. "That was incredible. Simon would have gone mad with joy. It's like they were dead and he brought them back to life." He closed his eyes. "He's gone now, you know. To that other world you talk about."

Ya Min leaned back with her face to the sky. "I am sorry, Gizhaa, that you cannot see your brother for now."

He reached across the sand and put his hand on top of hers. "Ya Min, is there some way you would consider…"

She pulled her hand away. "I am sorry, Gizhaa. I cannot marry you."

"Marry!" Gizhaa gasped. "We hardly know each other yet."

She sighed. "No, but you think marriage is the greatest joy you can achieve. And I cannot marry you. And I'm glad of that, but I'm sorry you must wait a little longer to see this… You think that if we could be together, we would never be separated and our union would overcome all loneliness and sorrow. But marriage is just a taste of what is to come. No matter how wonderful it is, it's still only a taste and it's never all it is hoped to be. When our two worlds become one, that union will truly never be separated, and it *will* overcome all loneliness and sorrow."

Gizhaa stood, his eyes fixed on the approaching boat. "Then I am sorry for my display of affection. Please forgive me."

Ya Min didn't move. "I once overheard your father say, 'The one who tells half the truth is hiding the truth.' The truth is that I do care for you, Gizhaa."

He knelt beside her. "Another wise man said, 'Even the most common of forces can lift the mightiest of burdens.' Until this perfect union you speak of comes, is it not possible that the common forces of affection and devotion might be enough to lift these heavy burdens we face?"

She tilted her head back and smiled. "Then you will join the team after all?" He didn't respond. "We can work together, Gizhaa, as long as you understand this: my heart belongs to the King forever."

Gizhaa studied the boat that was now mooring near shore. A dinghy dropped over the side, splashing the man onboard.

"I'm in," he said to Ya Min. He grabbed her hand to pull her up from the sand. "On your terms."

He shook her hand formally and then a wide grin spread across his face.

"Come and meet Jordan!"

chapter thirty

GABEKANA

"AT THE END OF THE TRAIL"

Jordan rowed to shore with quick, sure strokes of his oars. By the time he drew near, Gizhaa and Ya Min had taken their shoes off, rolled up their pant legs, and waded into the frigid water to grab hold of the dinghy.

While Gizhaa steadied the boat, Jordan leapt out and the two men grabbed each other in a long, hard hug. When they pulled away, Gizhaa's eyes were moist, but Jordan's smile was broad enough to be seen clear to the island. He was shorter than Gizhaa, but broader. His hair was so fair it was nearly white. His blue eyes were the colour of the lake water.

As Ya Min patiently held the boat steady, a bevy of questions flew back and forth without anyone moving from the ankle-deep water.

"Jordan, how are you? Where have you been for so long?"

"How is your family? Everyone well?"

"What brings you across the channel? Are you staying over?" Gizhaa shook himself. "Jordan, this is my friend, Ya Min. Ya Min, this a long-time friend of our family, Jordan. Let's get this on shore and warm up."

Gizhaa reached for the dinghy.

"Wait!" Ya Min interrupted breathlessly. "Your sailboat… I have never been sailing. Might we go for a ride?"

Jordan raised his eyebrows in delight. "I would love to take you." He turned to Gizhaa and asked cautiously, "Is Inaa around? I thought maybe she would like to go out. I've just rebuilt the boat completely!"

Gizhaa caught his breath and glanced at Ya Min, his stomach turning. "No, she's not. Maybe we can go another time—"

"No, no," Jordan cut in. "Let's just go for a quick ride about. We've already got our feet wet."

Ya Min nodded encouragingly, so the three stepped into the dinghy. As Jordan rowed them out to the sailboat, the sun began to sink lower in the sky, reflecting off the waves. *Didi*'s white haze touched the horizon ahead of them. Ya Min already seemed spellbound by the beauty.

Gizhaa leaned toward Jordan. "I'm thinking about taking a journey soon, but I need someone to watch the farm until my father returns. Any chance you'd like to come and stay for a while?"

Jordan didn't miss a stroke. "I've got a good farmhand in charge of things back home. I'd love to. When do I start?"

Gizhaa chuckled. There was a God in heaven.

Δ   Δ   Δ

Inaa leaned out over the railing of the ferry. It was her first day without the cast. She flexed her feet as the boat bobbed slowly over the waves. Her broken ankle had been complicated to treat, but her benefactors had seen that she had received the best medical care from an Immortal physician. His expertise, combined with her own regenerative function, had successfully repaired the break in a full moon cycle.

The fumes had so poisoned her mind that it had taken her nearly half that time to put together what had happened the day of the fire. As the yellow sunlight washed over her and the wind whipped her coat, she opened her eyes wide to avoid remembering the flames, the heat, and Tom. For the past two weeks, she had been hobbling about, trying to earn her way into the vestiges of the New York Revival, seemingly to no avail.

All she knew was that Tom was dead and the *Ohsh* had taken both her father and Gizhaa—whether dead or alive, she did not know. Now she was free of the cast and had promised herself one thing: that she would find them.

But today had been her breakthrough. An anonymous contact had arranged for her to meet a local recruiter.

As the ferry pulled up to the dock, Inaa's recruiter waited to collect her, and it was none other than Regent, the head of the New York Revival. He stood on the dock, sizing her up with growing appreciation as she stepped off the ramp. He didn't hide his interest.

She returned his subtle smile, coyly. "We meet again, Regent!"

He offered her his arm. "Welcome aboard. I assume you have grown to understand New York better since our last meeting?"

She tipped her chin. "I'm sure I have. It seems a bastion of progressive thinkers gather here, if I'm not mistaken. I'm hoping there might be a little room for me."

He chuckled. "Yes, I'm sure there is a room for you, Miss Inaa."

As they walked away, she fixed her gaze on the horizon and reminded herself chillingly, *I can get places none of the rest of them can.*

OJIBWE-ENGLISH DICTIONARY[38]

Note: There are a number of Ojibwe dialects spoken in North America. This particular dialect is used because of its extensive audio recordings preserved by the University of Minnesota.

Aaniin—hello

Ahaaw—okay/come on, here used as an expression

Aki—earth, land, ground

Anashinabe—the southern group of Anishinabe divided into what today are the Ojibwa, Odawa, and Potawatomi; the northern group along the Ottawa River divided into Algonquin, Nipissing, and the Mississaugas.

Baamaapii—until later

Baapagishkaa Aki—earthquake

Baawiting—Sault Ste. Marie, one of the first political centres for the Ojibwa as they moved west

Bawaajigan—dream

Bimaaji—saved/rescued

Biminizha'an—follow it along, pursue it

Boozhoo—greetings

Dagwaagin—fall, here referring to the fall harvest festival

Dasoozo—trapped, pinned down

Dibikigiizis—moon

---

38 *The Ojibwe People's Dictionary*, John D. Nichols, ed. University of Minnesota, Department of Indian Studies, 2015. Accessed: 2016–2017 (https://ojibwe.lib.umn.edu/).

Didibininjiibizon—ring, used here referring to a gas halo around the earth

Gaagige-Bimaadiziwin—everlasting life

Gabekana—at the end of the trail

Gagiinawishki—habitual liar

Gichi—prefix meaning big, great, very, quite

Giiwe—go home, return

Gikinoo'amaagoowin—teachings or lessons, used here for the evening storytelling

Gizhaadan—guard, watch over it

Gizhe-Manidoo—God, the Creator

Inaabam—see a certain way, as in a dream

Indawemaa—my sibling of the opposite sex

Ishkode—fire

Ishkodewidaabaan—train

Ishpiming—heaven

Maadaadizi—journey

Mazinikojigan—carving

Miigaadiwin—war

Miigiwewin—gift

Miigwech—thanks

Mizhakwad—clear

Naawayi—centre, here referring to the temple in Jerusalem

Nagamon—song

Nanda-Gikendan—seek to know it

Ningide—(it) thaws/melts

Nisayenh—older brother, here referring to First Nations

Nishiime—younger sibling, here referring to non-Native peoples

Nitamoozhaan—firstborn, here referring to the Jewish people

Odoodeman—clan system

Ogimaa—chief, here referring to Gichi-Ogimaa, the King

Ohshkagoonjing Giizis—crescent moon

Oodenawan—towns

Waaban—it is dawn

Waazakonenjigan—lamp, light

Wabunukeeg—daybreak people

Wanishin—lost

Wiidookaagewinini—helper

Anna Raddon decided to write her first novel at the age of 9 just to beat Gordon Korman's record. That story about a girl and a canoe accident never did get finished, but perhaps you will find vestiges of it in *After Miigaadiwin*. Decades later as an avid read-aloud mother, she found that, in this age of dystopia, books reconciling honest history with an imaginative future are needed.

Inspired by great Canadian authors, Raddon decided to write about places she knew. Awe-inspiring Canadian landscapes, from the shores of Lake Huron (where she resides alongside an Anishinabe First Nation) to the edges of the Arctic (where she summered in a remote village), became the backdrop of *After Miigaadiwin*.

A fanciful and irresistibly hopeful future came to life in her book. Raddon imagines a world where redemption and healing are tangible, where people and cultures honour each other and their Creator, and where a simple gift can change the world. *After Miigaadiwin* is her open-handed offering.